D0631508

GETTING OUT THE WORD

THE QUEER GIRL IS GOING TO BE OKAY

3 REASONS WE LOVE THIS BOOK

The South's Got Something to Say: Dale Walls centers queer love, joy, and growth without shying away from the realities of queer life in Texas

It's giving #tenderness: the story warms your heart with tales of queer love of all kinds—friends, family, and romantic partners amidst the highs and low of second-semester senior year of high school

Talent to watch: debut queer writer Dale Walls is a Lambda Literary Fellow and the creator of YouTube series Art in Color

PROMOTION HIGHLIGHTS

- Major physical ARC distribution
- Extensive earned media outreach
- LQ's social ambassador program
- Appearances at select festivals and cons
- Virtual and in-person events with indie booksellers
- Submit for all major awards
- Original #content across social platforms

THE
QUEER
GIRL
IS
GOING
TO BE
OKAY

LQ

LEVINE QUERIDO
MONTCLAIR · AMSTERDAM · HOBOKEN

THE QUEER GIRL IS GOING TO BE OKAY

· · · · · · · · · · · ·
· · · · · · · · · · · ·

DALE WALLS

This is an Arthur A. Levine book
Published by Levine Querido

LQ

LEVINE QUERIDO

www.levinequerido.com • info@levinequerido.com
Levine Querido is distributed by Chronicle Books LLC
Text copyright © 2023 by Dale Walls
All rights reserved Library of Congress Control Number: 2023931582
ISBN 978-1-64614-270-5
Printed and bound in U.S.A.

Published November 2023
First printing

To all the queer kids in the South.

THE
QUEER
GIRL
IS
GOING

TO BE
OKAY

ONE

Dawn hopped over the fence and landed flat on her face. Her heart raced as she looked down at her palms, which were muddy and scratched up from the patches of thorny weeds in the big yard.

She felt wet dirt on her right cheek and swiped the back of her hand across it, smearing even more mud across the skin.

"Come on!" Georgia motioned to Dawn through her rolled-down window, revving the engine of her old, dark green Toyota Camry.

Dawn tried to focus but her head felt fuzzy and the dew drops sprinkled all over her skin were making her even more uncomfortable than the dirt. Dawn looked up at the window she'd crawled from, the shed just below it where she'd scraped her knee trying to land, the grass below the shed, and finally, the fence separating the house from the rest of the street. She tilted her head up to the second story of the painted white house with its wooden slats and rustic cream siding and windows so big she couldn't imagine who needed to own a view of that much of the world.

Shaking out the leaves from her hair, she watched as a boy looked down out of the open window on the second floor at her splayed body, then looked quickly over his shoulder, then down at her again. Dawn raised her hand to wave goodbye, and just as it seemed the boy was going to wave back, he swung a fistful of her pink underwear out of the window, the crumpled fabric landing unceremoniously in the dirt next to her. The boy shut the window with an echoing snap that bounced off all the other big windows in the neighborhood of big houses.

Dawn propped herself up on her knees and bent her elbows until she was in a crouching position. Her skirt stopped mid-thigh and did nothing to protect her lower half from the chunks of mud now coating her legs. She reached across the wet grass to grab her underwear but after seeing the mud caking the soft pink cotton decided to abandon them in the yard.

"D, What are you doing? Hurry up! Edie has to be home soon." Dawn looked into the backseat of Georgia's car and saw Edie resting her forehead against the foggy glass. She knocked her head two times against the glass and tapped her index finger to her wrist as if to say *time to leave! Time!*

Dawn stood up and brushed the dirt off of the wet spots where her knees had touched the ground. She stumbled and leaned her tired body heavily against the white exterior of the Architectural Digest–ready home. The row of bushes separating the house from its neighbor rubbed against her and wet her clothes in odd, leaf-shaped patterns. Her knees ached from the fall but she tucked her tall frame beneath the bushes' cover and ran across the side of the yard to the safety of Georgia's car. She slipped into the passenger's seat and Georgia pulled off into the thick heat of the evening.

Carly Rae Jepsen crooned about love through the dashboard speakers while Dawn stared down at her mud-caked palms. Edie and Georgia stayed quiet as the song went on, and just as Carly was bursting into the chorus, Dawn decided she should speak.

"This was the last time. I swear."

"Uh huh." Georgia rolled down her window and stared out at the suburban traffic beneath the just-setting sun. Hondas of all kinds and colors rumbled next to moms in oversized SUVs and eight-seater vans.

"Dawn, you have to stop meeting up with this guy," Georgia lectured with quiet conviction.

"I know, I just said that."

"But you've definitely said the same thing before and yet here we are in River Oaks again waiting behind a bunch of bushes to pick you up from another absolutely garbage situation." Georgia gripped the steering wheel.

"He said his mom was home." Dawn shrugged in defense and went quiet again.

"Right." Georgia took a deep, heavy sigh and let her foot slowly rest on the gas as she came to a stop light. "Look, Dawn." She reached up to the passenger seat side and flipped down the mirror hanging there. "Honestly, look at yourself. You are gorgeous. You are soft. You are an angel." She paused and Dawn brushed her hair out of her face in the reflection, considering Georgia's words. "You are also covered in mud because a stupid boy you, I assume, don't even like that much told you to hop out of his literal window and jump over his six-foot fence into a mud pit like an episode of fucking *American Ninja Warrior*."

Dawn stared at herself in the tiny reflection. Mud streaks, she realized, were smattered through her waist-length walnut-brown hair and a few flecks had even landed in her teeth.

"What Georgia is trying to say is," Edie leaned forward from the backseat and rested her palms on Dawn and Georgia's right and left shoulders, "you are better than this. A lot better."

"Let me see your phone." Georgia reached out and held her open palm under Dawn's nose."Um, no? You're driving."

"You are not about to kill me," Edie chimed in from the back. "I did not survive seventeen years at my parents' house to go out texting and driving PSA style."

Georgia sighed again and craned her neck down the road, the lines of strip mall stores already turning off their flashing open signs.

"Just give it. I'll wait till that stoplight down there."

Dawn hesitantly pulled her phone out of her pocket, a small stripe of dirt streaked across its glass screen. She clicked it on, a picture of the beach scene from Alfonso Cuarón's *Y tu mamá también* flashing on her lockscreen before she unlocked it and rested it in Georgia's open palm.

Georgia cruised to the stoplight and pulled up Dawn's messages. At the top was a conversation with an unsaved number.

"This him?" Georgia turned the phone to Dawn.

Dawn bit her lip and looked out the window. She knew what had to be done for her own good. "Yeah. Yes, it is."

Edie leaned in from the back so she could see the screen, her deep brown skin glistening from the ribbons of moonlight beaming through the windshield.

In her attempt to press the contact icon, Georgia's thumb scrolled through the messages and landed on an image. "Not a dick pic, Dawn . . . not that."

Edie yelped as she dramatically covered her eyes and collapsed into the backseat.

Dawn's caramel cheeks went a dark red. "I didn't even ask for that! He just sent it!"

"Even more reason to do this." Georgia tapped to the contact page and pressed the word *block*. The message thread disappeared. "It was for your own mental and physical health, really."

Edie nodded her head in silent agreement in the rearview mirror.

"I know." Dawn sunk into her seat and stared out the window at the approaching highway ramp. Georgia started to pull off again, the glowing phone still clutched in her free hand.

"Holy shit." Georgia yelped, nearly dropping Dawn's phone.

Dawn looked up into oncoming traffic, heart racing in fear. But all the cars around them were at a standstill.

"What the heck, Geo. What?" Dawn noticed Georgia wasn't looking at traffic though, she was looking at the phone.

"Look. Look at the email that just came." She shoved Dawn's screen towards her face.

The email was so casual, Dawn almost didn't notice her life was changing.

"The subject said submission update from the Austin Film Festival. See?"

Georgia reached over to zoom in on the screen as she drove, her baby blue acrylic nails making a tapping noise as she moved her hand. Her blunt-cut black hair swished against Dawn's shoulder as she leaned over the dash to see the phone screen.

"Georgia!" Edie shrieked in panic from the backseat as the car in front of them screeched to a halt.

Dawn tried to keep her attention on the words as Georgia abruptly whipped into the far left lane.

"Oh my god. It says I'm through. I-I made it through to the second round with the excerpt I sent."

Georgia gasped. "What does that mean? When is the rest of the film due?" She reached for the phone again, but Dawn moved her hand away.

"Wait wait wait. You're driving. I'll just read it out loud." She focused intently on the words as they flashed across the screen.

Dear Dawn Salcedo,

It is with great pleasure that I notify you that your film THE QUEER GIRL IS GOING TO BE OKAY *has been selected for the second round of judging in the 30th Annual Austin Film Festival. Out of thousands of submissions, your work impressed our primary round of judges and will now be subject to a final round before the awards ceremony this April. Please submit the entire film to the link below no later than March 31st by 11:59 p.m. CDT.*

"March 31st?" Georgia exclaimed, swerving the car as she tilted over to try to see the screen. "That's a month away, babes. That's like three seconds from now. You better get on it."

"Let me finish reading!" Dawn concentrated on the words again.

Once the entire film is received, it will be considered for competition in the Student Documentary Feature category along with any "Best of" nominations it receives from the Grand Jury, and you will have a chance to win a full scholarship to the University of Texas at Austin Radio, Television, and Film Department!

On behalf of the Selection Committee, congratulations to you and your team.

Dawn remembered when she'd first found out about the competition. It had been a Friday. Senior year was full of Fridays. Another week waiting to hear back from colleges, another week taking classes whose subject matter seemed to fade in relevance by the hour. The flyer was simple enough, a bright red sheet of paper hanging off the bulletin board outside of her homeroom class:

Austin Film Festival: Submit your student film today and win a full scholarship to UT Austin! Details below.

Dawn had snatched the poster off the board before she'd even finished reading. She was going to get that scholarship if it killed her.

Sitting in the passenger seat, she fell into shock. The city sped by as she tried to understand the words on her screen. She was going to be a filmmaker like she'd always wanted. The years of watching long, strange films in her bedroom on her perpetually broken laptop were going to lead to something. All the little videos she made of her friends, the odd angles and clear stylistic imitations of much more expensive, much more important movies, were for a reason.

"That's huge, Dawn. I can't believe you're literally a famous filmmaker and my friend." Georgia tried to reach over and hug Dawn as she exited the highway but Edie reached into the front seat and stopped her.

"Are you trying to kill us?" Edie cried from the back. "Congratulations." She took a deep breath and settled back into the seat as Georgia refocused her attention on the road. "Oh, Georgia and I haven't even done our interviews for it yet. Ben needs to do theirs too so I'll remind them tonight. You still coming?"

Georgia pulled into her and Edie's neighborhood and slowed down to a crawl. She braked at a stop sign as two kids crossed, hunched half over from the weight of their backpacks.

"To Ben's birthday? Obviously," Dawn said, still staring at the message on her phone with wide eyes. "They only reminded us about it thirty times this week on top of your four hundred."

"We're a persistent couple, what can I say?" Edie smirked and grabbed for the door as Georgia pulled up to her house.

"I'm about to throw up. Y'all are so gross." Georgia pretended to hurl into the windshield as Edie slid out of the backseat and stood behind the car until Georgia popped the trunk with the lever by her feet.

"You know you love us." Edie slammed the trunk closed and threw a smile towards Georgia through the rearview mirror. "Dawn, you're coming on your own, right?"

Dawn replied, still distracted by her screen, "Yeah. I'll meet you and Georgia at the party."

Georgia pulled off as Edie disappeared into her house.

Dawn read the message then reread it. Even after Georgia had dropped her off at her house and she was alone on her front lawn with just the sound of her neighbors arguing through their kitchen window on the side of the house, she read it again. This was her opportunity to leave her home, to make her dream real. When she was a kid, curled into her mom watching VHS tapes of movies she wasn't old enough for, her eyes glowed with the magic of the stories on screen. She'd always wanted to tell her own stories just like that. Love crossed over into obsession in middle school, long days holding a shaky phone camera in front of her friends' faces and editing them together on whatever free software she could find at the library. Now, she had a project she was proud of and it was going to win her a scholarship to study film. Now, it was finally real. She was so close.

She was going to win that scholarship.

TWO

Tonight, Edie was going to lie to her parents for the second time in her whole life. Dinner was set, and the lamp-tinted lighting of the dining room was already closing in on her as she prepared her words. The lie bubbled up in her cheeks threatening to spill out of her lips too early.

Time was running low on the lie. She usually loved staring at the retro clock on her parents' dining room wall with its oddly shaped numbers and hues of orange, but now it just seemed to be mocking her with its insistent *tick tick tick*.

"Bow your heads and close your eyes." Edie was stunned by her father's voice, thunderous and cutting across the room, too caught up in her own thinking.

Her thoughts ran like rapidly unspooling thread as she grabbed her brother's hand on her left and mother's on her right.

"Dear Lord, thank you for blessing us with this meal, and placing your holy hands over it so that it shall fill us," he started.

Her eyes wandered around the table and met the people she called her family, each one of their heads dutifully tilted downward.

Her father's rounded lips spoke with fervor, the wiry black mustache above them moving up and down as he grew more passionate. Even sitting, he was staunch and heavy-gutted. He looked like a child's drawing of a Southern Baptist preacher.

Light played on her brother Marvin's clenched hands, his little fingers entwining hers tight like vines as he prayed. He looked as close to their father as any nine-year-old could get. He always got his hair cut just the same as their dad's. Even as early as five, he took pride in the militaristic straight lines cutting across his neck and down towards his cheeks.

Her mother was gorgeous; the complete opposite of Edie. All sharp lines and golden brown skin. When she laughed, her straight teeth showed. She had deep, rounded, coffee-no-creamer eyes, and greeted new people by holding out both hands as if to say *we already know each other, and you can trust me more than anyone else in the entire world.* Her bowed head let a single pressed curl fall against her cheek.

Edie caught sight of herself in the mirror above her father's head. She was unremarkable. She was dark brown, soft, lips like blowing soup cool.

"Dear Lord, please heal the sick and feed the poor. Please allow me to watch over my family and keep them safe. In Jesus' name, amen."

Her mother's hand squeezed tight as Edie listened to her father's closing words.

"Amen," they said in unison.

The light tinkling sound of metal scraping against dinner plates filled the room. Edie slid mashed potatoes onto her large plate as she gathered the lie up beneath her tongue.

She thought about her parents' goodness and how it made it hard to lie to them. They bragged about her good grades at church, took her to all her quiz bowl competitions without complaint, made sure she had all the opportunities to do better than well in all her classes, even getting her a tutor when she got an, according to them, extremely disappointing B+ on a calculus test. *They weren't giving out As?* her father had asked incredulously, just before dialing the number of one of the congregation members who taught math at the University of Houston.

"Can I go to Georgia's to work on a project tonight? It's due Monday." Her eyes settled on her plate as she waited for her words to play out. She'd left the lie until the last minute, because her parents were much more likely to say yes to a school emergency. Making sure she had straight As was their priority, even if it meant missing church events sometimes.

Edie's first lie took place at this table the summer before her junior year. She did it as a test, an experiment doomed to fail. Her parents were strict, but she was fifteen then, a reasonable age to ask for things just out of reach, she thought. She had asked her mother if she could go on a weekend road trip to a water park in San Antonio with a bunch of friends. There was no water park or road trip. She just wanted to go to a concert, make room for the possibility of getting drunk for the first time, and sleep over at a friend's house thereby avoiding being wasted in front of her parents. It hadn't worked, which is why she was back here again at the dining table, nervous, hopeful.

"It's too late," her father said. The night collapsed violently before her eyes. She hadn't planned for no. She had to push. She had to do something.

"Please. I-I have to get this done. It's huge for my grade." She poked at their weakness, her perfect academic record.

"Gaile?" Her father looked to his wife as if to get a second opinion. Hope began to build itself a makeshift home again in Edie's head.

Her mother evened her gaze. "What class is it for?"

"Physics. I really need to finish it tonight, because I won't have time this weekend with the test review." She thought adding more detail would enhance the quality of the lie and had planned out her words carefully over the past few weeks leading up to

Ben's party. Missing their birthday would be a disaster, so she had planned everything, even mentioning the fake physics project offhand earlier in the week during family dinner.

"Oh, yes. You can go, but you need to ask if you can sleep over. I don't want you biking home late by yourself."

Light burst from within her, and it was all she could do to stop from jumping up on the table and screaming in triumph. The lie worked and came with sleepover benefits.

"Okay. Can I go now?" She moved to pick up her plate and scoot her chair away from the table.

"Finish your food," her father huffed as he scraped his fork across his plate.

"But we have to get as much done as possible before we get too tired."

"I said it once, Edie." She began to shovel the potatoes and meat into her mouth with a swiftness. Her mother shot her a critical look, so she slowed down in an attempt to act normal. Her seat couldn't even get warm before she'd tossed her plate into the sink and gathered up the backpack she'd stuffed full of party clothes to pick from when she got to Georgia's.

Edie yanked her bike from the junk piled in the corner of her family's ever cluttered garage and pressed a button on the wall so that the huge metal door would open onto the driveway. Balancing her bike in one hand, she pressed another button on the outside and watched as the garage door came down slowly with achy metal noises. Edie mounter her bike and set off. She felt the quiet of the neighborhood in her breathing, in the wind brushing her cheeks, in her feet as they pedaled around and around. She looked up at the night stars and lost her balance as a few blinked back at her. There was too much pollution to see everything. Her heart raced from all the movement.

"I'm a liar," she whispered close to her chest.

"I lied," she screamed, pedaling hard. The wind caught her words and carried them down the sidewalk behind her.

Every time she got to leave her house, air rushed into her lungs like water through a gorge. The open night fell out beneath the wheels of her bike. She was some terrible, shaking particle finally returning to equilibrium. The moon washed her and made the night feel mystic.

Georgia's house was only a few blocks from hers. She could already see the outline of her body through the curtains of the front window as she biked up to the lawn. Its yellow façade greeted her familiarly. The door flaked white like the underside of an orange peel.

One hand gripping her backpack, Edie balanced the handle-bars of her bike as she swung her leg over the side. The wheels tipped over and the bike fell to the lawn. She rushed to the door she knew would be unlocked, already waiting for her.

Soft radio music drifted through the hallway leading to the kitchen. Edie let her finger drag along the mint-green walls as she hummed the tune: something she'd heard before but couldn't quite place. Pictures lining the hallway walls showed Georgia and her mom, Frankie, in black and white through the years. There was one picture where Frankie glowed twenty-something-years-old and smiling into Georgia's baby hair. In another, they both wore ski jackets and struggled to smile on a snow-covered moun-tainside, every picture a small story about how much they liked each other that day. In every single one, Frankie held Georgia like she was holding herself.

Everything about this house pitted itself against Edie's idea of her own house. She drowned in Frankie and Georgia's fishbowl world. Their colors and music and fantastical care for each other. She found it all romantic, the way they knew everything about each other.

Edie rounded the corner to see Frankie taking a frozen pasta dinner out of the microwave, Georgia perched on the counter next to her. Frankie floated around the kitchen to grab a paper towel, her movements somehow both clumsy and light in her floral wrap dress. "Edie, how are you?" she asked.

Edie warmed to Frankie's words.

"I'm good. Just tired from school stuff." She threw her arms around Georgia and slumped against her body. "They won't give us a break."

Georgia laughed. "We have to go get ready, Momma." She gave Frankie a fast kiss on the cheek.

"Make sure your phones are on, okay?" They both nodded and turned to leave for Georgia's room.

"Oh, and call me when you get there," Frankie yelled after them.

They fumbled down the hallway. Edie dumped her bag out on the bed and looked critically at the clothes that spilled out. She held them up against her body. A simple red crop top caught her attention.

"Too much?" Edie asked, holding it up.

Georgia turned away from the mirror where she'd been looking at her own potential outfit on a hanger against her body.

"Too little. In the best way possible." They laughed and settled into an easy quiet as they put their clothes on.

They'd always been this comfortable with each other. They'd met in middle school, the only two girls in an advanced writing course their school offered. Georgia wrote long stories about Korean girls suspiciously similar to herself falling in love and Edie couldn't help but ask her for every detail. *Does the dad ever find out about Callie's depression? When the cat runs away, does that mean something? What happens at the end?* Georgia answered every question like a professional, refusing to have holes in her stories. Even after the writing class was over for the year, Edie kept reading her work and asking for more chapters printed out on crisp white paper from the library printer. They became close friends over highlighted sentences and words crammed into tiny margins.

They ended up at the same high school, and when Georgia told her she had fallen in and out of love with a girl in a city far away over the summer break before ninth grade, Edie listened as if she were telling another one of her stories, every detail of the utmost importance.

Edie pulled the top over her head and tugged the fabric until it curved around her skin. The straps of the bra she'd been wearing looked silly peeking out under the crop top, so she slid it off beneath the top.

Georgia looked Edie up and down as she tugged at the shirt. "Do you think you'll ever let Ben meet your parents?"

Edie stopped adjusting the outfit around her body and looked up. "No."

"Edie," Georgia urged.

"I know, but it's not like I don't want to. It's my parents. The nonbinary thing." She frowned at her own words, the weight of them heavy as she slid on her skirt. She suddenly felt cold and fully unprepared for Ben's birthday party. "Ben said they were fine with it."

"Well sometimes, people lie when they're in love," Georgia muttered, her head stuck in the neck of a tank top with the word LOVER written out in black, a small white bow sewn to the dip of the neckline

"You think Ben is in love with me?" Edie turned to grab her shoes from the bed.

"What? You've been dating for like five months." Georgia pulled her head through a plain white dress and smoothed her hair down with both hands. "Have they not said it?"

"Not yet." Edie felt herself shrink down to the size of a crumbled straw wrapper at the admission. She slid her earrings in and shoved her feet into her shoes quickly and without much care. She could feel Georgia's gaze on her back but was too afraid to meet it.

Ben hadn't told her they loved her yet, because she hadn't let them. She liked Ben. She liked how they knew everything about her. She liked their freckles and unwillingness to say anything mean towards anyone. She couldn't love them though. Because loving them meant being exactly what she feared most, a disappointment to her parents. She thought of it as a problem for future Edie.

"It's okay, E." Georgia pulled Edie into a quick hug. "Let's go before the party dies a sad death."

They slipped out the door past Frankie and started out into the night.

THREE

February 28, Thirty-One Days to Deadline

Dawn shut the medicine cabinet and met her reflection in the mirror on the opposite side. She leaned into the mirror to get the lipstick just right. It looked good on her the way it did in the store. The thick red of it let her be exactly who she wanted to be, who she was on her way to becoming. A fearless beauty. Her dust-brown hair settled in a soft pool around her naked collarbones.

As she moved to her bedroom, she let her mind wander to outfits. She'd picked something out two nights ago but worried the spontaneity she wanted to project would be ruined by the premeditation. She let the thought go and grabbed the top she'd placed at the front of the closet. She yanked it from its place on the hanger and let the shimmery silver material curve around her flat chest and settle on her form.

She always thought of her body as something to get along with, a well-meaning coworker at a job she wasn't allowed to quit. She borrowed Edie and Georgia's clothes every now and then but was too tall for anything to fit her correctly. As she leaned into the closet, a clear divide revealed itself between her old clothes piled into a small mountain on the left and her new wardrobe. She looked at herself in the top again and shut the door.

She saw her room as dreamy and elegant despite the messiness of it. She liked its smallness, the single window, how there was nothing for her to do except read and think and then read again. She shimmied on some jeans and stuffed a bag with a jacket, some pajamas, her wallet, and keys then stepped out into the hallway.

There were only three rooms in her home besides the kitchen so anything that happened in the house happened everywhere.

She treaded into the living room and moved her hand to the doorknob. Dawn looked around the space. The cool blue of a single fluorescent lamp played against the empty living room like a shadow box. One sofa, one chair, two bookshelves bookless and longing. The emptiness of it felt like a second body in the room.

"I'm leaving, Papa."

She stood and listened and noticed her breath. One inhale. Two. Three. No reply came from the echoing walls of her little house. The low glow of night bathed her brown skin slowly as she shut the door behind her.

The top of the parking garage was warm and light with wind. People crowded around each other, dancing and gossiping about all that had happened between the last party and this one. The neon lights coming from people's phones, the tacky outfits, the crooked teeth; they played frantically in her wide eyes and she tried to adjust to all the stimulation. Dirty cigarette butts burned out beneath her feet and the familiarity of it all warmed her to the evening.

As she stood looking for familiar faces, namely Georgia and Edie, the parking garage became crowded and hot with the presence of wandering bodies. Small iron railings along the edge of the garage created lines in the scene of the city spread out below. People Dawn recognized and didn't recognize let themselves fall in and out of her view.

Dawn turned her head towards the sound of her name and saw Georgia motioning for her to come over, a simple white fringe dress tinkling frantically against her body as she moved her hand back and forth. Edie trailed behind with Ben. They were wearing a bright pink sash that said "Birthday Girl," the "Girl" crossed out in Sharpie and replaced with a poorly scribbled "Person" on top of their typical uniform of a tie-dye shirt and jeans cut short above their knees.

Dawn hadn't seen Edie and Georgia since that afternoon and thought they looked so good. Edie wore an apple-red crop top that dipped just above her belly button where a flowing white skirt draped downward to her feet, and Georgia's dress and matching earrings gave her a fairy-like look. Much better than the sweat-pants-as-daywear monsters second semester of senior year had turned them all into. The night was open, and she felt its potential energy buzzing deep beneath her skin.

She exchanged hugs with everyone and told Ben happy birthday. She couldn't afford a present for them but noticed the lack of gifts around and felt grateful. Georgia and Dawn made faces as Edie and Ben got lost in each other's kisses and moved towards the makeshift dance floor.

"I've missed you," Georgia said as she gathered both of Dawn's hands into her palms.

Dawn saw Georgia and Edie as guiding lights in the dank sewer drain of Alsbury High School. She'd met Edie wandering the halls of Alsbury a few days after she'd transferred there sophomore year. Georgia was her warmup partner the very first volleyball practice she'd ever attended the next semester. They were both so bad. They'd spend entire practices shoving volleyballs under their shirts, pretending they were rich pregnant housewives of River Oaks. Ben was nice too; they'd met when Edie brought them as a plus-one to watch *Paris Is Burning* together for the third time at Georgia's house. The most important people in Dawn's life seemed to appear during her first moments in new spaces. She thought it was exciting and romantic that she could be just a car ride away from some new, unknowable love.

"Are you okay? Do you want to dance?" Georgia's voice was scratchy and strained against the music so that Dawn only caught the words *want* and *dance*.

Dawn wanted nothing more. She needed to dance and feel her body as worthy of movement, as capable of something good beyond her own understanding, excused from its innumerable failures with boys, with mirrors, with itself. She saw Edie and Ben enveloped into each other across the floor and grabbed Georgia's hand so they could move towards the mass of dancing bodies.

After what felt like hours of music flowing from the top of her head and into the rest of her limbs, Dawn caught another sight of Edie and Ben dancing sweetly across the dance floor and began to feel her body and feet aching as she grew tired of thrashing around to the fast-paced, angry beat of the latest song. She wandered towards the edge of the garage quietly. Dawn looked up and saw a single constellation through the city's clouds, maybe Orion's Belt. Looking around again, she saw Georgia and Jill Moger talking on the lawn chairs set up in the corner. Dawn had seen them flirting at parties for months but Georgia still hadn't said anything to her or Edie about it yet. Georgia didn't usually mention girls until she was sure about them, so Dawn and Edie had a running bet on when she would bring Jill up. Dawn watched as Jill let her butt-length licorice hair swing out to drape over Georgia's lap as she whispered something in her ear.

Dawn swung her legs out over the edge of the building and reached her hand out towards the bumbling lights of the city. Here is the skin, she thought. Here is the hand. Here is the thumb and the forefinger. Here is the moon. Here is the body swimming over the night. Here is the sound of every weed creeping up through the hot, Houston cement.

"Soda?" A gentle hand came into her view and then a golden boy.

"With alcohol?" Dawn smiled up towards him.

"Nope. Ben thought it'd be a bad idea to mix drinks with several people hundreds of feet above the ground."

She quickly looked him up and down as he bent down to her level. The warm lights of the parking garage shined against his eyes and illuminated their green and brown flecks, his smile edging gently at sharp cheekbones. Against the noise of the party, his voice cut her up and melted her down again. She let her eyes wander over his just-unfolded clothing and sandy brown hair as he ushered one of the plastic red cups to her hands.

She brought the drink to her lips and downed it all in one gulp. In an attempt to place the cup on the ledge, it wobbled from its place and slipped to the shadows below. She watched it all the way until it hit the ground and got swept into the street.

"Ben is a very smart kid."

"You're Dawn, right?" He looked at her and settled comfortably into a spot beside her on the ledge. Their thighs touched and she held in a ridiculous scream at the warm feeling of their skin being together.

She nodded.

He seemed to be humming all around her with the electricity of the night inside of him. His prettiness made her tired, she felt so extremely aware of how she looked to him, so alert, but she liked the feeling of fatigue.

She watched his fingers press into the other cup, the fingernails like waning crescent moons. She couldn't keep herself from imaging his hand on her wrist, thigh, waist, pressing into her, crushing. She liked the feeling of worms turning over the dirt of her stomach as he spoke.

"I'm Knox. Ben told me you were making a movie or something?"

"Yeah," she offered dully.

Every day she spent hours writing out ideas for the film in her notebook or editing clips she'd already recorded. She wanted so badly to share her friends' stories.

"What's it about?"

"Queer love."

This was true and untrue. It was so much more. It was a documentary about something she wanted but couldn't have. She found herself desperate to document queer love and all its caveats and inconveniences. She wanted to identify it, hold it, know that it could be hers one day. Among all the love in the world, did some of it not rest in the hands of a few lucky queer people?

The idea of her documentary felt powerful and correct in her mind. She wanted to tell a story she thought couldn't be told by anyone else. Or, if it could, she hadn't seen it yet. She didn't care if it wasn't perfect, she just needed it to exist. Love was like a Christmas list of gifts she knew were too expensive but that she couldn't stop stupidly asking for year after year anyway.

For the past four months, she'd been filming her friends responding to questions about love and queerness. She wanted to know everything. Breakups, hookups, how to ask someone out, how queer love looks, why people were afraid of her and her body and her beauty. She needed to know everything.

Dawn wanted love to surround her like flurried pollen in April. If she couldn't have it, at least she could witness it. She could hold it right in front of her in digital intervals of light, sound, and color.

"Like Scorsese or Kubrick?" he asked.

"More like Chytilová and Jennie Livingston become best friends and make a documentary," Dawn laughed, regretting dropping her cup, her hands feeling empty now.

"Who?" His head tilted slightly to the right like a child's.

"Yikes." The party seemed to get louder around them as they talked. Dawn tried hard to focus on his words but kept getting distracted by the music and the little dent in his cheek that appeared whenever he smiled at her.

"What's it called?"

"What?"

"The documentary." He asked, his smile curving its way up again to the dent and sending Dawn's mind into a haze.

"Um, *The Queer Girl Is Going to Be Okay*. I mean, it's not all about queer girls—"

"Oh, cool."

"Like, I interview nonbinary people and gay cis people and lesbians, pretty much anybody I'm friends with. It's just, when I started making it, I did these really shitty videos of my two best friends who are girls and myself on my phone camera, and the idea kind of just went from there so the title stuck." Dawn could hear herself talking too much but sensed that he was really listening, taking in each and every word with a small nod. It was a new and unfamiliar feeling and she loved it immediately.

"Hmm, well since you're letting just *any* gay in, how can I, a queer who loves, be in it?"

"We aren't friends yet," Dawn said. And yet she couldn't stop herself from liking everything about him immediately. She liked to think he was born on the elevator up to this party and had emerged on the other side of the doors fresh and untouched by all the ugliness she knew could store itself inside the hearts of real-world teenage boys.

"But we could be."

"I'll think about it," she laughed, trying to play it cool.

"Well, while you're thinking about it, do you want to maybe get out of here?" he said, his now empty cup spinning between his busy fingers.

Dawn looked around for the right answer. There was Edie, Georgia, Ben, the party. She couldn't leave them for some boy she'd just met. She'd promised herself to stop doing that. She lifted her head from the soaking bucket of hazy thoughts and squeezed out all the excess into the chilly night.

"I can't," she said. *Stupid, stupid, stupid*, she thought.

"Too bad. What about Saturday? I live next to Gremler Market. We could hang out there."

"Yeah, that sounds good." Her heart knocked against her chest hard and fast. She didn't like it but couldn't help but place her hand over her rib cage to try to remember the intensity of the feeling for later when she thought of this moment. Knox stood, his hand brushing her leg as he moved from the ledge.

"I'll see you around?" He walked backwards towards the still-moving crowd of hot, dancing bodies. He smiled again, waiting for her response.

"Yeah," Dawn breathed out. She watched him disappear into the mass of people and Dawn felt her chest expanding unreasonably beneath her shirt.

Midnight came and went and stragglers began to plan a mass exodus to Whataburger for late-night burgers and fries.

Ben, Edie, and Georgia came to sit with Dawn in a grouping of pink lawn chairs she'd laid claim to as people emptied from the garage.

"Congrats, D. Edie told me about the film festival." Ben smiled at her and toyed with the rings on Edie's fingers as they held hands over the arms of the plastic chairs.

"Oh, thanks. I'm starting to realize how stressed I actually am. Like, I need to win." Dawn closed her eyes tight and tried to quiet the thoughts those words brought up in her.

Ben lit up. "Wait, didn't you win that short film fest last year for your video about the gym teacher's art car with the clowns all over it?"

"Oh yeah, that was incredible. You got this. Easy," added Edie.

"Yeah, but that didn't have a full ride to film school as the prize," Dawn replied with a deep breath.

Ben pursed their lips into a small circle and let a whistle out. "Jesus, wow."

"Exactly. I could even get somebody to take care of my dad."

The group quieted. Dawn never talked about her dad or really anything that happened after the girls dropped her off at her front door in the afternoons after school, or in the evenings after jumping out of some guy's window. Not even on those late nights when the moon is high and nineties songs are blaring from the radio of somebody's Toyota Corolla and everybody's worst secrets and fears come out in whispers over the hum of the engine.

They didn't mind this. Dawn always seemed to have everything under control, so they didn't push her for information.

"What, like you'd use your savings?" asked Georgia.

"I mean, I have a couple thousand dollars from when I worked at the bookstore and babysitting for that rich family in West University." Dawn tried to do some quick math in her head but ended up with a jumble of numbers floating in the blank space.

"I thought that was for college," said Edie, always the reasonable voice.

"My dad needs a caretaker," Dawn uttered out. "Either I find a way to pay for one and college, or I have to stay home."

"As in, not go to school?" Georgia asked, her voice approaching a screech. "Dawn, no. You've been talking about film school since the literal day we met. I remember thinking, this girl talks a lot about movies."

"I know, I know. I applied to a bunch of schools, but even if I get in somewhere, I don't know if they're going to give me any money."

Dawn looked around and noticed that the four of them were the only ones left at the party.

"So, what's the deal with your friend Knox?" She tried to sound casual and not completely obsessed.

"What do you mean?" Ben questioned, folding their legs over and squeaking in the lawn chair.

"Like, what's he about? What's his deal?" Dawn asked again.

"Oh," Ben exclaimed, recognition flowing over their face. "He's nice. Not straight, I think. Listens to a lot of Kim Petras. We met at a soccer camp thing when I was younger. He's a really good baker. Like, he would bring all these pastries for everyone to eat after practice and they were so good, so we asked where he got them one day, turns out he'd been making them. That was wild. I mean really, there was an eclair that I still think about to this d—"

"Babe, focus. We need crush info, not his whole life story." Edie placed a light hand on Ben's now fidgeting hands.

"Oh. No, yeah. He's nice, I guess. Sorry, I don't really know him super well," they said, pulling their phone from their pocket with their free hand.

"A nice baker who listens to my favorite German pop princess. Good to know." Dawn tried not to get too ahead of herself as Ben held their phone up to the circle with the time flashing on the center of the glowing screen.

"Time to go for me." Dawn bent her knees to stand from the chair.

"I'm taking you home, right?" Georgia asked, standing up from her seat with a small groan.

Dawn nodded and looked towards Edie and Ben.

"Are y'all good?"

"Yeah. We're just going to go to my place," Ben answered.

"Happy birthday, my star. Love you, E." Dawn bent down to give Ben a hug and then Edie. "See you Monday, Ben?"

"Second period Physics. My favorite waste of time." Ben laughed and grabbed Edie's hand again.

Georgia and Dawn made sure they had their phones and disappeared from the parking garage.

FOUR

The ride home was silent except for the occasional slurping noise of a lemon-lime soda Ben had picked up from Whataburger on the way home.

"You okay?" Ben asked. Edie stared at Ben's lips as they formed the *o*, then *a*. She thought about their objectively perfect mouth and the way they only ever drove with one hand.

It was easy to love them when they always smelled like mint and said things like "what the heck is up" when they really just meant hello. Their crooked singing voice on early mornings before homeroom, bending notes to fit where they obviously didn't.

"I just like you," Edie breathed out with a light sigh.

Ben turned to look at Edie as they exited the highway to their neighborhood.

"I have a gift for you when we get to my house," Ben professed to the quiet car.

"It's your birthday. You can't have a gift for me," Edie uttered, mocking offense. "It's not allowed."

"It's not a big gift, don't worry. Actually, I'll just tell you."

Edie laughed. They could never hold secrets or surprises. Ben's capacity for secrets was like a cup of water already spilling over on itself.

"I bought us pillows that are lavender-scented." Ben smiled wide and stared as Edie's face went from expectant to confused.

"Because . . ."

"Because you said mine were too flat," Ben exclaimed. Their speech began to rush in explanation. "I saw some fluffy ones at the store and they said 'scented.' I remembered you said a while back when we were walking by that elementary school and saw that lavender bush, you said it was your favorite. So, I don't know. Is that dumb?" They looked up at Edie for a response.

"No, not at all. Thank you." Edie felt something welling up in her chest but tried to let it snuff out like a dying flame. She was not going to say I love you. She was not going to admit to herself that she was not the person her parents wanted her to be. She knew she wasn't but still, saying the words out loud would be the final step.

"Yeah, no problem."As they pulled off to the feeder road, they reached their right hand to rest on Edie's thigh.

"Hey, is it okay if I go home?" asked Edie, drawing a heart on the heat-fogged window with her finger.

"Oh. What's wrong?" Ben tried to hide their disappointment but Edie could hear it in every word.

"Nothing. I'm just not sure if I told my parents I was staying overnight somewhere. You know how they are." She cursed herself for lying to them. The guilt was a leaden blanket over her whole body.

"No problem." Ben turned the wheel quietly, heading in the opposite direction of their house. They were silent but Edie could feel their sadness.

"I'm sorry. I don't want them to get upset. It's just easier."

Edie hated upsetting her parents, or, she liked them not being upset with her. She loved when they beamed at her, approval lacing their words as they bragged about her to fellow churchgoers of Sundays. It felt good, almost like she could make up for the biggest failure of all, her queerness. When they approved of her, she could almost see it cancelling out her relationship with Ben, her personhood. *Yes, it's true. I'm queer,* she could imagine herself saying one day when she was braver and stronger. *But, hey! Remember? I was valedictorian! I got into Cornell! All your friends think I'm a golden child! You used to really like me. Doesn't that mean something? Doesn't it? Doesn't that count for anything?*

"No, I get it," Ben said. Another moment went by with the air massive and silent between them. "I think if they met me, they'd get it. We could probably hang out way more." They stared out at the changing streetlights and kept driving and driving.

"Yeah maybe." Which was her cheap way of ending the conversation where she was comfortable. Ben crept the car to a stop around the corner from Edie's house and put it in park. They turned to Edie as she twisted to pick up her purse from the backseat.

"Happy birthday, Ben." They kissed for way too long and the lights from the house they were parked in front of came on like a flood.

They laughed and shared another fast kiss.

"I love you." Ben went red at the realization of their words. They said it like it was nothing. Like it was another way to say goodbye.

Edie grabbed the door handle and looked out at the rows of suburban houses. She turned back to them and looked at their downturned face.

"I hope you had a really good day," she murmured, the sound of a sprinkler coming on in the neighbor's lawn making the words soft and muddy.

She got out of the car fast, afraid to look back at Ben's face. As she listened to Ben pull off into the neighborhood, Edie leered up at the night sky where scattered stars twinkled through the city's light pollution.

A few steps towards her house and she realized she'd left her bike and backpack at Georgia's house. She turned around and began the long walk.

On Dawn's ride home with Georgia, everything in her mind was Saturday with Knox. Nothing was anything else. The nasty gum that got stuck on her shoe when she got out of the car was Saturday. The men at the bus stop she walked past who drenched her in glares were Saturday. Her home was Saturday.

Walking through the chipping green frame of her front door, Dawn felt like she could collapse from tiredness. Something sleepy seeped into her skin as the stuffed air of the place pushed up against her. It disappeared after a moment.

Dawn always thought that people could never really know what their own home smelled like. They're too close to it. Dawn liked to imagine her house smelled like the torn wet petals she stepped on when crossing in front of her neighbor's house after it rained. The brutal pink of them emitted a sweet dying smell that she loved.

In reality, her home reeked of sweat and heavy warm odors, dank scents and dust easily caught in the yellowing carpet.

"Dawn?"

Sound swept from the bedroom into the open space where Dawn stood. Her father's voice was hymnal-like, all monotone low rumbling. She kept quiet for several seconds. *Saturday, Saturday, Saturday.*

"Dawn? You bring home some food?"

Nothing. She took a breath and let the silence settle in a moment too long.

"Yeah."

"Don't say *yeah*. Say *yes*. You know your mother hated that."

Even from bed, his voice echoed weak demand. Settling her purse onto the kitchen counter, Dawn played with the idea of leaving to hook up with a guy she'd met on some app a few weeks ago. They'd hung out a few times, and though she didn't like him, she liked validation and warmth and closing her eyes really tight so that she could pretend she was in a honeymoon house in Maine with the seaside lapping at a cliff's edge and not some bedroom in the Heights with a boy who did not love her. She was too young for him or maybe he was too old for her, she was still deciding.

"Come in here. I haven't seen you."

The lights in his bedroom were turned off, a TV in the corner playing old episodes of *Wheel of Fortune* between long blocks of infomercials. It was his favorite show. It was all he did when he was in one of his depressive states.

He lay with the blankets messily wrapped around him, two strips of shallow light from a streetlamp coming in from behind the deep purple curtain across the only window. The low glow played against his light brown skin. The rest of the room was filled with newspapers and little projects he'd never finished: model airplanes, birdhouses, a ramp for something to slide down. The scene made Dawn sad like a movie would.

Peter Salcedo used to be a man with his chest out to the world. Every morning was cold orange juice and a project to be completed by sundown. She liked to remember him this way, as he was before her mother's death her freshman year.

"What did you get?"

"Chicken from Whataburger." She stepped forward to the bed.

"You look thin."

"I'm fine."

She pulled his right hand from beneath the swathing and extended it towards her. His long nails were yellow around the curved edges.

She grabbed his hand, careful to place his fingers in her palm like a child's. His skin was cold despite the blankets. This is the one thing that had not changed about him. *Cold hands,* he would always say, *are a sign that my insides are as warm as can be.* This never made sense to Dawn, even now.

"You really do look a little skinny."

"I'm fine. Have you left the bed today?"

He shook his head no. "Too tired. Maybe tomorrow."

"Okay, Papa. I have to go."

She dropped his hand and watched as it flopped stiffly to the bed.

The door of his bedroom shut behind her like clockwork. She shot a message to the boy in the Heights and watched as his response popped up on the screen seconds later. The chicken sat stupidly on the counter where it would remain greasy and uneaten until she came home again early in the morning.

FIVE

I guess I knew in seventh grade. This girl, Katie Stuckey, she would eat these oranges in her packed lunch, the mini ones. She was my best friend, or, we were good friends. And she would do this thing where she would peel the little orange in one whole peel. I found it so intriguing. Sexy, maybe. I'm not sure. Her fingers were always a little sticky after lunch. All the peel would be stuck under her fingernails so that it looked like she'd painted her nails orange but only at the tip. I died to hold her hand. I would make up games just to touch her fingertips. I guess I just thought no one else in the world could peel an orange in one go. So, yeah. That was it. Katie Stuckey. Katie Stuckey. Ka-tie Stuck-ey. It's like a song, right?

"Georgia, you are so amazing," Dawn said turning off her camera and looking up from the small digital screen.

Dawn had set up the old band room at Alsbury as a studio for her film. The empty room served as a quiet space for interviews. It was all the way at the end of the English wing, so no one ever walked in on her during filming. She'd hung up an orange vinyl background on poles, and the hue brought Georgia's skin a bright-ness even in all the dust and somber of the classroom.

Georgia looked as though she were sitting for a portrait. Each interview had a different background color, and Dawn thought orange was perfect for her. She tried to match each color to the person who was talking. Some of her friends were a bright blue, some a dingy yellow. Georgia's answers were bold and direct, so the sunny color made sense behind her. She didn't feel the need to nestle her truth into the ellipses between her words.

"Thank you so much for coming."

"No problem," she offered. "Any excuse to talk about myself."

Georgia slid off of the round stool and let her feet hit the white and black speckled linoleum.

"Very funny." Georgia's interview was shorter than many of the others Dawn had filmed. Some people stretched on and on about their lives, their intimacies. Dawn was always surprised at how open people could be in front of the camera, as if she had stepped out of the room, and now, they were talking to themselves or God or some friend who knew them deeply and terribly.

"Are you excited for Saturday?" asked Georgia, a small smirk sneaking its way onto the edge of her smile. "With Knox?"

"Not really. I mean, I am, but I don't want to be," Dawn sighed as she looked around for the camera case. Her hand moved to the lens, the body, the plush case and all its compartments.

She took apart the camera delicately and placed it back into its bag. Each piece had a place, and she knew each one like children she had to tuck into bed.

She finished and all her little failures began to knock against each other in her head like marbles. Boys and girls with their expectations and soft hands and words digging into Dawn like a shovel into dry earth.

Their names were a found poem of disappointments in her head.

Brian
Sergei
Alexia
Marco
Mother
Fucking
Assholes

Hoping was for nice girls. For girls who were going to marry the first person who was nice back. She didn't let herself do it. It was a luxury owned primarily by girls who didn't know better because they didn't have to. Who didn't know that all boys want is to stick their hands in your mouth and make you cry. Dawn felt she knew this thoroughly, a veteran of late nights spent in backseats and bedrooms that all seemed to smell like the same armpit slathered in the same deodorant over and over again.

"I'm just so tired of all these high expectations leading to nothing because people are so fucking scared of me. It's like, why did you ask me out?"

Dawn wondered if she meant this. Maybe she liked the constant game of *I lose, you win*. Maybe under several layers of chill and Saran Wrap, her heart was beating too hard and fast to be ignored by mediocre boys. Maybe she wanted the attention so badly she was willing to suffer the multitude of hurts and losses that came with it.

None of the answers seemed right. She needed respect and sweetness. An avalanche of gentle love needed to slide down the mountain of her stupid, ever-present want. Georgia interrupted her thoughts.

"But also, Ben says he's pretty cool, so just give him a chance before you decide he hates you."

Georgia helped Dawn pick up the equipment with overly careful movements.

"I know. Are you going to Government?"

"Nah, I'm gonna skip. I have to go to the library. Want to come?"

"Can't. I have to do some prep for my meeting with the college counselor next week." Georgia moved to the corner of the room where a dusty drum kit and a stack of horn cases rested. "Text me how the date goes though, okay?" She snatched her bag from the floor and slung it over one shoulder with ease.

After a quick hug, Dawn watched her spill out into the hall during the busy passing period.

Dawn fixed her own bags on her shoulder and tried to escape the deep well of thoughts that seemed to occupy every single moment since Knox had asked her out. She would be fine. She had to be.

To Georgia, Alsbury High School was the stuff of nightmares. It was a public school she'd tested to get into, something the school district called a magnet program. Every student was constantly slammed with homework and advanced courses, the school administration's attempt at keeping up Alsbury's image of high performance and academic excellence.

Georgia was dreading her meeting with the counselor. Every upperclassman had three mandatory talks with Alsbury's college counselor, Mrs. Jimenez, and since the end of senior year was approaching, her last one was next week. She had been rejected from every single school she applied to except one, and even that was not an actual acceptance, but a waitlist. A sentence without a period. She had no idea what to do next.

Almost everyone at Alsbury got into great schools, even the kids who didn't try very hard. It was just that kind of place. People fought to keep their spots in the top ten percent, and for the most part, everyone took everything about school very seriously. Extracurriculars were not just fun activities students enjoyed and cared about, but competitive résumé boosters to impress colleges. If you weren't president or vice president of the Future Medical Professionals of America Club or Math Honor Society, or at least trying to obtain either position, you might as well not even show up. Freshman year, Georgia tried hard to fit in, forgetting about her middle school writing days, securing her spot as secretary of Alsbury's intersectional feminism club, struggling with Edie's help to maintain B grades in subjects that made no sense to her. The difficulty of classes increased sophomore year, and she found herself flailing, her only success a creative writing elective Alsbury offered once a week. She was happy there, good at every new form introduced by the kind but overworked English teacher, excited to float away into her own made up worlds every time she entered the classroom.

All Georgia ever wanted to do was write. She applied to English programs and a few biology programs at different universities because she thought that's what she was supposed to do. It got her absolutely nowhere. All she had to her name was a waitlist spot with no guarantee. She was an underachiever among stars. Her worst fear was being left behind while Edie and Dawn traveled far away for school and made new friends. They'd both already gotten into several colleges and Edie had even picked one, Cornell. She suddenly felt incredibly upset with herself for not putting in more work.

Georgia split off to the school's entrance and began to walk out to her car.

The walls of the school were painted a sickly teal and had yellow tiles lining the ceiling and floor. Alsbury didn't really have a mascot since no one played any sports, but there was a huge rhino mural painted on the wall towards the entrance, so maybe that was it. She wouldn't describe her experience as a bad one, she'd met great people and been challenged over and over, but still, Alsbury was this huge thing dragging her down for the last four years, a set of endless academic expectations she couldn't live up to. Edie and Dawn were the only good things about it.

She pulled out her phone and started a text to Jill, the girl she'd recently decided was wonderful and even potentially her favorite person. She sat down on a bench near the school's parking lot to send the message, a precaution she took ever since chipping her tooth after tripping while text-walking.

As soon as she started to type, a message popped up.

> **JILL:** *how's your day going, bub?*
> **GEORGIA:** *good! heading home early, tho. i feel gross. think i need to apply 2 more schools??*
> **JILL:** *ew, college*
> **GEORGIA:** *we get it, junior.*
> **JILL:** *do u wanna come over tonight? we never finished moonrise kingdom*
> **GEORGIA:** *hell yeah. u know how i love reckless adolescent love. i need to finish some notes for art history first tho. 9?*
> **JILL:** *yeah. i'll get snacks. byeeee bby*

Everything was easy with Jill. They liked all the same things: Wes Anderson, street tacos, expressionist paintings, and narrative poems with metaphors about bodies of water.

Georgia liked being liked. They'd met in feminism club where Georgia opened up a meeting once with a rant about the lack of women in the AP English Literature syllabus. Jill fiercely agreed with her argument and shared her number so they could recommend books they actually wanted to read to each other. They'd been talking every day since.

She had dark hair that Georgia liked to call her nest because of the way she tended to stuff the sleek black mass under a baseball cap to control its unruly length. She was pretty, ivory skin sprinkled with peach-colored birthmarks in the oddest shapes along her arms and legs.

Georgia pushed her phone into her pocket and pulled her carabiner of keys from her belt loop to unlock her car. She needed to go home and think of a new plan.

SIX

March 8, Twenty-Three Days to Deadline

Gremler Market sat nestled behind a small farming settlement off the Sam Houston Tollway. Vendors set up their stock early Saturday mornings in the hopes that passersby would pull off of the tollway, make a full loop, and buy fresh fruit and local honey. The sign peeking out from behind the settlement was faded and ugly. Pale red letters read *Saturday Farmer's Market* over wood panels that had ceased to fit the term "white" several years ago. Dawn sat beneath the sign on an equally downtrodden white bench. She was early by five minutes, a lesson her mother taught her: five minutes early for a date is on time, and on time is late. Part of her didn't want him to come.

Dawn had spent the morning looking at herself over and over again in the mirror. The denim fabric of her skirt hit her ankles and made her feel like she could twirl and become more beautiful with each rotation. Her t-shirt was white and tucked into the waistband. She hoped the look implied a certain cool girl carelessness.

She wanted to be a cool girl. One of the confident ones, a pink lip gloss type of gorgeous. She wanted to revel in her kitchen hips, the open cabinet of her stocked with whatever it is boys and men thought they wanted. She wanted grace, which she defined as one's ability to share one's body with others.

Instead, she was stuck in front of a disappointing mirror that grew more and more unbearable each second she let it hold her gaze.

No outfit was good enough, no laugh loud enough. She smiled at her reflection, leaning into some imaginary joke Knox would tell her. *That's hilarious. Do you see how beautiful my teeth are? How my cheeks curve up and make me gentle, even desirable?* Each grin revealed the same her again and again, the same skirt, same body, so she did what all girls have to do at some point; she settled.

A hundred people must have passed her in the twenty-five minutes she waited on that bench.

The sun dragged itself across the market stopping just overhead the sign as though to mock Dawn. She didn't want to call. She didn't want to face rejection head on. For now, she was a girl with a date that was late, and hopefully, with a very good excuse.

She picked up her phone anyway and listened as the ring went on and on.

"Hello?"

"He didn't show, Geo."

Her voice went up then down again. *He didn't show.*

>   didn't

He   show.

She could hear the whine, the tiredness in her voice.

"God, that sucks. You're at Gremler, right?"

"Yeah. It's fucking hot."

"I can be there in twenty minutes. Want to go to Ruby Nails?"

Dawn looked up at the sun and squinted into its yellow heat. A pity pedicure could save her.

"I've never loved you more, you actual angel. I might walk around for a little bit while I'm waiting, so just text me when you get close."

"Totally. See you in twenty, twenty-five max. Love you."

As they exchanged goodbyes and hung up, Dawn settled into her newest disappointment. Another boy who was afraid of her, or didn't understand who she was, or respect her enough to say he just didn't like her.

The bench grew hotter beneath her thighs. She stood to leave and began to move into the maze of vendors.

"Dawn!"

Unfortunately, he looked perfect. Knox was more gorgeous than she remembered. The yellow stripes on his shirt made him seem boyish, innocent even.

"I'm so sorry. I had to take my little sister to her friend's house, but her friend hadn't made it back home from the grocery store yet. I couldn't just let her sit out there in the lawn, you know? She's only fourteen, so." He stuffed his hands in the pockets of his baby blue corduroy shorts as he said this, his eyes meeting the ground.

Relief ripped across Dawn's chest like rain.

"And my stupid phone never works. I mean, you have my number, but I don't have yours, and—" Dawn interrupted his rushed speech.

"It's okay. Let me text my friend really quick." And she meant it. Suddenly everything was okay.

She searched his eyes for some hint of a lie and found nothing but apologetic pleading. It was then that she finally noticed how tall he was. He was much taller than her, a rarity given her almost six-foot stature.

She texted Georgia quickly and let the smell of mangoes overwhelm her as they began to walk side by side into the stalls of fruit.

"Have you ever been here? They have the best pineapple."

"I don't think so."

"We gotta get some." He grabbed her hand and pulled her towards a makeshift wooden counter decorated with vines of fake orange flowers. She wondered if she was supposed to be so happy already. She wondered if she was supposed to feel his palm against hers all the way up past her wrist, past her shoulder, and straight into her already warming chest.

"Can I get two please?" Knox smiled towards the woman and pointed past her to the pineapples on the shelf behind her as she absentmindedly chopped strawberries and placed the bits into small plastic containers.

" ¿Qué?"

Dawn pointed behind her to the pineapples lined up.

"Dos piñas, por favor. ¿Cuánto cuesta?"

The woman's gaze turned. She began to speak to Dawn in rapid Spanish, the ends of words clipped off and thrown away as she rushed through sentences. Dawn kept up despite her infrequent use of the language.

The woman asked her where she was from, if she came to the market often. They talked about the heat and the Mexican treats she sold. She gave Dawn a free cocada. The golden brown, sticky mass was wrapped loose in wax paper and felt soft in Dawn's hand as she pulled four dollars out of her pocket.

The woman looked at the money, smiled at Dawn, and turned her stout figure to grab the fruit. She began slicing away the hard exterior and Dawn turned back to Knox. She'd almost forgotten he was there; she was so caught up in the conversation. It felt like childhood. Like speaking to her mother, or, her mother's ghost. A small, warm feeling came over her and she smiled to herself.

"We should go sit down or something. I think it might take a second." Dawn felt confidence bubbling up to the surface. She put his hand in hers and walked to the other side of the alley of stands.

"You speak Spanish?" He looked at her with amazement.

"My mom does, or, she used to."

"That's so cool. I barely made it through freshman year Spanish with Ms. Spain."

"You had a Spanish teacher named Spain?"

"Yeah, but she was from Bogotá and she didn't let you forget it." He lengthened the *o*'s and pronounced the *a* as *ah*. Dawn's laugh floated between them.

She felt herself drifting in and out of the details of Knox. First his lips, a gentle curve leading up to laugh lines at the edges of his eyelids.

She racked her mind for things to say. What did boys like to talk about when they didn't just want to sleep with you? She couldn't remember. They usually just talked at her. But now, here was Knox with his questions and interest in who she was as a person.

She wanted to ask him about his school, his life, but felt too shy like splashing into the shallow end of a huge pool. He mentioned his job, a lab technician working with plants. He went to school for botany. Dawn imagined him watering pots of exotic, colorful flowers in a high-tech room filled with greenery that went on for miles. He went on and on and Dawn kept putting more and more of the pieces together.

Knox was from Austin. When he was in high school, his whole family moved to Houston for his dad's job. He had met Ben in an intramural soccer league. Their party was the first time they'd ever hung out outside of practice. He was a freshman at the University of Houston. He played drums poorly and had an older brother, Mitchell, and a younger sister named Sarina. The one he'd been late for. She was fourteen, moody, and always liked to be right.

"Who *are* you?" Dawn interjected after a while. A confused look dashed across Knox's features. She instantly went red. What she meant was, *you seem very mature and interesting, setting you apart from almost every man I interact with daily at Alsbury.*

"¡Piñas!" the woman yelled from behind the counter. Dawn was grateful for the interruption of her silly question.

"Oh, I can grab it." She began to gather up her skirt and stand.

"No, I got it." He walked towards the woman holding out the expertly cut bright yellow fruits with a stack of folded napkins. He was so confident. She could tell even from behind, his back only curving forward slightly as if inviting the world in through his shoulders.

"Do you want to keep walking?" He held out a fork to her while balancing his own with the fruit.

"Sure." They began to weave into the sounds of the market. Vendors crouched beneath the blue tarps shading their merchandise surrounded by dolls and electronics. Dawn let little trinkets and shoes catch her attention while she thought about the good feeling bubbling up in her stomach.

"So, tell me some more about your movie." He tapped his fork against hers as another piece disappeared behind his lips.

"My what?" She snapped back to his voice, her thought frenzied between his soft, pink lips.

"Your documentary." As he spoke, the juice rolled down his chin and onto the back of his hands in pulps. She looked away to straighten out her thoughts.

"Oh. It's mostly a film about my friends. I just ask them what it's like to be queer or just LGBT+ in general. What it means for their sense of self, their family, their idea of community. Then, I ask them what it means to be queer and have love, want love. Whatever."

"That's pretty cool."

"I just feel like I ask myself these questions all the time, but everything is so personal, and everyone has their own answer. I want to hear what other people have to say. I want other people *to hear* what other people have to say. Does that make sense?" Dawn felt herself talking too much but couldn't stop.

"Yeah. It's like reading somebody else's diary so you can compare notes from your diary." He eyed her up and down as if for approval. *He really wanted to understand,* she thought.

"Something like that." As their conversation fell deeper into Dawn's work, Knox reached his hand over hers to hold hands. She almost stopped walking as his fingers reached for her palm but managed to relax as he intertwined their fingers.

"I have a surprise. I mean, I just came up with it, but it's still a surprise." He let go of her hand and moved behind her, placing both his palms over her eyes. She could feel him breathing against the back of her neck and tried to concentrate hard on pretending she was the kind of person that liked surprises.

They shuffled forward slowly for a few seconds and made a slight turn to the right. He lifted his hands.

"Pick some out." Dawn let her eyes adjust to the shaded area filled with bundles of flowers for sale. This was sweet. A sweet boy was doing something sweet for her.

Dawn began moving up and down the aisles smelling each bouquet. She got so close her lips touched the petals.

"I think marigolds are my favorite." She reached for the flowers and let the orange folds brush against her cheeks and hair.

"They're all yours for the small price of spending more time with me." Dawn looked up at him with a smile.

"If you want to, I mean." He thumbed the bottom of his shirt.

"That sounds nice." She took the flowers to the counter and imagined all the things she didn't normally allow herself to do.

She didn't say yes to dates. She didn't have fun on the dates she did say yes to. She didn't bring boys to her house. She didn't like the unpredictability of firsts. First moments, first dates, first boys. She wanted to be comfortable at all times. To know and be known. She liked to turn her camera on and know what was on the other side. She liked to think that Knox could be on the other side.

"Let's get out of here." Dawn held the flowers to her chest as Knox gathered her other hand gently. The warm afternoon fell against their backs and settled there.

SEVEN

The next week at school, Dawn had a bad idea. It occurred to her in English class, Edie and Georgia stuffed into too-small desks on either side of her.

Their teacher had handed out a worksheet and then stepped out to talk to the principal at the beginning of class and never returned, twenty minutes and then thirty passed without her presence, students quietly working on the assignment.

"I should buy a dress for the awards ceremony," Dawn said in no particular direction.

Dawn had been pressing herself as thin as paper trying to edit her interviews into some semblance of a full-length documentary for days. Ever since she'd been notified that she had a chance of winning a scholarship and prize money, she'd obsessively stared at her computer every night, eyes glazed over, trying to create something perfect. She needed to relax for a moment and indulge in some unwarranted optimism.

Georgia looked up from the book of Jericho Brown poems she'd been reading in place of the grammar assignment they were supposed to be working on. "Absolutely you should."

"Shopping trip?" inquired Edie. " I think I already have an excuse to be at school late today. I just need to be dropped off around the corner from my place because my parents think I'm with Joyce Abo doing Model UN stuff."

"Love that. I can drive us," Georgia offered. "I don't have anything today except that stupid physics project, but I think it's due midnight tomorrow."

"Nobody's started," reassured Dawn with an easy shrug. Edie nodded in agreement though Dawn was sure she was just being nice and had in fact already finished the project flawlessly in classic Edie fashion.

"I'm thinking something elegant and flowing, memorable and pretty, in case I win."

"Okay, Miranda Priestly. And I think you mean *when* you win, which you will," insisted Georgia.

"Please." Dawn sighed and reached for her backpack, where the untouched physics assignment sat smushed between two notebooks.

"It's called manifesting, duh," retorted Georgia.

Dawn looked down at the sheet of paper with its long list of requirements. "I need to manifest an A on this physics project."

Georgia shot her a look.

"Okay, okay." She flipped the paper over and took a deep breath. "I will win. And when I win, I will be wearing a nice dress from the Galleria."

Georgia practically shot up from her desk. "Yes, yes, and yes. I'm interested. I'm involved. I am a woman seeking an Orange Julius from the food court."

Edie tapped her pen against the desk a few times in thought. "Are you finished with all the interviews except ours? Ben told me to ask you again in case you needed AV help."

"How dare you ask such a thing," Dawn glowered in a flat tone.

"What?" Edie looked up suddenly, worried she'd said the wrong thing.

The line of Dawn's lips broke into a smile and she laughed as Edie's face went from one of concern to annoyance. "E, I'm totally kidding. Yeah, it's coming along okay. It's been just days and days using my old computer trying to make something happen with the edits. Sometimes it literally crashes right in the middle of my work. It feels like some sort of cruel cosmic joke at this point."

"Babe, just use one of ours." Georgia scrunched her eyebrows into that soft upward arrow of concern Dawn was so familiar with. "Or at least the computer lab upstairs."

"I know, but I've already edited over half the interviews I've done. I'm in so deep on my busted little laptop, bless her heart."

"What about an external hard drive?" Edie wrote her name at the top of the English assignment and leaned on her desk. "I think you can move stuff even if it's already edited. Or like, in a software."

"Are you kidding? Those things are like a hundred dollars, probably more. I can't get that *and* a dress and keep saving for someone to help out with my dad when I leave."

"We'll figure something out, D." Georgia leaned over to look at Edie's paper and began writing the answers on her own blank sheet. Dawn pulled out her own English assignment and did the same.

"It's fine, I just need to keep going," Dawn sighed as the class bell began to ring.

Georgia and Dawn quickly finished copying down Edie's answers to the assignment, their usual routine for mind-numbing classwork.

"Meet after last period?" Edie snatched up the finished papers and shuffled them into a neat stack.

"Yeah, I'll just pull my car around. Or, you guys can come to the garage with me."

"We'll just walk up with you, right D?"

Dawn nodded in agreement as she slung her bag over her right shoulder. "I gotta go meet some AV guys to help me with editing stuff. See you guys after French."

"Love you." Georgia rushed off to meet Jill for an early lunch.

"Love you, my little angel babies," crooned Dawn.

"Love you." Edie slapped the assignments onto their English teacher's desk and slipped out of class, peeling to the right to meet Ben before next period.

Edie thought back to her call with Ben call the night before. Ben had been a hovering blur of pixels on her screen as they Facetimed. They started by saying sorry, that they didn't want to pressure her into saying I love you but that it had come out like a huge bursting dam. Edie had laughed and so had Ben. They were back to normal. Everything was normal for now.

Edie walked the stairs of Alsbury with her hands gripped tight around her backpack straps. Her gait became a skip as she made her way up the stairs to the math wing where the rooftop garden faced the brightly lit hallway. Edie pushed her way through the glass doors to the garden and found Ben hunched over their phone on the huge concrete steps that lined the rows and rows of Texas wildflowers. It was their favorite spot to meet, just between both their fourth period classes on the second floor, always swirling with butterflies or lizards depending on the season.

"My darling, I've been looking for you everywhere." Edie brought the back of her hand up to her forehead, a damsel finally stumbling upon her suitor.

"My love!" Ben feigned an accent stuck somewhere between British and Australian. "I thought you'd never return." They dramatically dropped their phone and outstretched their arms to greet Edie with a hug.

"What's up, nerd?" Edie settled into a seat beside them.

"Just getting sucked into some articles about linguistics stuff, what about you?"

"Dawn wants to get a dress for the film festival, so we're going to the Galleria after school. What was your linguistic thing about?"

"You really want to know?" Ben asked.

"Duh. Can't have you outsmarting me," Edie teased. "I'm the brains in the relationship."

Given permission to spew their nerdy facts, Ben launched in. "Okay, actually, it's really cool. There's this thing called the bouba/kiki effect," Ben's eyebrows shot up as they talked, their words rushing to keep up with their enthusiasm.

"Uh huh."

"And basically, this German guy in the twenties was like trying to figure out if there was some connection between speech sounds and the visual shapes of objects. So fast forward and this other experimenter was like, we should look into that. So, he did an experiment where they showed people one spiky shape, and one blobby shape and asked them which one is bouba and which one is kiki. And like 90 percent of people said that said the blobby one was bouba and the spiky one was kiki."

"Oh, so it's like how your brain associates abstract stuff with words and shapes in the same way?" Edie asked, not completely understanding everything but trying her hardest.

"Exactly. Ugh, I knew I picked you for a reason." Ben kissed her on the cheek and laughed.

"So, which one am I?" Edie asked.

"Which what?"

"Shape." She said.

"Kiki, obviously."

"Oh good. I was worried we were not on the same page, my little Bouba." Edie tapped Ben lightly on the nose.

"I'm obviously Bouba." Ben looked down at their phone where they'd dropped it before and saw the time. "Oops, we gotta go. Fourth already started."

"Okay, call tonight?" Edie asked.

"Obviously." Ben smiled.

They quickly hugged and Ben started down the hall. Edie picked up her bag and walked in the opposite direction.

Ben yelled over their shoulder, "Bye, Kiki!"

Edie tilted her head down towards her feet and smiled. "Bye, Bouba."

The Galleria appeared over the highway as the girls listened to the final moments of a podcast they all loved, *Food 4 Thot*. The topic of that week's episode was queer-coded cartoon villains.

As they pulled into the mall's underground parking lot, Dawn declared her favorite villain as Maleficent while Edie and Georgia got stuck between Ursula and Scar.

They floated between a section of designer stores looking at things they and their mothers and their mother's mothers could never afford let alone want to buy.

Dawn's mother and father used to bring her to the Galleria on her birthday and let her pick out one thing. The date fell in late November, close enough to Christmas so that all her cards and gifts from family members seemed to imply that they should act as both. *Happy birthday and Merry Christmas to my lovely cousin. $10 so you can buy a new toy!*

She'd go straight for the Build-A-Bear every year without fail. She'd slowly built up a collection of roller-skating unicorns and dogs that wore intricate leather jackets. All of them were stuffed to perfection and emitted her three- or four- or seven-year-old voice when you pressed the plush foot or paw.

My name is Albert and I'm six. Today is my birthday.

Her mother's voice would emerge from the scratchy, now-old audio machine right after Dawn's.

Mommy and Daddy love you. Happy birthday!

They were her most prized possessions. She kept them all in the back of her closet, only bringing them out on particularly draining nights when she needed to be tucked in by her mother's kind tone, the gentle singsong of her voice.

Dawn shook loose from her memories and found herself in front of the window of a store she'd never seen before, some boutique. A single midnight-black dress shimmered in the display, the ground around it covered in fake clouds made of cotton glinting with silver glitter, which made the dress look even more angelic and sleek.

"Dawn, I think that dress was literally made for you. Holy shit," said Georgia turning to walk into the store.

Dawn froze and looked at the glittering fabric then shifted her gaze to the glowing letters of the storefront. *MOSSÉ* they read in neon-white lettering. She'd never heard of it, which probably meant it was too expensive for her to even walk into. A stout security guard stood at the entrance, eyes pointed out towards mall patrons, another sign she most likely couldn't afford a keychain let alone a dress from this place.

"I'm not going in there just to disappoint myself with some three-thousand-dollar dress."

Georgia rolled her eyes. "It could be on sale. You don't know! Plus, it's perfect. Come on." Georgia grabbed her by both hands and began to walk backwards into the abyss of too-nice clothing as Edie disappeared into a small section of intentionally ripped jeans at the front of the store.

As they moved past the security guard into the dimly lit store, Dawn went red, worried he'd heard their conversation.

"Please, Geo. I need to be realistic about—"

She went silent at the row of gorgeous gowns in the center of the space arranged in a spiral leading to her dress, the black dress. As she moved closer, she noticed how the dress was particularly well lit, the mannequin bent into an awkward, impossible pose. Headless, her arms squared forward, legs akimbo, as if to say *beauty hurts more than you could ever believe.*

Edie emerged from a rack of pastel orange cashmere sweaters.

"That's so pretty. You would murder in that dress. I would actually let you kill me in that dress." Edie laughed at her own joke as Dawn stepped forward to touch the fabric of the skirted lower half.

Two thin strips split into an impossibly low V-neck triangle and flowed downward in a silken form that cut just above the mannequin's ankles. Because she was tall, the dress would stop, below her knees instead. Dawn walked around to the back of the pedestal to find the dark blue tag hanging off the back of the gown by a single thick white thread. She picked it up and turned it over to find the price.

Her eyes met the number and she accidentally let out a little yelp.

"Oh no," she whined and looked up at Edie and Georgia with a visible pout. "The price is not cute or quirky. Y'all, can we please just get out of here?"

"Let me see," reasoned Edie reaching out for the tag, which was now swinging back and forth across the mannequin's back where Dawn had dropped it. "Oh, it's not *horrible*. I mean, it's a lot, but . . . it's not impossible." She tried to even her voice.

Georgia peered over at the number with its two zeros. "How much do you have to spend? We can help you."

"Thank you, but no freaking way. I'm not asking you guys to buy me a dress." Dawn sighed and started to think of other places they could go.

"We'd do that literally even if you weren't winning any award. You know that," Georgia declared, looking to Edie who started nodding instantly.

"At least try it on, D. It's the perfect dress for you. Seriously." Edie insisted.

"Fine," resigned Dawn. "But if my butt doesn't look perfect you both owe me froyo for emotional trauma."

They found the rack with the black dress on it and fingered through for Dawn's size. Luckily, her height helped her a bit in the looking-good-in-clothing-she-had-no-business-wearing department. She pulled her size and started looking to the back of the store for dressing rooms.

A woman who'd been hovering near the girls the whole time they'd been in the store emerged from behind a display of jewelry and walked Dawn to a row of fuzzy, emerald-green curtains that seemed to reach all the way to the ceiling. She gestured to Dawn with both hands as if she were marshalling a plane.

Dawn settled the dress on a hook next to the small, gold-framed mirror leaning against the far wall of the dressing room.

"Let me know if you'd like to try on anything else or another size," Her voice came through the other side of the curtain. "Need anything, ladies?" Dawn imagined she was talking to Georgia and Edie who'd planted themselves on a huge, pink velvet couch facing the dressing rooms. Dawn listened to the woman's footsteps fade to the other side of the store.

"Ugh, I can't wait for Austin," voiced Georgia from the other side of the curtain as Dawn reached for the hanger. "I found a couple of poetry readings that are actually happening the same weekend as the film fest. I guess writers come into town to see the films and end up arranging a bunch of events around the festival."

Dawn unzipped the side of the dress and tried to step into it but tripped over her own foot.

"Great, so we can eat good food Knox suggested, go to some readings, watch Dawn win like a hundred thousand dollars, and then turn back around. Very chill weekend." Edie chuckled as Dawn lifted the dress over herself, a new tactic.

Her first date with Knox had been on her mind lately, his softness, the plush curve of his smile. She tried to keep the overrunning thoughts of him to a minimum, the film her first priority, but she couldn't help the creeping up, the little daydreams of holding his hand. They'd been texting, his excitement for Austin fueling her own.

"Exactly. I can't believe we have to wait another three weeks. If I have to listen to Principal Ramos tell us how great 'we' all did on some standardized test one more time, I'm going to scream." Georgia muttered. "Who is 'we'? I didn't see you take the SATs, sir."

"It's a full scholarship, by the way. Plus, five thousand dollars for film projects that I can spend however I want," Dawn said, finally getting the zipper up.

"It's already yours, queen. I'm claiming it in the name of the Lord." Dawn could imagine Edie reaching a hand up towards the sky in feigned worship.

"Thank you, E. I need the power of any and all available higher powers." She tugged at the bottom of the dress and attempted to get the neckline to rest on her chest in a smooth pattern. "Last night while I was editing, I freaked out because I thought I'd lost my escapulario that my dad gave me for luck when I was younger. I mean, full-tilt breakdown."

"What's that?" Georgia asked.

"Oh, it's like this piece of cloth that was apparently blessed by a priest. You wear it around your neck. I used to wear mine all the time then I don't know, I kind of just stopped. But last night I was in this editing haze and I just was like, wait a minute, where is it?"

"You find it?" Edie asked, concern lacing her words.

Dawn paused before answering, her eyes trained on her body in the small mirror in the dressing room. "Yeah, it was in my book drawer. I guess I used it as a bookmark for some Toni Morrison book I forgot to finish."

Dawn pushed aside the green fabric curtain to reveal herself in the gown. Looking down, Dawn noticed how it kissed her stomach and thighs so that she appeared rounded and tall.

"Wow. I mean, absolutely wow." Edie shot up from her seat.

"Incredible, amazing, genius, never the same, never been done before, not afraid to reference or not reference, daring, put it in a blender, pour it out the blender, drink the juice, stunning. I *mean*."

"I . . . don't know what any of that meant, like, on a constructive level, but thank you, Geo, for the contribution."

To her left was a mirror that folded into three panels. Dawn turned to it and watched herself frown and jut out her waist from three angles. Three dresses on three girls.

"What's wrong?" Edie asked, her eyes on Dawn's back.

"Nothing is wrong which is why this absolutely sucks. I look like a model and I can't buy this dress." Dawn put her hands on both sides of her face like an old Hollywood actress in distress.

"You always look like a model," sighed Edie in that motherly tone she often didn't even notice she was using.

"You know what I mean. If I bought this, it'd totally eat the money I've been saving for my dad to get some help. Well, not completely, but, like, a lot."

"Get the dress, D. This is literally the best you've ever looked and we're not leaving the store without it." Georgia insisted.

"The best? Ouch." Dawn laughed and twirled in the dress again.

"You know what I mean." Georgia rolled her eyes and leaned into Edie with a laugh.

"I can't afford it." Dawn gritted out, frustration rising in her voice.

"Then we will buy it, obviously," offered Edie. "You just owe us shitty cafeteria pizza until the end of time, or like, until graduation."

Dawn looked back into the three-faced mirror again. Georgia was right, she looked incredible and, more importantly, felt like the movie director she fantasized about being. If she didn't buy it now, she never would. If she didn't make dumb decisions now, she'd end up old and sad with no stories to tell.

"Okay, but I'm going to buy it. I'll figure something out later."

She went back into the dressing room and quickly peeled the dress away from her body. It fell to the floor in a slump and Dawn stepped out and put her clothes back on, somehow a new person now, the kind that would buy an incredible, expensive dress. She wanted to hurry up and make a rash decision. She couldn't get to the counter fast enough, the small woman trailing behind her to ring up the dress.

Dawn swiped her card and felt her stomach drop to the pits of hell then pick back up again as the woman gently folded the black fabric and wrapped it in a thin white paper with silvery foil.

She slipped the wrapped dress into a sleek, dark blue shopping bag with MOSSÉ embossed in white on its side and slid it across the counter towards Dawn.

The girls walked out of the store and emerged into the still-gleaming rows of shops and pretzel stands reeking of butter and salt.

EIGHT

March 12, Nineteen Days to Deadline

Georgia pulled into the parking lot and stared at the dirty white building ahead of her. She'd run over the curb by a few inches and tried to ignore the sound of her bumper collecting yet another scrape.

"Good one, bud." Jill laughed lightly at Georgia's blunder. Georgia looked over at Jill in the passenger's seat, her hand rest-ing across her bare waist at the thin strip of skin where her crop top ended. The three golden rings Jill was wearing pressed cold marks against her stomach in the heat of the car. Georgia shifted into park and let out a deep sigh.

"I'm a good driver, I swear," she moaned.

"You know that's what all bad drivers say, right?"

"Yeah but I'm different," Georgia said with a smirk. "I've only been in three accidents and two of them weren't my fault."

"Ohhh. Right," taunted Jill, finally looking around at the rusted white building. "What is this?"

"Something fun." Georgia unlocked the doors and looked out at the quiet, empty parking lot.

"You're so lucky you're cute."

"You're so lucky I'm cute."

"I am."

They kissed quickly and the radio kept playing some sad song by The Smiths. Georgia pulled back after a moment of breathing in Jill's skin and looked her in the eye.

What a perfect person, she thought, tracing the lines of Jill's strawberry-round nose, her birthmarks irregular kisses all over her skin, black hair like a secret down her back. Georgia was excited to share something she thought was beautiful with a person she thought was beautiful.

Georgia brushed her cheek against Jill's neck then slowly brought her lips up to her dangling gold earrings and whispered, "Get out of my car."

Jill let out a little giggle as Georgia pulled away and picked up her bag from the floor of the passenger seat.

Two squirrels lay out flat on the curb, exhausted from the sun. Georgia tugged at the bottom of her jean shorts where the fabric had become plastered to the sweat of her thighs against the blistering cracked leather car seats.

"Come here." She reached her right hand out to grab Jill and swung her around in a circle in the parking lot.

"Hey!" Jill tilted her head back and laughed into the hot air. "What are you doing?"

Georgia kept spinning her around and around as the glazed day burned their bare legs and the backs of their necks. She finally stopped and let Jill's hand go so that she stumbled and had to lean over for balance.

"Good. Now we're ready to see the art."

"Art?" Jill looked around at the parking lot full of nothing. The plain white building didn't even have a door.

"This way." They held hands again and Georgia led her out of the parking lot to the building next door, which was stout and gray and had dark windows that didn't allow passersby to see inside. Jill looked up at the gray façade as Georgia walked towards the door. The neon-green lights lining the edge of the garage made it look like an abandoned roller-skating rink from the eighties.

"What does this have to do with making me dizzy?"

"Nothing, I just thought that would be fun."

"Georgia."

"Jill." Georgia smiled and opened the door.

Inside, a stuffy guard sat at a desk that was too low to the ground. Though the room was dark, they could see his mustache and brown skin glowing blue and orange from a light that came from the opening just ahead.

He barely looked up from a crossword he was working on to speak.

"No pictures, please. Enjoy yourselves."

"Thanks!" offered Georgia cheerily as she pulled Jill ahead. They passed under a gray archway and into a dark room. Georgia's eyes adjusted to the dark to reveal a large concrete room, empty except for what seemed like fifty or sixty colorful fluorescent lights lining the right and left walls. They were in rainbow order and shone like tubes of lightning against the shadows of the dark room.

"Whoa." Jill let her eyes run along the walls of color as she tried to understand what she was looking at.

"Fun, right?"

Jill didn't answer. She ran alongside the wall so that each light glittered against her skin as she passed. They flickered over her body and lit her up one colorful beam after the other. Georgia laughed and watched her glow like the moon.

She ran after Jill and felt her feelings growing bigger, something she thought was impossible. How can you like someone more when the cup is already full?

Georgia caught up as Jill slowed down in the middle of the room.

"What do you think?"

"What is this?" she asked breathlessly, the darkness painting her a deep shade of blue.

"An art installation. The artist's name is Dan Flavin, I think."

"It's incredible." Jill's voice echoed and she giggled at the sudden rupture of noise.

"Yeah. He designed it right before he died. It's part of the Menil."

"That little museum by the park?" She twirled again and the colors bounced off of her in shifting shades.

"Uh huh."

"Wow." Georgia watched as Jill tilted her head up slowly to the shaded sky light above them. Despite the sun being out, the room maintained a dimness that allowed the art to glow. Georgia couldn't help but lose track of the light, the room, instead keeping her eyes on Jill.

"It feels like you should dance, right? Don't the lights just make you want to dance?" Jill shimmied and did two poorly turned pirouettes on her right foot, lightly bumping into the wall.

"Not really." Georgia let out a laugh as Jill peeled herself from the wall. "I think most people just look."

"I mean, we could do that too." Georgia's hand latched onto Jill's as she giggled and settled down. They walked from one end of the space to the other and took in the changing colors and monumental quiet.

"I was so nervous you were taking me to a skating rink." Jill whispered.

"Why are you whispering?" whispered Georgia.

"It feels right." Jill shrugged, her eyes big at the room before them.

"Okay," Georgia replied, keeping her voice low. "Why were you scared?"

"I don't know how to skate." Jill smiled and lightly tapped her thumb twice on Georgia's tightly grasping hand.

Georgia snorted out a laugh and heard the echo boom back at her.

"Are you serious?"

"Yeah. I never learned." She tilted her head down so that the rainbow swished through her hair in colorful spirals.

"Good to know. I promise I will never take you skating. Unless you want to learn, of course."

"Thank god. No, I do not want to bust my face open in front of the cutest person I know, thank you very much." Jill smiled and Georgia felt warm all across her chest.

They made it to the edge of the room when Jill noticed a corner with white lights emitting a soft glow from the other side.

"There's more?" She looked at Georgia and tugged on her hand.

"I don't remember. I've only been here once with Dawn. She knows way more about cool art stuff around the city.

Jill dragged Georgia around the corner and discovered a much smaller room with white tubes of light arranged in small shapes like triangles and slants along the wall.

"This is so nice."

Jill rocked back and forth on her toes and Georgia noticed the hair on her legs and the scuff marks on her white sneakers and the way she said "nice" like it was a name. She leaned in to kiss her on the cheek and felt Jill's skin ice cold beneath her lips.

They stared into the bright lights and tried to make sense of their abstract shapes.

"It's like a skyline." Jill turned to Georgia after looking at the installation in front of them.

"Or a pyramid."

"Two girl giants kissing," she gasped.

"It's their first date." Georgia wrapped her arms around Jill and rocked them back and forth together in the neon darkness.

"Absolutely." They laughed and walked back to the main room where the rainbow of lights went on and on before them. They walked to the middle of the room and laid down beneath the skylight.

Georgia closed her eyes and tried to remember the details of the moment. She put her hand over Jill's and told herself to remember how soft the skin of the back of her hand was. How warm she was. How loud her breathing was as it slowed and slowed. She wanted to remember that she could be happy like this. She was capable of liking someone this hard.

She opened her eyes to look over at Jill and saw that her head was turned towards her. Her hair spilled over onto the concrete as she rested her palm behind her head.

"What?" Georgia traced the corners of Jill's face with her eyes. She looked at the world in Jill and the world looked back.

"I just like spending time with you."

"Oh," Georgia squeaked out, just barely feeling Jill's breath against her cheeks. "Me too."

"Hey." Jill propped herself up on her elbow and leaned over so that her hair draped into Georgia's face and tickled her skin. "You want to go somewhere where we can scream?"

Georgia didn't even know what that meant but nodded vigorously towards Jill, who was already smiling so that her teeth showed at the edges. She felt out of breath as Jill tilted her head down so that her hair became a comfortable forest canopy over her head, wild and dark.

Georgia swung open the door to let her walk ahead. The moon was shimmering now, shy behind a few dark clouds.

Georgia began to walk towards the parking lot where her car sat but Jill turned in the opposite direction. Georgia hesitated to follow but saw that look in Jill's eye that meant she was confident and sure and definitely knew what she was doing. Georgia loved that look.

"Come on. Trust me." Jill grabbed her hand and led her across the street and past a couple of apartment complexes where twenty-somethings walked around with their overly eager dogs. They passed a coffee shop and laundromat that looked more like a night club than a place to wash clothes. Georgia began to hear traffic but couldn't place the noise.

The sound of hundreds of cars passing by echoed in her ears but she didn't see a highway. Jill tugged at her hand as Georgia stopped to orient herself on the sidewalk.

"Almost there. I promise."

They walked past another apartment complex and suddenly emerged on a towering white bridge over Highway 59.

The wind whipped Georgia's hair over her eyes and she turned to Jill with a smile. The city looked magical and dirty and massive below them, cars rushing past in both directions. Georgia always thought of Texas highways as sort of ridiculous with their six lanes going both ways, cars speeding around you if you go any less than twenty miles over the speed limit. From this angle, though, it all made sense. Dirt-splattered eighteen wheelers and trucks from the same four car dealers appeared then quickly disappeared below them just as fast.

Georgia waved down at a car and jumped when it honked back at her.

"You're a natural." Jill laughed at Georgia's surprise.

"People honk at you?"

"Yeah. Watch." Jill waved her arms wildly above her head and danced a little at the sound of the city. Three different cars honked at her in what seemed like seconds.

Georgia felt like she was in a movie. It was too perfect, Jill's face glowing as the sun went down on her skin and the city turned into headlights and office building windows.

"Hey. You said there would be screaming," Georgia smirked

"Well, what do you want to scream?" Jill's nose just barely twitched as she spoke, something Georgia hadn't noticed until this very moment.

"I don't know."

"How about a secret? If you scream it, the wind will take it and the cars will drive away with your secret. It's like you won't have to hold it inside anymore because it's part of the world afterwards."

"Oh. Let me think." Georgia went quiet for a long time. Nothing would come up and she felt embarrassed as she watched Jill watch her think.

Jill rested a hand on her shoulder. "I'll go first."

Georgia blinked as Jill turned to the edge of the bridge again and ceremoniously placed her hands on her hips.

"I got a 71 on my AP Chemistry test this week and I don't care!" Jill's words got cut short by the wind and the sound of cars scraping by below. Her scream disappeared into the sun as did her secret. It was perfect.

Jill beamed as she turned back to Georgia.

"See? Easy."

"What am I supposed to say?"

"Anything. There are no rules. "

Georgia abruptly turned to the road and cupped her hands around her mouth like a bullhorn.

"I'm scared I'm not going to get into any colleges and my friends will disappear into the ether!"

"I'm not good at cooking and it's literally just measuring things!"

"Sometimes I write angry poems about people and almost email them but then I don't!"

"I hate my hair!"

"I hate my smile!"

"I hate Instagram but I can't delete it because what if I miss something!"

"I hate that I'm expected to be something so quickly! I'm a child!"

Georgia and Jill collapsed into laughter at their words. They sat down on the ledge beside the fence overlooking the passing cars. Georgia turned towards Jill and realized, finally, how grounding she was. She was someone she could trust with her failure. She didn't have to give anything to her. She didn't have to say the right thing to her. She just had to be.

Wind continuously brushed their hair into their faces and they watched silently as car after car after flatbed truck flowed beneath the overpass.

"I'm really scared about school," Georgia finally breathed out, her hand sliding into Jill's.

"You're going to do just fine, babe. You have the skill, you have the creativity, and you're also very cute." Jill raised their intertwined hands to rest beneath her chin and gave Georgia's knuckles a chilly kiss.

"What about if I get in?"

"Then that would be incredible. That's what you want, right?"

"Yes. I mean, no." A semi-truck honked its horn long and low as Georgia tried to gather her feelings. "Well, what about us, is what I meant. You're going to have another year of school."

"Nothing will happen to us. We're going to keep being together. I'm going to come see you."

There was that confidence again, that certainty Jill had that Georgia loved. She wasn't scared of anything. Not thousands of miles, not love over the phone, not endings.

"You will?" Georgia asked.

"Of course, sweetie. I love you."

"I love you too." Georgia squeezed Jill's hands and Jill squeezed back. They looked at each other as the early evening dusk closed around them. Jill pulled Georgia into her until they were one wind-chilled body.

The evening was officially over as dim turned to darkness all around them on top of the bridge. The cars kept coming, kept honking, even as they turned their backs to the freeway and left the traffic behind.

They started to walk back to Georgia's car, linking pinkies, and were quiet besides each other. Georgia felt a warmth in her stomach that was both overwhelming and comforting at the same time. Their secrets were sacred and required silence and space. Georgia thought of all the things she screamed into the air and what Jill let out too. It might have been the sweetest thing that had happened to her all year. Jill's presence beside her was soft like the underside of a petal.

Jill was easy to speak to, easy to like. Jill cared for her like her best friends did but then there was the mixing of their breaths when they pressed their foreheads together, the intoxicating wetness of Jill's lips slightly parted on her waiting collarbone. Georgia wondered if everyone had little loves like this, had dates where they forgot about their problems or who they were supposed to be for moments at a time, so wrapped up in how lovely everything was. She was sure they hadn't invented queer love, but part of her questioned it. Had everyone been feeling this limitless and never told her? She read books, plays, short stories about infatuation, of course, even written them, but this was different because it was her own.

Jill slid into the passenger seat and reached her hand out to rest on Georgia's as she shifted the car into reverse then pulled out of the lot.

The night died behind them as Georgia drove into the traffic with love at her side.

NINE

My name is Ben Price, I'm seventeen years old, and I'm nonbinary. Was that right, D? Just my name and age?

I guess love is something I'm still trying to figure out, or understand. It took me a long time to date anyone, well, relatively long time. I'm only seventeen, I guess. I just needed time to figure out my own identity. I was really confused about how I wanted to present, I didn't understand who I was or what I wanted for myself, so I don't think I could have, like, brought somebody into that. I mean, that feels like a fundamentally queer thing to me. To want to know your otherness before you can know someone else's.

Queer love, to me, is like when you cut the gift-wrapping paper and the scissors catch and it makes that slick cutting sound and slides all the way down smooth. It's like that with Edie. She saved my life. That's completely fully true. I never thought I'd be the type of person to say, like, oh this person is my better half. This person is like . . . the love of my life. Yeah. The love of my life.

Edie was slumped over Ben on their bed reading a copy of David Sedaris's latest collection of essays. She'd developed an obsession with him after hearing someone reading an essay of his on the radio. She looked him up after hearing the story and quickly devoured everything she could about him, every book, every interview. She could name his husband, sisters, hometown, favorite foods.

She had always been this way, liking things, ideas, and people too much too quickly to the point of quiet obsession. Bands she'd only heard once, facts about space, a fashion designer whose clothing she liked but would never be able to buy; they all got caught in her mind until she meticulously searched and read about them, gorged and exhausted with knowledge.

Even realizing she was queer at age thirteen, Edie tracked down dozens of books and websites about LGBT rights, read whole novels under her blankets at night about white boys in the Midwest being disowned by their Catholic families, and pored over plays with girls kissing in every other scene. None of it fit her individual feelings and story exactly, but she considered it valuable research regardless. It all made her into who she was.

Ben was doing something on their phone, but their eyes were glazed over to the point of not looking at all. Even though it was late at night, she knew she could fit in a few more pages before she had to head home. Her parents wouldn't start looking for her until eight.

"Edie," Ben whispered.

"Shhh." She had just gotten to the end of an essay and had only a few pages left. She was usually at UN club at this time but it had been cancelled so she went to Ben's.

"Okay."

Edie tried to keep her focus on the page but couldn't, afraid she'd been too harsh. She watched their lips part in hesitation and then close again. Edie already knew what they were going to ask. They wanted to come over. She retrained her eyes on the book, pretending to read, pretending to have something else to think about. A few moments passed and Edie peeked up as Ben finally tried again to open their mouth with more conviction.

"I have something to say," they ushered out the words from their lips quickly.

"What?" she asked gingerly, placing her book face down on the bed. She looked up at Ben and waited.

"Not to say, but to ask."

"Shoot." She held her breath. They looked nervous, their nails digging into a loose strand on their faded jeans.

"I wanted to know," they paused and inhaled deeply. "Do you think I could come meet your parents or something, sometime." The words stuttered out uncertainly, Ben still not meeting Edie's eyes.

Edie froze. She didn't say anything as her mind went blank. Her hand slid beneath the book and she picked it up as if to begin reading again.

"Nope," she voiced, the book blocking her face.

"What? Why not?" Ben's voice dragged to a whine, like some injured animal.

"Why would you even ask that?" She rested the book against her face so that the pages touched her lips and muffled her voice as she spoke.

"Stop avoiding the question, and please put the book down, babe." Ben's words sounded more insistent now, almost upset. Edie suddenly grew tired. So tired she could barely get out words anymore. Being wrong was exhausting.

"What question? I don't know what you're asking me." She let her eyes wander around the room to the rows of swimming, debate, and dance trophies Ben had lining their dresser. They were always winning something. She concentrated hard on the plaques and saw that they all said First Place. She tried to remember how many debates and dance competitions she'd sat in the audience for. She could feel the heat of Ben's gaze on her as she thought about all of this. They were getting angry.

"I'm asking you why you're ashamed of me." Hot tears began to form at the corner of their eyes. They swiped their wrist quickly across their face as if to catch the crying before it started.

"I'm not." She wasn't. At least, she didn't think so. She wanted to be her own person, but she wasn't. Not yet, anyway. Their silent nods of approval when she got good grades or stayed in on weekends instead of asking to attend a school event or a birthday still meant something to her. Introducing them to Ben would crumble the façade she'd been delicately building since the day when she was thirteen when she'd realized she was a disappointment in the biggest way she could possibly be, a failure of literal biblical law.

"Of course you are. What other reason is there? You don't even really like me. I'm just like—like some sort of fucking game to you." Ben stood up and pushed off the covers from the bed in frustration.

"Ben." Edie was surprised at their sudden redness, the shrillness of their voice as their anger gained momentum.

"What, Edie? Am I wrong?"

"Fine," she said, finally letting go of the breath she'd been holding in, afraid. "You want to know the truth?"

"God, not the truth. That would just be way too much."

"What does that even mean?" She stood up and looked at them as if for the first time.

"It means you don't know how to be real about anything. It means your parents' 'holier than thou' attitude has forced you to lie about every single fucking thing. It means you don't tell the truth unless it's absolutely necessary."

It was true. Everything they said was absolutely true. Watching Ben hold back tears, she decided to be honest for once. "They don't know that you're nonbinary, and they will hate you automatically when they find out. They'll act like they like you, but as soon as you leave, you're done for. We're over."

In her home, there was no Ben. There was Ben in her thoughts but never on her tongue. There was Ben in a whisper. There was Ben beneath their sheets on early Monday afternoons. There was Ben across from her at a restaurant she knew her parents would never go to. She couldn't conceptualize them to be something said out loud past her doorstep.

She wanted to be honest, to be open and free from judgement. Part of her hated the lying. She knew God didn't hate her, but her parents were another story. She could already see their downturned lips, thin lines of disappointment at her supposed sin.

"Is that it?" They lightened.

Edie nodded, tired of all the yelling. She finally looked up and felt exhausted by all the truth in the room. *This is the part where they break up with me*, she thought.

"That's not a big deal." They softened, the room becoming suddenly less hot, less energetic.

"It's not?" She let herself relax at their words.

"No. I can just not mention it." Edie grew hopeful. If they lied to her parents everything would be fine and she could keep hiding them and their identity.

"Really? Like just use different pronouns?"

"Yeah, wait. I mean, no. I don't want to do that." They stumbled over their words. They sat down again on the bed and looked at Edie questioningly.

"Why not? It's a perfect plan."

"No. I don't want to use pronouns I'm not comfortable with. I think maybe just not saying them would be better."

"But you just said you would! I need you to."

Edie heard herself and felt ridiculous. She was stuck with her parents, stuck with the selfish, anxious self they brought out in her. She was ever desperate for acceptance she knew she'd never get if she told them the truth. Edie knew college could be better, but for now, she was just some stupid, wanting child, hopeless for the last glimmers of her parents' love for a version of her that didn't actually exist.

"I'm not doing that, Edie. I worked way too hard to be comfortable with myself just to lie to more people in an attempt for them to like me or accept me. You of all people should understand that." Their words ran on without a breath, small scissors cutting into Edie's perfectly round plan. They waited to speak again. "I think we need to take a break. Like, a long one."

Edie started to cry. She wiped the corners of her sweater against her eyes again and again, making the tears worse and reddening her skin.

"From each other?"

"Yes. Please go." They looked away from her and kept their eyes on the abandoned copy of *Calypso* that had fallen to the floor.

Edie picked up her book and backpack. When she leaned over, the snot dribbled out of her nose and onto the blue rug. She tried to cover it up by wiping her shirt across her upper lip again and again but it was useless. She left without looking back at them. The sidewalk scuffed beneath her sneakers as she walked down to her bike parked by the neighborhood pool. The sun went down across the cream-colored houses, and Edie was left with nothing.

Edie loved Ben. She knew it as soon as she started her walk home. To Edie, love was Ben's untethered laughter expanding over Edie's body like a rush of water through a busted dam. Their t-shirt curving up when they reached for their locker to reveal just one earthly inch of pudge. Love was long. Love lived on Danica Street and drove a shitty red car. Love missed sixth-period Advanced Calculus to make out with Edie after lunch for four days in a row. Love was the plot of a B movie. Love kicked Edie in the chest and left her bleeding on the searing Texas concrete like love is so apt to do.

TEN

March 13, Eighteen Days to Deadline

I think trying to find queer love in Texas is weird. It's like a massive small town. Everyone knows each other, or at least, of each other. Like, somebody can pull up a queer person on Instagram from three cities away and you already have seven mutual followers and three of them are your ex-girlfriends. It's kind of awful. Anyway, I like love, I like hearing about love. I'll read any book about love. It doesn't have to be queer, or even realistic. It could be about a flower and a bee who are deeply involved. I'm weak for any story about yearning. Wanting.

I have a crush right now. I think it's sweet to want someone you don't really know yet. Crushes are nice because they make life interesting. You can get through a single day just thinking about crushes. You can have your crush from the bus, crush from fourth-period Biology, crush from the soccer team. Maybe that's just me though. It's like writing a story about a made-up person. Loving someone is trickier. You can see all the mistakes they make. You can see how ordinarily fucked up they are just like you and everyone else you've ever known deeply. But I guess the knowing is a kind of love as well.

Georgia watched as her mother tied her hair up in the reflection of their small bathroom mirror. Frankie was wearing a simple A-line dress, the yellow of it radiating through the space. Her makeup was light and hinted at an unspoken effort. Georgia spotted herself in the mirror as her mother's eyes caught her in the reflection. She grabbed a small pin from the counter and placed it in Frankie's hair. Her mother lifted her hand and gently rested it upon her head where the pin was placed.

"Is this trying too hard?" Frankie asked.

Georgia firmly shook her head and thought of all the ways her mother's beauty was different from her own.

Their noses were just the same, two soft question marks curving down to meet their lips. Georgia's lips went up softly at the ends like ocean meeting mountainside. Frankie's naturally downturned lips sang sad songs without even opening, and Georgia had spent her life trying to pull their edges upward with every bad joke she could muster.

Her mother's cream skin folded tight around her eyelids and made her look too young for children or anything else she'd endured in the past thirty-five years. Frankie had given birth to Georgia at eighteen and had accidentally created her twin, a twoness they both delighted in even when silently moving around each other in their home. Georgia called her mother Frankie because they were best friends, two women for whom nothing and no one else mattered.

When high school came and other girls began to boldly whisper their hatred for their mothers, Georgia struggled to understand. She examined Frankie closely during those days, watched her buzz around the house filling vases with flowers she'd stolen from neighborhood parks, listened to her hum the same Nirvana songs over and over again in the kitchen as she shoved one onion pancake after another into her eager mouth, followed her mother's hands as she typed up words on her computer then deleted them, editing papers and essays and articles for anyone who needed it and would pay enough so she could cover the bills. She couldn't see anything in her mother to hate or even dislike. She just saw Frankie.

"Thank you," Frankie said turning away from the mirror. "You're going to like him. I already know it."

"We don't fight," joked Georgia.

"We make nice." They both said, laughing.

"That's my girl. We don't fight. We make nice." It was something Frankie used to say to Georgia when she was in elementary school. Sometime around second grade, she started scuffling with some of the other kids at school who made fun of her for her lunches. Her mother didn't know how to cook much, most of her lunches containing anchovies straight from the can and leftovers from the two Korean restaurants her mother liked in the strip mall next to their house. The kids would laugh as she pulled out the takeout containers while they grabbed for their Tupperware and thermoses of perfectly squared sandwiches and cut fruit.

Every day before her mother dropped her off at the front gates, she would pull the rearview mirror down to look at Georgia in the backseat and say *We don't fight*. Georgia would reply *We make nice*. Georgia didn't like being difficult. She saw the way her mother tried so hard.

We don't fight. We make nice. Georgia never asked how it started or where her mother had heard it. Sometimes they still said it to calm each other down.

The doorbell rang and all the lightness drained from her mother's eyes and was swiftly replaced with panic. Georgia watched as Frankie attempted to bounce lightly from the kitchen to the front door but her knees wouldn't let her be graceful.

Frankie cracked the door and revealed a man too tall to fit under its frame.

Simone was a skyscraper of a middle-aged man with sunken eyes hidden behind thick, blue-rimmed glasses. Georgia immediately associated his look with that of a mildly successful writer from the sixties. He wore gray, pleated pants, and a lime-green knitted pullover. He fingered a book in one hand and lilies in the other.

He leaned across the mantle to kiss Frankie on the cheek and accidentally dropped the book at Georgia's feet. They both bent to pick it up, but his hands met it before hers could. He stuffed the book under his already sweat-stained pits.

"You must be Georgia." He reached his hand towards her, but his height forced his hand to angle down towards hers awkwardly so that their fingers touched rather than their palms.

"These are for you." He stretched the lilies towards Frankie, and Georgia could see the nervous energy seeping down his neck, up his wrist, and straight into the noisy crinkled plastic of the bouquet.

"Thank you. Come in, come in. I'm going to put these in some water." Frankie left them to stare at each other like two cowboys facing off in a Western, both ready to win or lose something, though it was unclear exactly what.

"Frank told me you like writing. I got you this." He pulled the book from under his arm and offered it. Georgia eyed the cover. It was someone she'd never heard of before. She quickly turned it over to read the backside. Two of her favorite poets had written reviews. Simone's approval rating was inching up.

"I have a project coming up on contemporary poetry, so this'll be good to use." She let a smile slip. He wasn't the worst, so far.

"I have some more books you could borrow if you want. I mean, this one is a gift, but, you can borrow others." He pushed his toes into the doormat as he spoke. "I'm not sure they're what you're looking for. Do you know Hull?"

She nodded her head. Of course, she knew Lynda Hull. She was one of her favorite poets. She had two of her books on her bedside table in that exact moment.

"What's your favorite?"

"I memorized a lot of poems from *Star Ledger* a long time ago, so that's probably my favorite."

"Huh. Well, you know if you like her, Nikky Finney is really good. Or, you wouldn't happen to like Siken, would you? I mean, none of them are very similar, actually, but I just thought—"

Georgia watched as his heavy tongue pushed his words up against his bottom teeth as they spilled out so that everything he said felt rushed and excitable.

Georgia hesitated to like him, then decided he was okay. Not many men came through the front door expecting a date with her mother. Maybe two or three over the last eighteen years of her life. She wanted her mother to be happy, to laugh in a way she couldn't with her, romantically, sweetly.

Simone was passing the test, so far. He was kind and read good poetry. She started in on another question but was cut off.

Frankie rounded the corner, fresh gloss glistening on her heart-shaped lips.

"You kids don't have too much fun," Georgia joked towards her mother.

Frankie flashed her a smile as they slipped out the door.

"You either, missy," her mother retorted, the night wind catching her words as the door shut.

Georgia squished her feet into the cool tile of the entrance as her mind wandered away from her mother. The sudden emptiness of the space scared her into a quiet anxiety.

The final days of college acceptances and rejections were around the corner and she couldn't keep herself from using every spare moment to think about how much of a failure she'd been throughout high school. She never made good grades or ran any clubs or tried very hard in anything. She just kept showing up and now it was senior year and she was belly up, gutted again and again by every university she liked.

She stood in the kitchen until hunger pushed her to make a snack. She grabbed a bag of popcorn from the pantry and watched it spin around in the orange microwave light as her head clouded more and more with each kernel pop.

Georgia's mother never pressured her to do well in school and rarely asked about her grades. Now that she thought about it, she hadn't brought home a report card in years. Grades were an unspoken occurrence, maybe because Frankie assumed she was doing well.

She snatched the hot bag by the corners and wandered into her bedroom, the butter dripping down the paper and onto the hall-way carpet as she walked. She settled into her bed and opened her laptop to a series of opened tabs she'd never closed but also never looked at. Poems Dawn had sent her, a scathing review of a pho place she loved, and illegal links to every episode of a TV show she thought she might have wanted to watch several months ago. She minimized the window with all the tabs and opened a completely new one to create a false sense of newness and organization. She typed in her email and opened the folder she'd titled *College Stuff* to view the messages from all the schools she applied to.

She looked at all the decision emails and individual pages with their apologies and regrets and encouragements. There they were one after the other laughing at her with their lack of animated confetti and congratulations.

She opened a new tab with her Kenyon College waitlist. The page was simple enough, a letter letting her know she was waitlisted and a link where she could upload additional material.

She'd really wanted to get into Kenyon. She'd applied for the English program because she'd heard it had a creative writing emphasis and regularly brought really talented writers to campus to give talks and teach workshops.

She clicked to the section where she could upload additional materials. She hadn't really looked before because she was so sad about not getting in. She guessed the section was available to waitlisted applicants in case they'd achieved something acceptance-worthy since turning in the application and wanted to let the university know. Reading through the short list of guidelines, she saw that she could upload creative writing samples.

She quickly opened up a folder of her computer stuffed with writing snippets from different projects over the years and tried to think of what showed off her skills the best. The deadline to upload materials was about to pass, but she decided she would try anyway. Imagining herself sitting in lush green grass poring over a new book of poetry on Kenyon's campus, she sifted through project after project.

A ten-minute play she'd written last year followed three girls as they prepared for prom night. The characters were based off of Edie, Dawn, and herself. When she showed it to them last summer, they both told her she should apply to creative writing programs for college, they told her she was meant to be a writer. By the time deadlines came around, she hadn't applied to any. English, sure, but no creative writing programs. She was too nervous.

She'd only ever let Edie and Dawn read her words as well as the one English teacher. She wasn't she sure she had the talent to exist in rooms with real writers, people who published their work online and won awards like Scholastic and YoungArts. She was a closet poet, a covert playwright.

This was her last chance, though. Being shy hadn't worked. She needed to put her writing forward just to see what could happen. She uploaded the short play into the supplemental materials section and pressed submit before she could regret it. She opened up another window to her email.

Tell me what you think, babe. Sent this to Kenyon to see if it helps me get off the waitlist. Putting my best writerly foot forward. xxGeo

She shot off the email to Jill.

Closing out both tabs, Georgia picked up the book Simone had brought her.

Hours later, Georgia heard the garage mechanically straining to come up and then a car door open and shut again in the front of the house. Her mother's muffled voice mingled with someone else's—Simone. The noise kept getting closer and closer until the back door creaked, signaling their entrance.

She kicked the blankets off her feet and moved her laptop to the side, but then changed her mind and settled back into the warmth. She liked knowing the sound of her own home, so familiar with it she could feel its every movement.

She slowed her breathing and stopped squirming to listen to her mother's voice against Simone's.

"Which door did you say?" Simone's voice echoed down the hallway towards her room.

"Second on the right." Her mother's sound ghosted around the house as Georgia listened to Simone's footsteps approach. Georgia could tell he went too far for the bathroom when the tile went silent and the sounds of his footsteps changed to scuffling across carpet. The sound of her bedroom doorknob turning startled her out of the thought. Simone opened the door.

"Hey there, Georgie." Simone faltered against her door frame. He'd removed his lime-green knitted pullover and now bore only a disheveled white button-up. His pleated pants were unbuttoned at the top as if after dinner he'd been so full he needed to let his belly air out and forgotten to close it back in. His glasses were smudged with fingerprints. Georgia felt nervous at his drunkenness. He seemed so different from the man she'd met just hours earlier.

"Hey, Simone. How was the dinner?" She didn't know what else to ask him. She thought she might yell for her mother but waited for him to move from his swaying position at her door.

His left hand slid up her door frame as he leaned his weight against it for support. The moment felt strange, but Georgia couldn't get herself to move. His eyes refused to focus on her as he moved further into the room, stumbling over his own heft.

"Georgie Porgie, it was blue. Your mother is blue." He dropped his voice to a whisper as a glowing yellow light ran past her window, a neighbor's passing car. "Shhhh, don't tell Frankie. I think I had a better time talking to you about books than I had with her all night."

Georgia's laugh went up and down like a child's windup toy, artificial, uncomfortable. Simone walked towards the bed and lodged his knee onto her blankets. Each movement he made suddenly felt like cockroaches congregating over every inch of her exposed skin.

He pointed to a book on her bedside table. It was the one he gave her. "Oh man, she's good." His breath reeked of cheap alcohol. Something she would have blindly tasted at a party sophomore year.

"I know, you told me." She whispered, surprised at her own quietness.

"My favorite is "Jackson Hotel." Do you know that one?" He leaned in as he said this and ruined everything and made her feel dumb and still and unable to push him away. Nothing bad was happening but still she didn't like his unnecessary closeness.

"Yeah. I like that one a lot, actually." Her breath slowed and slowed as she watched his mouth move sloppily, delayed.

"*I watch her fade down the street until she is a smudge, violent in the circle of my breath. A figure so small I could cup her in my hands,*" he recited, his eyes trying hard to focus on Georgia's. He reached out his hand to her. "Do you like me?"

The right words caught themselves on the way up her throat. She could only muster up the first thing that came to mind. "I don't like anyone."

"Well that's too bad because I think I really like you."

Georgia soaked in quiet embarrassment.

"Simone? Are you okay?" Her mother's voice drifted in from the hallway, startling them both like a sudden earthquake.

"Be there in a second, Frank." He smiled at her as he said it. He let his outstretched hand drop to his side.

Simone stared into Georgia. With his eyes, he slipped under her tank top and laid bare his wants across her stomach, warm and flat. He wanted her and she wanted to evaporate into nothing. He lifted his knee so that the bed squeaked of relief from his weight. And then he was gone.

Georgia caught her breath as the door closed behind him and listened to muffled goodbyes and kisses at the front of the house. Her mother's footsteps trailed back into the hallway until she heard a light knocking on her door.

Her heart pounded against her shirt, some huge unbearable drum. She caught hold of the blankets on her bed and then let go again. Georgia swallowed the previous moment like a bitter pill and told her mother to come in.

Frankie glided across the carpeting and splayed her body dramatically across the foot of Georgia's bed, a renaissance Venus. Her cheeks warmed up red before she'd even said a word.

"What did you think?" She was like a schoolgirl asking her friends about a new love interest, waiting and overly in need of approval. She looked happy, the real kind. It took Georgia about two seconds to decide what she was going to say. She gave Frankie what she wanted, what Georgia thought she deserved. .

"He seems great," she mustered. She tried not to let her voice flatten out like dough under a pressing palm the way it wanted to.

Her mother's impatient energy turned to excitement. "Really? Great?" Georgia could tell her mother couldn't help from jumping up a little at the words.

"You seem good together." Frankie was practically dancing. Calming after a moment, she turned away with a smile.

"Thanks, my little button. Come on and help get me out of this thing." Frankie gestured blindly behind her back towards her dress zipper as she sat up on the bed.

Georgia moved to help her out of her summer dress. They both caught sight of themselves on the bed in the full-length mirror shoved in the corner of the room and Georgia saw two people trying to help each other as best as they could.

ELEVEN

March 14, Seventeen Days to Deadline

Friday afternoon, Georgia sat in an uncomfortable chair in the administrator's office. She was bored out of her mind and began to fidget with things she dug up from the bottom of her backpack. She found a note from Jill. It was a crude drawing of one of their teachers wearing a beret and holding an oversized baguette in his cartoon hands. Georgia couldn't remember the joke, but she remembered laughing. She liked Jill a lot. She liked how simple Jill's life was. Two parents, a cat named Moseby, a rainbow flag slung high above her bed surrounded by posters with quotes from famous feminists. She had confidence, a certainty about everything she did.

Jill walked like she had someplace to be, even if she was just moving from one end of a classroom to the other. Georgia still couldn't tell if she wanted to be with her or just slowly become like her over time, or both.

A voice came from the doorway Georgia was settled beside.

"Miss Graham. Please enter," the voice insisted.

She gathered up her bag and found herself across from Alsbury's college counselor.

Georgia winced as the seat opposite the counselor screeched as she pulled the chair away from the desk to sit. She was face to face with Mrs. Jimenez, her natural enemy since the sophomore year college preparedness assembly.

Mrs. Jimenez shuffled a few papers around her desk and met Georgia's eyes over her turquoise, square glasses.

"I really can't help you at this point Miss Graham."

"I know." Georgia dug her jagged, freshly bitten fingernails into her thigh as the wall clock moved slow and loud next to the window just above the counselor's nest of deep brown hair.

She brought her attention back to Mrs. Jimenez's glare. Georgia watched her lips tighten until they were lemon-soured into a perfectly unhappy circle beneath her nose.

"It's always *I know, I know, I know* with you. But you know what, Miss Graham? You don't. And at this rate, you are headed for absolutely nowhere. I don't think that's a place you want to go. Am I correct or incorrect?"

"Correct. I know." She sighed at having repeated herself. Everything she said and did felt stupid in front of this woman.

Of course she wanted to get into a good school so her mother wouldn't have to worry about her. She did everything for her mother. Her whole life was about making things easy for Frankie so she could relax in small and infrequent ways, something Georgia knew her mother rarely indulged in. Watching her mother try to get by alone was like watching a wind-up toy in perpetual motion, only ever stopping to wind up again and again. She would never intentionally add to her mother's stress.

"How many colleges did you even apply to?" Disappointment sputtered out of her like some sort of machine built to ruin Georgia's day.

"Five." Wrong answer again. She could see it in Jimenez's narrowed, squinting eyes.

"With your grades," she trailed off. She took a deep breath in, exhausted with Georgia. "You just don't care, do you?"

"I do." Georgia thought about it hard for a moment. She really did care. She wanted to go to school. She wanted to write. She wanted to leave the city and try something new.

"Act like it, Miss Graham."

"I was waitlisted at Kenyon. I uploaded some creative writing as my supplemental material," she muttered.

"Oh, you write?" Jimenez toyed with a pen on the edge of her desk. She bit into it.

"Yes. Poetry, mostly."

"Are you good?" She chewed hard on the pen so that Georgia thought the thing might bust open and spill ink all over the place.

Georgia started to nod, but Jimenez was already looking away. She closed the file of information in front of her as if to signal to Georgia that the meeting was over. Georgia scuffled from the chair and turned to leave the room, defeated.

"Good luck. Please send in the next student," Mrs. Jimenez called after her.

She wandered down the empty hallway considering Jimenez's words. As she stirred around the corridor, she found herself growing angry with her mother. Why did she have to like Simone? Why hadn't she been checking on her report cards? Why didn't she tell her to do her freaking homework? What kind of mom was she anyway? Her life was falling apart, Simone was a creep, and it was, she'd decided, completely her mother's fault.

TWELVE

March 21, Ten Days to Deadline

Dawn's eyes went blurry with the searing blue of the screen. How many hours had it been? Two? Seven? The sky pushed a soft blue glow through her tiny window. Almost sunrise. Her room was a wreck. A plate of tortilla chips with melted cheese on top sat rifled through on her dresser. Next to her bed sat a cup of chocolate milk she'd made with syrup and almond milk like a crazed monster sometime around four in the morning. She was perched on top of her covers, not wanting to get tempted by the warmth of her sheets in the night.

All this and she still had hours of unedited footage and audio to cut together into some semblance of a movie. She could see the light at the end of the documentary tunnel, but it was dim and achingly far away. From editing together B-roll of friends in the hallways holding hands to cutting out all the *uhhhs* and *umms* from each talking head interview, Dawn was deep in the weeds.

Her phone buzzed with her morning alarm. It was time to wake up and she hadn't closed her eyes in almost forty-eight hours. The screen glowed to reveal three notifications, two of them missed calls from Edie. She swiped to type out a message.

hey e! sorry i missed your calls. i was in an editing hole. see u in gov.

The message sent and the phone started ringing immediately.

"Edie?"

"D! Are you okay?" Edie's voice crackled sleepily through the phone.

Dawn sighed and tried not to sound as gross as she felt. "Yeah, I just got super caught up in editing last night."

"Oh, good. I was just worried. I feel like you've been sequestered in a documentary-making cave. Just checking in." Dawn started to move around her room picking up clothing from the floor and putting things back into place on her desk.

"Aw, thanks. But no, yeah, I'm really good actually. Things are coming together for once. I'm pretty happy with the work I've been doing. What's up with you?" Dawn measured her words through the phone. Edie hadn't said much about Ben since last week. All Dawn knew was that they were on a break after their fight. Edie could be kind of cold when it came to emotional stuff, so she didn't want to push too hard.

"Literally nothing at all. I'm just like, emotionally bored."

"What do you mean?" Dawn sat down again and tried to focus on Edie's voice completely. She could tell she had been struggling for the past few days. She barely even talked in class anymore.

"Like, I used to just give so much attention to Ben. More than I noticed, I think. And now, I only have myself to think about and it's so boring."

"Not only do I respect that sentiment, I fully understand it. Sometimes I think I want a partner just so I can have something to do." Dawn startled herself with her words but put away the thoughts that came up alongside them.

"Is that weird?" Edie's voice was low on the line, the sound of her packing for school almost louder than her speech.

"Absolutely not."

"It's not like I waited around for them or didn't have a life. It's just . . ."

Edie took a pause so long that Dawn didn't know if she was even still on the phone.

"They added to your feelings. You had more to feel with them," she offered.

"Exactly. Georgia told me I should use the extra energy on self-care, but I already cared about myself with Ben. We were together *and* I loved myself. We talked on the phone for hours *and* I painted my nails, you know? Now I just have really nice nails." She let out a little laugh.

"It's going to be okay, E." Dawn didn't know this but figured it was an alright thing to say. She was never great at comforting people, even close friends she desperately wanted to help.

Edie's breathing receded to a shallow whimper through the speaker.

"Dawn?"

"Yes."

"I'm actually kind of a mess right now." Her words caught and her breath came out in slow patches. Dawn always saw Edie as the solid foundation of their group. When no one else had it together, she did. When they went to the beach, she had the sunblock and towels. She had wit and foresight and gentleness. Now, she was a ball of anxious thought and sadness.

"That's okay."

"I gotta go," Dawn heard Edie rustle some papers on the other end of the line. "Thanks for listening to me literally cry about nothing." She sniffled and calmed down as the sun rose outside Dawn's window and painted her room a dull orange.

"It's not nothing."

"Okay, fine. Cry about love or whatever the word is for liking someone so much that not talking to them actively ruins your day." Edie laughed quietly through the snot caught in her throat.

"Anytime. I mean that. Georgia and I are trying to go out for lunch. You coming?"

"No thanks. I have some extra work to do for that English assignment due at midnight."

"Oh my god. I literally forgot about that."

"Yup." Edie replied.

"Yikes. Okay, see you in Gov. Love ya mean it."

"Love ya mean it," Edie repeated plainly.

When Dawn hung up, the other notification from that morning popped up on her phone. It was an email from a name she didn't recognize: Collin Rees.

She slid her finger across the screen to open the message.

Dear Dawn,

Hi! My name is Collin Rees, and we are competing against each other in the Austin Film Festival. I saw your clip on the finalists site and am completely obsessed. The way you seem to be crafting a story of love is unpredictable and disappointing and lovely, just like the real thing (I think). I don't know if you saw my clips on the site, but my film is about queerness too, kind of. It's about my little brother. He's trans, and living in Austin near the capitol with all this fucked legislation has been weird. My parents are really . . . going through it. I thought I'd document our lives.

I saw so much of myself and my life in your movie. I think my friends and I are all on some weird search for something that doesn't really exist in the right way for us yet. I just wanted to reach out and say all of this and also wish you good luck.

Best,
Collin Rees

P.S. Here is my phone number if you ever want to talk about documentaries or just life.

Dawn d idn't really know anyone in Austin and quickly decided that she wanted to be friends. She remembered seeing his thirty-second excerpt on the finalist website and instantly liking his work. Maybe he'd be nice.

She pasted the phone number he'd put in the email into a new text box on her phone:

hey collin, it's dawn. thank for emailing I'd love to talk about documentaries n stuff. hmu!

She saved his name as Collin with the movie clapper emoji so she could remember him.

Dawn tossed her phone into a tote bag from under her bed and grabbed her laptop. She gathered up the food wrappers and dirty dishes from her bed and drawer and made her way to the kitchen.

Her dad was in his room. He still hadn't left the house coming up on two and a half weeks. Last time he went out, she didn't see him for four days. He said he'd gone all the way to El Paso to pick up some vegetables and she still didn't know why or where the food ended up because it certainly wasn't in their kitchen. He had that look in his eyes when he said it, so unfocused and excited at the same time.

Her mother was so good at understanding him during these times, but Dawn was lost. She was the child. She was supposed to be taken care of.

She curled an apple from the countertop in her fist and stuffed her computer into the tote bag on her shoulder along with a pen and a few notebooks for school.

If editing the documentary didn't kill her, trying to graduate definitely would.

THIRTEEN

March 22, Nine Days to Deadline

The sun melted the girls down as they sat in the Fiesta Mart parking lot Saturday afternoon. The heat was angry, hissing at everything it touched. Edie and Georgia rocked back and forth on coin-slot mechanical horses as Dawn lazily spun on the baby carousel. Her knees were tucked uncomfortably to her stomach so she could fit into the machine. Georgia watched as Dawn rested her just-bought chocolate ice cream pint to her forehead to feel the cool.

Brown sludge melted down Dawn's hands as she spoke. "Guys, I have some news." She spun excruciatingly slowly in another circle on the carousel as she made her announcement.

"What?" Edie asked, already sweating.

Dawn had dragged them out for a day of errands she needed to run, which had met its midway point with all of them buying pints of ice cream in Fiesta and promptly realizing there was nowhere to sit in front of the store. Georgia felt like the sun was draining all the energy directly from her skin.

"Guess." Dawn licked her bottom lip to catch the ice cream dribbling down her chin and laughed.

"Ugh, why?" Georgia whined; her least favorite game was guessing things that she would definitely find out anyway. "You finished the documentary," she posited impatiently.

"God, I wish. Guess again."

"You're going to start wearing pantsuits to project your dominance as a modern woman." Georgia smirked.

"You know my thighs are too big for that." The girls rolled their eyes.

Both rides stopped at almost the exact same time. The festive songs crunchily spilling out of their sound boxes died down as they rolled to a standstill. Dawn fished around her jeans' pockets for quarters. "You guys have more coins?"

"Just tell us!" Edie shook her hand and the strawberry pint she was holding spilled onto the sidewalk and oozed outwards in a pink clump on the sizzling concrete.

"Okay, chill. So, you know how I applied to NYU for film and TV?"

Edie jumped off her horse and crowded around Dawn to give her a hug. "You got in!"

They screamed and attracted the attention of two older men walking into the store and a woman rolling her cart out to a container of watermelons resting atop a set of broken pallets.

"Dawn, we might be going to the same place! Well, like, four hours away, but basically the same place," Edie exclaimed.

"I know. I can't believe it. I mean, I doubt I'm getting financial aid, but yeah. I'll find out in a few days," Dawn said.

"Well you don't both have to sound so freaking excited to get away from me." Georgia sat alone, still on the machine. She tried to mask her sadness but felt that it was too obvious. Now, they were both leaving her, officially.

"Never," said Dawn setting her ice cream down.

"Never," Georgia repeated back mockingly.

"I'm serious," Dawn said as she reached her pinky out towards the other girls. The chocolate from her fudge ice cream covered her hand in little dribbles of brown-colored sugar.

"Pinky promise we'll video call you and write letters and everything no matter where you are. I mean, I can't even technically go so, you know."

"Pinky promise." Georgia reached out her hand towards theirs. She didn't like being the odd one out. Even if they called every day, even if Dawn ended up somewhere else, she'd still be far away, leaving Georgia alone with nothing to do. She had to get into a school.

They locked their fingers together and laughed at the ridiculousness of the scene, of each other. Edie and Dawn chucked their ice cream in a nearby trash can while Georgia worked her lemon sorbet over for the cold, sugary soup at the bottom.

"We need to have a senior trip or something," she muttered between slurps. The last bits of ice dripped down her arm and freckled the parking lot.

"What, like, go to Europe and find ourselves like the River Oaks kids?" Dawn asked as she raised an eyebrow.

"Okay, no, obviously we don't have the cash money for that. Something chill so we can be together before we all disperse into the trenches of university life. What if we went to Galveston?"

"When? After graduation?"

"No, like right now." She stood in front of Edie and Dawn so that they couldn't walk any further. "I mean, we're not going to France, we're not going to hike up some trail and kiss nature and realize we're specks in the universe, so let's just go to the beach. It's so hot."

"It's not even graduation yet," Edie pointed out.

"Forget the senior trip thing. Now, I just want to go to the ocean. Today. Right now." Georgia was practically buzzing with the idea. "We can go into the store and buy snacks for the ride and the beach."

"What about swimsuits?"

"I always keep one in the back of Georgia's car, duh," sang Dawn, a cheeky smile planting itself on her lips.

Georgia scrunched her brows together, puzzled. "Since when? For what?

"Since forever! A lady can never be too sure. Are y'all wearing bras?"

Georgia and Edie pulled the collars of their shirts away from them and looked down. They nodded in unison.

"Then just wear that. I think if we leave now, we can get back by tonight before Edie's parents freak out. We might even get back by, like, six."

"I'm down." Georgia responded, already turning back towards the store.

Edie stared up at the sun. Georgia could see her calculating all the things that could go wrong as if the numbers and statistics were floating just above her tilted head.

"Are you sure we'll be back by six or seven at the latest?"

"Yeah. It's only an hour drive. We can stay for like," Dawn started to do the math on her hands slowly, "four hours. Or we can leave early if we have to."

Georgia knew that Edie was strong, but she had been struggling. She needed to get out of her cycle of thinking about Ben, crying, doing homework, then thinking about them some more. Now that she'd gotten over the few days when she acted like she didn't care, she was like a bird running into the same cage wall over and over again, trapped in her sadness.

"Yeah, okay. Let's do it. But I swear, if we don't get animal crackers for the road, I'm changing my mind."

Dawn squeezed them both into a hug. "Your wish is my command. Let's go!"

They all rushed into the store to grab food for the car ride and the beach. After ransacking the snack aisle for animal crackers,

Oreos, and trail mix, they all crammed into Georgia's car. Edie rolled her window down in the backseat and let the trapped heat escape through the crack.

Chloe x Halle spilled out of Georgia's busted dash that, after many years of working fine, now only played CDs. When it broke, the girls had spent a week burning homemade CDs filled with perfect songs for the road. They had ridiculous titles written out in red and black Sharpie like *Songs for Running Down a Hill in a Long White Dress* and *Solange Saved My Life and So Will This Playlist*. Edie was going to miss these little moments, the stink of oil refineries along Highway 288 coming in through the window and filling the car as the music played on.

....
....

The waves bruised the crumbling shore harsh and fast on Jamaica Beach, a strip of land along Galveston Island where the Gulf of Mexico kissed the edge of southeast Texas. The highway faced the water and mossy grass grew alongside it in thick patches before the sand. Houston families usually crowded its shores during holidays, but when the girls arrived, it was all but empty save for a few parents hoping to occupy their nearly naked kids running along the seaweed scattered sands for a few hours over the weekend.

Dawn was wearing a cherry red bikini with a bow at the midpoint above her ribs and a matching one tied over her butt. She stamped across the beach, each footstep pressed into the sand another strut on an imaginary runway.

"I am as free as the wind on this beach," she ceremoniously pronounced to no one. The waves thinned for a moment and caught her words.

"Hot!" encouraged Edie from her spot under a blue and white parasol that, seemingly abandoned, she'd reclaimed for the three of them.

"Did you just quote *Paris Is Burning*?" Georgia asked, her head tilting towards the sun to face Dawn.

"Maybe," yelled Dawn from across the sand. She'd always loved the documentary. Her favorite scene was when Brooke and Carmen Xtravaganza frolicked across the sand of some New York shore in jean shorts so extremely cut off at the thigh that they might as well have been denim underwear. Brooke talked about being trans and feeling free as she danced around the beach. It was one of the most beautiful moments Dawn had ever seen in a documentary. "I am what I am, Georgia."

Dawn kicked the sand at her feet and placed her hand over her forehead to keep the sun out of her eyes. She looked out at the massive body of water. It reminded her of her childhood. The way her dad would drive them far out with nothing but two fishing poles, a cooler, and a bag of pretzels and Coca Cola in the backseat. He'd rest his palm behind her head while she sat in the front seat to make sure the poles didn't swing in her direction when they hit bumps on the highway. She would fall asleep pretending his hand was a giant's and she was as small as a flower.

These adventures were always just him and her. Dawn was the youngest of four. Her step-siblings were adults with jobs and children. They were the result of some first marriage of her dad's Dawn knew almost nothing about. Her father was older than anyone she knew in real life, seventy-two, or maybe seventy-three, she couldn't remember. His mood swings started when she was in middle school. He'd disappear often and forget things constantly. Her birthday, her name, where he'd put his keys, car, papers for work. Then he'd reappear with things, a new car the family couldn't afford, trash he'd collected for a business idea he hadn't quite figured out yet.

Things hadn't really started to fall apart until Dawn's mother died. He retreated into nothingness and could barely keep the days of the week straight. His upswings were like fires to put out, the smoke stinking up everything for weeks afterwards.

On the fishing trips, she never caught anything or even really helped. Except with the worms. Her job was to pick out a container of them from the island's corner store and put them on her father's golden hooks. She'd liked watching them squirm between her fingers before she slipped their fat bodies onto the hook, dark red and angry.

She splashed out and in on the edge of the water, her toes getting lost below the lapping waves. The water in Galveston was a murky, dark green. Not romantic or even beautiful, but always colder than the brutal Texas heat, so accepted for its flaws. The same body of water she'd fished in with her father a lifetime ago.

The waves tired her eventually, and she joined the girls at their spot next to the umbrella.

"You guys know Jill?" Georgia asked after a moment of relaxed quiet.

"Your girlfriend, Jill?" Dawn chimed in, giddy.

"The girl, Jill, who you are dating and who you are in fact in love with, Jill?" Edie laughed while lodging her book down into the sand. She propped herself up on her elbow to look at Georgia expectantly.

"First of all, relax. Second of all, yes. I mean, no. But basically, yes." She stumbled over her words and looked down at all of their sand-filled socks piled at the edge of the towel.

"What's up, G?" Dawn placed her fingers on Georgia's knee as if scandalized by the potential for gossip. "Literally do not skip a single detail. We've been waiting for you to say something for weeks."

"Y'all, I don't know. It's just really easy." Georgia smiled a little as she went on. "We have so little in common, but it just totally works. I mean, we have the important things in common, like taste in poetry and love of antique vases, of course. We've gone on a couple dates and stuff and we talk about poems and cooking and good TV shows. And she's so smart and so kind. Like, I told her about this book I really like, the one I mentioned to you D, about queer clubs in Brooklyn? And she got it from the library and read it the next day." Geo brought her fingers up in front of her nose and snapped. "Just like that. The next day."

"Wow. That's serious."

"Yeah, the last time someone recommended me a book I didn't get past the dedication," Edie laughed. "I'm so happy for you."

"I don't really know what's supposed to happen when we graduate, though. It's like we're going to be on two different planes. Like physical planes, you know?" Georgia's face bent into a near pout.

"That's hard. You could always text and try to keep it up if you're that serious about her," added Edie.

"Yeah, I don't know. It just feels like summer is the end of everything. Houston just evaporates and we're supposed to become new people in new cities. I mean, assuming I get into any colleges."

Dawn sat up and looked at Georgia straight on. "Of course you will, G."

"God, I hope. I sent off some new writing to Kenyon."

"Do you have any?"

"What, like, with me?" Dawn nodded "Alright, I have some. But, they're not great."

"Shut up, they're always great."

"Read them! Read them!" Edie and Dawn chanted in unison until Georgia stumbled into a standing position, the waves crashing behind her.

"Okay, fine. I have one called "Teen Superstars Scream Fire Over 59 Highway." It's about us." She held her phone in one hand and raised the other majestically towards the dimming sky.

2AM the Waffle House is packed
Teenage bodies glowing golden
Gray parking lot of possibility

We have hotboxed the car
With the words of Stevie Nicks
The smoke of her words fishing into the folds

Of our brain matter
Convincing us we are in love
With love
With life
With each other

Policemen watch the moon,
watch us, our fears touch
Mine sounds like my mother's
Yours sounds like a father's imitation of a mother's song
rushed and virulent

3AM mourning broke across our headrests like rain

Us with our young skin
twinkling mouths
Pearl beneath clam shell tongues

4AM we settle under our own somber fires
Our flames innocent and shy, only incidentally to blame
for the housefires
Lives not lost between red lights
We have so much summer left inside

Georgia bowed and the girls clapped. The waves crashed softer now, just barely lapping sweetly at the sand. The sun started to ease down and Georgia collapsed into a cuddle with the girls on her striped towel. A long silence reached out between them as they breathed in the warm air.

Dawn reached her right arm up towards her face to look at her watch. It was getting late. "I think we need to go soon."

"Yeah, I was just going to say. I'm sorry we can't stay longer," said Edie as she stood up and started to dust off her shoes.

They all got up and cleaned themselves off one last time in the water. All the boats on the horizon were gone now, either back to the dock or made invisible specks by the darkness.

They beat their sand-filled shoes against the wooden steps leading up to the parking lot and rinsed their toes in a faucet attached to a metal pole. They stuffed their wet feet uncomfortably into their damp socks and trampled across the searing asphalt.

In the car ride home, thirty minutes vanished. An hour. The Houston skyline appeared outside the passenger seat window, majestic and glinting orange from the dying sun's reflection.

FOURTEEN

COLLIN: *Whatcha up to?*

DAWN: *babysitting my teacher's aggressively adorable baby. his name is juno, can you believe?*

COLLIN: *That is a perfect name. Hope I'm not interrupting.*

DAWN: *don't worry. he's already asleep. i'm Very Responsible.*

COLLIN: *I guess technically I've been babysitting since my brother was born. The pay is shit tho. 0 bucks an hour and no health benefits.*

DAWN: *sounds like a good time. how does he feel about your doc?*

COLLIN: *I think he likes the attention. he's so much younger than me, so we don't really hang out a lot. Good excuse to spend time together.*

DAWN: *that's so cute! i kind of wish i had a sibling around my age. my step siblings are all adults, I hardly know them. i don't think my best friends would ever tell me, but i'm pretty sure i have a severe case of only child syndrome.*

COLLIN: *Really?? I don't get that from you at all. I mean I guess we've only talked over text (like every day haha) but I would have assumed you had some little siblings running around. You seem like somebody who takes care of people.*

DAWN: *seriously?? wow. i guess that's a good thing. honestlyyyy, if i had little brothers and sisters i would just make them watch movies with me. watching documentaries about sans serif fonts alone can be . . . a yikes*

COLLIN: *I can imagine lol. I would definitely watch Helvetica themed movies with you.*

DAWN: *really?*

COLLIN: *Hell yeah. Jeff Morales actually has a new movie out this weekend streaming if you want to do a facetime/watch party thing? I think you can stream it. I heard it's very queer and very sad.*

DAWN: *say no more.*

COLLIN: *I'll send you the link :~)*

DAWN: *who is he? :~)*

Collin 🎬 has sent a link.

COLLIN: *Cool guy, duh.*

DAWN: *oh wait! this is that movie with samira wiley and the girlfriend in kansas!*

COLLIN: *Yeah, you free? I just realized the link says the livestream is Sunday only.*

DAWN: *yup see ya there! or virtually anyway lol*

COLLIN: *Cool. It'll be nice to do something unrelated to the doc. Yesterday I spent four hours editing :/*

DAWN: *someone who understands my pain!! my friends think i'm like a perfectionist or something. like . . . no . . . that's just how long this stupid thing takes!!*

COLLIN: *Can't wait until we have people to edit for us haha.*

DAWN: *seriously. i'm so nervous for the fest. which day of the week is the deadline to turn in the final version again?? think it's a friday. i feel like I have a lot of time but i know i don't. yikes*

COLLIN: *Next week on Friday. It's kind of haunting me. I think I can get it done though.*

DAWN: *can't wait to see you.*

DAWN: *WAIT OMG*

COLLIN: *What?*

DAWN: *i just realized i have no idea what you look like. i was trying to picture meeting you at the fest and then I Realized. lollll*

COLLIN: *Wow haha. I feel like we're already in so deep. I think I text you more than some of my best friends at this point. Erm I don't have Instagram but I can send something.*

DAWN: *eh if you want. i love the mystery. you could be a serial killer which is kind of exciting.*

COLLIN: *What does a serial killer look like?*

DAWN: *send a pic and we'll find out :)*

COLLIN: *Very funny. Just a sec let me find something dashingly handsome yet humble. First impressions are important.*

DAWN: *i expect nothing less than a Dior campaign.*

COLLIN: *Collin 🎬 has sent an image.*

DAWN: *YOU'RE A BRUNETTE??! dawn salcedo has left the chat.*

COLLIN: *Baby, I was born this way.*

DAWN: *i'm just kidding. a charming cinephile in big glasses, just as I suspected. The freckles were a surprising twist.*

COLLIN: *I like to keep you on your toes.*

DAWN: *i'm practically tipping over.*

DAWN: *juno's parents (aka my teacher and her surprisingly buff husband??) just got home. gotta go edit like a madwoman. byeeeee*

COLLIN: *Later skater.*

Dawn grabbed her money and left the house quietly as her teacher and her husband stumbled around just barely drunk on a night out alone. She spent the entire bus ride texting pictures of Bimini Bon-Boulash to the groupchat she had with Edie and Georgia and was warm in her room before eleven o'clock.

Dawn put her phone in her backpack and zipped it all the way then put her backpack in the closet. She did this to keep herself from getting distracted by questions that occurred to her randomly, or texts. One second she was asking herself *what was the name of that girl in* The Outsiders? *Peach? Carmen?* then suddenly two hours later she was six articles and two Wikipedia pages deep into the history of the hanky code. She was proactively saving herself from herself.

She pulled out her laptop and began the slow process of rewatching interviews she'd filmed earlier that month of students from other schools around the city. Friends of friends in the same band room where she filmed all the talking heads appeared on screen as she downloaded their clips and dragged the videos into the editing suite. She tried to find a font she liked for the chyron at the bottom of everyone's interview displaying their names and ages but was struggling to figure out what she wanted the film to look like overall. After talking to Collin, she'd changed a few things around with the narrative structure of the film, and Dawn was seeing the end product come together more and more. He gave her some editing tricks and told her about movies she might like that reminded him of her work.

Dawn liked talking to Collin. He was comfortable and almost nice to a fault. He always texted in full sentences. They texted each other now for no reason at all and Dawn couldn't help but feel nice every time she saw his name pop up with the little emoji right beside it.

She kept watching clips, like unboxings that revealed different scenes from stranger's lives, then closing the box again only to open up another and then another.

I actually met my partner at White Linen Night in the Heights, can you believe that? Isn't that the most obnoxious thing you've ever heard? We were both buying vintage pottery.

I don't know who I am yet. I think queerness is about constantly unburying yourself from this huge dirt pile. It's like, me, I made the hole. I put the dirt in. And I'm probably going to spend my whole twenties digging for some semblance of a full person under there. It's kind of sad but also kind of relieving.

Do you like my skirt? I wore it because my friend said she dressed nice for her interview. This is my first time wearing a skirt to school. It feels scary and totally exciting too. Is that dumb?

One time when we were arguing, my mom told me that some celebrity on TV said his mom asked him not to come out of the closet until after she died. I asked if that's what she wanted me to do. She said she didn't know. I think I was fourteen. I'm sixteen now.

Sometimes I think I've made him up. That's how perfect my boyfriend is. On our first date, I told him I was kind of a germaphobe, and at the end, he held one of those swinging trash cans open for me so I didn't have to touch it. That's how I knew.

When we first kissed, it was like an elevator that couldn't stop on any one floor. Up and up and up and up.

I feel like my body is always in the line of fire. So many people have questions about how my body moves and works, what clothing I put on it and how it slouches or bends. All I want is to be. I want to put on the clothes that make me feel pretty. I want to walk with my shoulders

back and my head high. It's a casual violence. That's it.
A casual violence other people have towards me.

Editing the documentary, she played each clip over and over again until she felt like the stories were her own. Maybe *she* had met her boyfriend on Tumblr. Maybe *she* had been the one to go to the same craft store three days in a row trying to get the cashier with the blue hair to pay attention to her.

But they weren't and she hadn't.

She thought about Knox and his slouching shoulders and quiet laugh. Was he just another story she was telling herself? The date had been fun, easy, easier than almost anything she'd done with anyone else so far. She remembered him bending down to pick up a fallen doll from the shelf of a vendor's stall full of toys. A little girl in yellow begged him to hand it to her and he did with a smile. The feeling Dawn had felt in her stomach at that moment was undeniable.

Dawn didn't want to get ahead of herself but of course she loved to. She loved to imagine futures that might never happen. Knox was the start of her own potential love story. If she were interviewing herself, she'd say they'd met at a party and fallen into each other like dominoes.

The night stretched out like tired limbs and Dawn's eyes got heavier every second. She wanted to be done but knew it was a process that required time and attention. She wanted to have a real movie, but the finished thing was so far ahead of her she could barely imagine it. Each little shuffle was an inch towards a very blurry finish line.

She had all the motivation in the world. Edie and Georgia constantly encouraged her to interview and edit as though she were making something that was really important to them. People that she had interviewed constantly asked her how it was going. See-ing her father unable to take care of himself pushed her like nothing else. The scholarship and extra money would basically save her. Even Collin with his documentary tips and late-night texts about movies and dumb jokes shifted her into high gear. Dawn was going to finish her documentary and win the competition even if it took every night of her young life.

FIFTEEN

Dawn watched Knox's hands turn slowly on the worn leather steering wheel and wondered where they were going. He had texted her that morning with a proposal for a surprise second date. *Dress fancy, but not too fancy*, the text read, accompanied by a ghost emoji. She had no idea what it meant, so she borrowed Georgia's too-small tenth-grade-formal dress and placed her expectations at a comfortable height where she could see them.

He'd picked her up in his truck, an old silver Ford he said belonged to his older brother who'd left it at home for Knox when he went away to college. He was wearing black dress pants and a plain, white button-down underneath a mustard-yellow cardigan. Dawn thought he looked like he was going birdwatching in a private New York City garden in 1940. She let herself laugh quietly at the thought as she looked around at the city outside the window.

The bright green tulle dress she had on felt a little silly now that she was looking down at it splayed across her thighs. What if we're just going to get pizza or something, she thought. Slashes of streetlamps cut across Knox's sharp jaw as he drove further and further into East Downtown.

She'd come to this part of town once to take photos of Edie for some media class assignment. The stout industrial buildings were mostly covered in graffiti. There were portraits of civil rights activists and men who'd been unjustly gunned down by police.

Collages, flowers, and murals saying, "EVERYTHING IS GOING TO BE ALRIGHT" and "LOVE THE EARTH" covered every inch of concrete and brick.

Dawn straightened out the front of her dress across her lap and debated asking how close they were to the mystery location. Their first date confirmed that he wasn't a serial killer, but one could never be too sure, she thought as she checked her phone to make sure Georgia and Edie had her location pinged. They always did this, tracked each other when they went out with anyone new. Sometimes, she even checked in on their locations at night to make sure they were in the right place. Not because she was worried, but because she could. It was a ritual she enjoyed like nothing else.

"Almost there," Knox said, as if reading her mind. He turned to look at her as they made another corner and she decided everything was going to be fine.

He crept into an empty lot and parked next to a small steel building that seemed to glow softly from the inside. She could see something orange and bright through the dirt-worn windows.

"Come on." Knox cut the engine. He got out of the car and Dawn sat in silence for a moment as he came around to her side of the truck to open her door. Dawn listened to his keys jingling and thought of all the bad things that could happen in the coming moments. She had been with boys who wanted to hurt her. She could see it in their eyes like fire approaching a stream of gasoline. She braced herself for the worst but then stopped herself from spiraling downward in her head. Knox was good and normal and sweet. *Please, please, please let this be normal and good and sweet.*

"Should I be scared?" she tried to let out a joking laugh.

"Just trust me." He smiled and she melted again. She took a deep breath and repeated his words to herself: *Just trust him. Just trust him. This will be normal and good and sweet.*

They held hands during the short walk, and after a while ended up standing before a busted open window on the building's far right side.

Knox approached the window, and without pausing, climbed through, his huge sneakers and broad shoulders barely touching the window's edges as he shimmied through to the other side. He looked back at Dawn and reached his hand out.

"Are you kidding?"

"No, not at all. The surprise is in here."

"If you murder me, I'm going to be so annoyed," Dawn whined.

She grabbed his hand and stretched her right leg through the window and buckled forward slightly, almost catching her dress on the window's jagged glass edge.

"Here, hold my arm." Dawn struggled for a moment to avoid the glass but pulled herself up and over eventually, her nails digging into the fabric of his cardigan.

The first thing she noticed was candles.

They lined the windowsills, the floor, every surface glowed with orange and yellow flames of varying shapes and sizes. There were half-burned jars, candlesticks, Halloween-themed wax holders shaped like ghosts and pumpkins.

"I picked up as many as I could from a bunch of different thrift stores." Knox watched her as she looked around the large, echoing room, where a picnic was spread out before them.

Dawn went quiet.

"What do you think?"

She couldn't think of anything to say. Silence gripped her as a million thoughts crossed her mind simultaneously. Her first thought was that she did not deserve this act of affection. No one had ever done anything so nice for her. She wanted to cry, or maybe call Georgia and Edie, or somehow talk to her mom about what to do when boys were too nice to even believe.

"You hate it. Wow, that is . . . super embarrassing. Um, we can go somewhere else if you want. I have another place we can go." Knox tripped over his words and hurriedly turned back to the window they'd come in through.

Dawn finally looked away from the picnic and turned to grab his arm. He looked her in the eye as she gripped him, searching. Dawn almost laughed at how amazing he looked. This kind of boy had always been a punchline to a joke she liked to tell herself late at night. Amazing boy likes girl. Girl is dumb enough to believe it. Girl gets made to look like an idiot in the end.

"No. I love it. I absolutely love it. It's almost too nice. I mean, I don't know what to say. I love it." She looked him in his eyes as she said this, hoping to get across all that she couldn't say out loud.

Knox relaxed again, his shoulders relaxing down from the hunched position they'd taken just moments earlier. He lowered her hand from his arm and squeezed his palm around hers. His hands were sticky with nervousness, but Dawn liked the feeling of warmth anyway.

"Come on." She let him guide her to the blanket where they both kneeled down to sit against the plush material.

"You look incredible by the way. Sorry I didn't say that before, I was kind of anxious about the whole breaking and entering thing," he laughed.

"You too."

"Oh, thanks. I thought dress pants would be both fancy and good for the floor. Sorry, I should have told you we were going to be sitting on the ground."

"It's okay. I think the fluff of my tulle is protecting me."

"Good." He settled into a firm sitting position. "Okay, so here's what I've prepared for our evening." He gestured to the plates in front of them both. "I have labored over a luxurious dinner of peanut butter sandwiches and saltine crackers and grapes. Also, a baguette that was on sale at Trader Joe's." Dawn laughed and reached for a grape to pop into her mouth as he continued.

"For dessert," He reached into the basket and pulled out a small cake that fit perfectly into his gathered palms, "we have my miniature version of Mary Berry's Victoria sponge cake. Strawberries instead of raspberries, because I'm not a monster."

He set the cake down and sucked the icing that had escaped to his pinky off between his perfectly rounded lips. He wiped his wet hand on the back of his pants.

"Oh, I forgot. I brought a little speaker for music too." He tossed the phone with the music app open at Dawn so that it landed in the fluff of her skirt with a dull thud.

"Pick something."

"Oh god. Like what?" Dawn hesitantly grabbed the phone and began to scroll through his music. The usual suspects: Gus Dapperton, Kim Petras, Charli XCX, too much Tame Impala to count.

"Something good." He shrugged and focused on the food arrangement.

A little bit of panic set in and Dawn's thoughts raced at the pressure of setting the right vibe. She had to create the perfect mood. Romantic, but not too romantic. Lowkey but not sleepy. Memorable and good yet soft and sweet.

"You okay?" He looked at her while pouring cider into two glasses that had somehow appeared while she was staring down at the waiting search bar.

"Yeah. I just don't want to play the wrong thing."

"No worries. Here, I'll pick something. And if you hate it, we'll just change it."

An old Frank Ocean song flowed into the echoing room.

"Alright, I think everything is ready," Knox said.

Dawn reached for her sandwich.

"How's the movie going?" he asked between chews of his first bite.

Dawn spoke before taking a bite. "Good. I'm getting down to the final interviews. I hate hate *hate* editing, but I have to do it."

"That's so cool. Cool that you're interviewing people like Ben."

"Like Ben, how?"

"Like, genderless. He's kind of like you."

"They," Dawn replied quickly, moving on to the more important mistake. "And I'm not like Ben." She watched his head tilt to the side again. "I'm a girl."

"Hmm." He took a sip of his cider.

Dawn watched his unmoving expression and tried to think of a way to push forward, to keep talking about anything else. "It's nice, though, to feel how close I am to having something real and complete."

"I can't imagine. I don't know anything about how movies are made. Or, documentaries, if there's a difference," Knox shrugged.

"And there is," Dawn interrupted between bites. She covered her mouth with the back of her hand.

Knox let out a little laugh. "Of course. Do you have a favorite?"

"What, documentary? That's impossible, but I did just see *The Price of the Ticket* which was really good. It's about James Baldwin. I don't know if you could really even call it a documentary."

"Who's James Baldwin?"

"Oh no," she glowered. "Are you joking?" Dawn immediately regretted her words as he shook his head. She knew that people hated when you act like they're supposed to know everything all the time. It was one of her worst habits, expecting everyone to know the exact same things she did.

"Um, he's a famous gay, black writer and activist. He kind of just like, left America for Paris for most of his life because he was sick of racism and homophobia, but then when civil rights started popping off in the late fifties, he came back. I have a few of his books, so you could borrow some if you want."

"That's so cool. Unrelated, but I saw this film one time called *Toast* that I'm pretty sure is my favorite movie of all time. It's about a famous chef. Helena Bonham Carter plays his evil step-mom. They have to beat each other in cooking competitions to win the affection of the dad. It's kind of incredible."

"I've never seen it, but I want to immediately. I have a running list of movies I want to see that's approaching ridiculous lengths."

"How many?"

"Definitely over a hundred," Dawn confessed. "Honestly, it's a lot of classic movies that I feel like I'm *supposed* to have seen at this point as a self-professed movie connoisseur."

"Wow. You're going to kill me." Knox gritted his teeth into a smile.

"What, why?"

"I've never seen *Forrest Gump*."

"Dude, *I've* never seen *Forrest Gump*." Dawn searched around and found the glass of cider Knox poured for her. She downed it and looked at Knox with a smirk.

"No way. You know, if we watched it together, you could cross it off your list."

"Is that a third date proposal I hear?" She put the glass down then picked it back up, her hands still nervous as she toyed with the rim.

"Absolutely." Dawn smiled up at him when he said this, and felt peanut butter smeared on the bottom edge of her lip.

"You have a little something." Knox reached out and let his thumb brush against her chin.

He brought his hand back and Dawn saw the bit of spread on his finger. He licked the peanut butter off with a smile.

"You ready for dessert?"

Dawn's mind wandered several places, and she couldn't keep pace with the question.

"Yes. I'm- yes."

He laid the cake out, cut her a slice, and slid the plate towards her.

Dawn reached down and brought the plate to her chest. She ushered the fork to her lips, careful not to spill anything on her clothing. She brought her lips, which she knew by now were only covered by a spottily faded lipstick, around a small bite. The flavor was tart and sweet all at the same time. The strawberries and icing mixed on her tongue like a frantic and wonderful dance. It was as near perfect as it could possibly be.

Knox watched her as she finished the first bite. He hadn't even picked up his plate yet, nervous and anticipating critique.

"It's very correct. It's right." Dawn slid the fork out of her mouth and went for another bite.

The second bite of cake hit her mouth and she started tapping her outstretched foot in a little rhythm against the edge of the blanket.

"That good? Good enough for a little happy dance?" Knox nodded at her foot.

"Oh, god. I didn't even realize I was doing that. I always used to jump around when I was a kid when my mom would make, like, macaroni or spaghetti for me after school. Bad habit, I think."

"That's so cute. You're really cute." His eyebrows furrowed as he picked up his plate.

Dawn blushed and stuffed another piece in her mouth.

The night drew on and Dawn grew more comfortable sitting across from him. They talked more about school and how Knox wanted to build his own solar-powered greenhouses for communities that didn't have ways to grow food.

She felt herself liking him more and more with every reverberating laugh, every snap of his fingers he made when he couldn't quite remember the name of something but had it on the tip of his tongue.

"You know," *snap snap snap,* "the girl who used to be on *Suite Life of Zack and Cody* who played the nerd. Then she was the mean girl in uh," *snap snap snap,* "*High School Musical.*"

"Oh, queen and popstar Ashley Tisdale? Of 2007 pop hit "He Said She Said" fame?"

"Yes! Exactly! How did you know that?" Again, his eyes, orbs of bright amazement Dawn couldn't look away from.

"I cared . . . way too much about *High School Musical.*" She tilted her head down and smiled, her plate now empty and crested in crumbs.

"I've never actually seen it all the way through, I think. Wait no. I saw the first one but not the other ones."

"You know what? You're probably fine."

He laughed and Dawn noticed his lips again. His fully lined up smile with one bottom tooth sticking out imperfectly which of course made Dawn fall in love with him even more.

The night went on like water down a drain. They talked and talked until just a few candles remained, the rest blown out with a series of drafts that wafted in through the open windows.

They'd inched closer and closer as they spoke until there was no room to deny how badly Dawn wanted to kiss him.

"Did you want to maybe head out and go somewhere else?" he asked, his breath now spilling into Dawn's as she tried to keep her heartbeat from vibrating through every inch of her skin.

"Um, yeah. We could go . . ."

She tried to think clearly, but his skin was touching hers in three different places and she couldn't hold on to any thought long enough to make sense of it.

"To yours?" he asked.

"To my house. If you want," she shuddered quietly.

"Yeah?" He brought his hand up to brush her hair behind her ear and for a moment she thought she'd actually stopped breathing. He leaned in closer and dipped his head down so that they were level. He gently touched his forehead to hers and their lips lightly brushed.

This close, the smell of crushed strawberry jam on his tongue swirled around her head before settling at the tip of her nose.

As Dawn debated leaning in to bridge the final gap between their lips, Knox kissed her.

As his lips moved against hers, she felt warm and honey-sweet. The good feeling gripped her like a rubber band pulled tight.

Knox pulled away and looked her in her eyes. She looked back and saw kindness, a boy offering his sweetness to her. He stood up and grabbed Dawn's hand to help her stand. She stumbled a bit over her tulle and fell into him so that her hands landed flat on either side of his chest with a gentle push. He held her there for a moment, letting the few remaining candles play in her eyes. She felt the perfection of the date all around her.

They blew out the candles, grabbed the basket and blanket, and pulled off into the late evening.

SIXTEEN

March 24, Seven Days to Deadline

Now that Knox was here, Dawn saw her room as small and unimportant. Nothing in it gave the idea that an interesting and fully formed person might live inside. She had a ratty blue bedspread and white dresser drawer. On top of the dresser sat two small containers filled with clip-on earrings she had worn so many times she'd forgotten where any of them had come from. A television that had stopped showing actual channels sometime between elementary school and this exact moment sat buzzing hushed static ceaselessly in the corner. She kept it on because she liked the white noise in the background.

As they sat together on her bed, she watched Knox move his eyes over her empty walls, the TV glowing soft against his skin. She'd never brought anyone she was interested in here before and hesitantly watched him observing all the nothing. The marigolds from their first date sat on a makeshift shelf beside her bed. She became excruciatingly aware of the winding springs of her mattress pushing upward into her thighs and the cheapness of the bed.

They sat close enough to each other to make her nervous but far enough to make her want more. The wanting made her feel childish. She untangled herself from the comforter and walked across the room.

She stood in front of her dresser and bent down to the bottom drawer where she kept her books.

"Do you like poetry?" she asked.

"Sure, I guess. I mean, I don't know much about it."

"My friend Georgia got me into it."

She stood up and walked back to the bed where Knox had comfortably trapped himself in the blanket atop her sheets. With one hand grasping the book, she used the other to join him under the warmth. In an attempt to get comfortable, her hand brushed against his knee and she drew back. Their eyes met, and he smiled but said nothing. Her stomach turned over again and again. She tried to concentrate on the book and let her thumb fall over several pages until it met a worn space where the binding had bent backwards and broken.

When I see you pass by, my indolent darling,
To the sound of music that the ceiling deadens,
Pausing in your slow and harmonious movements,
Turning here and there the boredom of your gaze;

When I study, in the gaslight which colors it,
Your pale forehead, embellished with a morbid charm,
Where the torches of evening kindle a dawn,
And your eyes alluring as a portrait's,

I say within: "How fair she is! How strangely fresh!"
Huge, massive memory, royal, heavy tower,
Crowns her; her heart bruised like a peach
Is ripe like her body for a skillful lover.

Knox stared at her as she looked up from the page. "It's Baudelaire," she whispered.

His hand moved to her cheek. Everything in the room suddenly became a question. His palm gentle against her face was a question. His eyes as he leaned into Dawn were a question. His fingers as he moved the book to the side of the pulled-back sheets asked several questions, and Dawn felt the answer to all of them was yes.

She leaned in, she leaned in, she leaned in.

There were several uncertain pauses between their lips as they kissed. Dawn didn't know what would happen next, and something about his gentleness told her he didn't either. They kissed again. His bottom lip became wet as it met her open mouth then moved down to brush against her neck. The questions kept coming.

He moved his fingertips underneath her tulle so that both his hands surrounded the softness of her stomach on either side. Tilting forward, he nestled his nose into her neck and placed a single kiss above the collar of the dress.

She helped him take off the dress completely and let it slide lazily from the sheets to the floor. Some part of her was mortified to be seen, the other impatient and comfortable beneath the warmth of his palms.

His hands squeezed softly at the space below her ribs.

"Wait, why are you wearing a bra?" The sentence rolled off of his tongue and into Dawn's mind like a single, shining marble.

"What?"

"Your bra. You don't have boobs."

"I-I know. And I don't really want them."

Dawn crossed her arms across her nearly naked chest without thinking. She held the whole world in her mouth and felt afraid to let a single river out. She was not going to cry in front of this stupid boy. He didn't deserve to see her wide open.

"Then—"

"It's just— This is just. It's how I dress." She could hear herself becoming defensive and hated every second. No one needed to know why she was a revelation in her own right. Why she did or did not want things for herself, for her body.

"No, I know. It's just like kind of a weird thing for a guy to do."

"Wh—"

"I mean, I get that you like to wear skirts and stuff but like, the bra is kind of extreme. Like no one even sees that. I mean, I'm seeing it, but—"

"I'm not a guy."

"What?"

"I'm a girl. A trans girl."

He slipped his hand into the lining of her underwear which had become exposed in their fumbling. As she realized that while she was naked he was still completely dressed, she suddenly felt incredibly stupid. Stupid for letting him into the bedroom, stupid for the whole day. She didn't push his hand away in objection, but turned to look at the blank walls of her room.

"I mean, not really." He pulled his finger back to let the band of her underwear snap against her hip.

"Get out." She went red and could feel anger and frustration building up in her chest.

"Come on. I mean we could still . . . you know."

"I said get out!"

He pushed the sheets off and looked at her for what felt like years.

"Get out! Get out! Get out!" Her pleas became desperate and strained. He moved from the bed without a word.

The ugly, full sound of her oncoming tears fell over the room as the door slammed closed. She hadn't even begun to cry fully and already felt tiredness envelop her body. She listened for the front door. When it finally latched, she wrapped the blanket tight all around herself and tried to disappear. Through the small slit of light where her eyes peeked out from the fabric, she saw the marigolds.

She leaned over to the platform they sat on, picked them up, and threw them against the door with a yell that reverberated back up the walls and into the broken glass. The sound of her own anger scared her. It was as if she'd been meaning to scream for months.

....
....

Dawn turned the camera on and positioned herself on the bed. She looked into the flipped viewfinder to spot herself amongst the blankets and make sure she was in focus. Moonlight trickled in through her window in waves and touched her skin all over. She was her own favorite color.

I thought love was about being the best possible punching bag, and I was wrong. I know that now.

Queer love is untouchable. If I didn't know so many people in relationships, I'd swear it didn't fucking exist. I mean, I love my friends more than anything. That's its own love, community love, the kind you need when your parents can't see you for who you are. But that's not what I'm talking about. I'm talking about romantic, gotta have it, everything reminds me of you you you, capital L love. Being me is lonely. It's very lonely. I don't know if love can fix it but I'm almost certain it has the potential to. It will.

This documentary is about representation but it's also about a lot more than that. It's about making queer people human. It's about youth, it's about a universal feeling. Everyone knows what love is. It's nice because the definition is so different from person to person. That's what I'm interested in. The difference. The variation. The ways love can exist in the world from a kiss to an orange peel.

SEVENTEEN

March 25, Six Days to Deadline

Houston suburbs seemed so spacious and quiet to Georgia that they somehow had their own sound. Perfectly manicured trees rustling, small and large dogs barking in their very own yards, the squelching tires of cars pulling into driveways, all of them the exact same. Georgia parked her car in the lot of a neighborhood pool.

They set out on their own three-woman parade to a party that was going to be lame but nonetheless needed their presence. As their high school went, everyone was going to be there simply because there was nothing else to do that weekend.

"You know what? Fuck him," Georgia muttered, her strides way too big for Edie and Dawn to keep up.

"Who, Knox? I know. I just thought he was so nice," Dawn whined over the sound of a passing car.

"Not everyone who's attractive and interesting is nice," Georgia preached, attempting an air of wisdom.

"Of course I know he's awful, I just don't like making mistakes, even if the mistake is another person."

"You've never done anything wrong in your life."

"You know what's weird? Even after all that, I still kind of want to be in love. Is that weird? Like, I want to match clothes with someone. Is that ugly?" Dawn cringed at her own words.

"Yes and yes, but I support you. I want that for you." Georgia laughed.

"Okay, good."

"So what's up with that guy you've been texting from the film festival," Georgia asked, finally slowing down enough at the end of a short block for Edie and Dawn to get in step with her on the sidewalk.

"Collin?" Georgia watched a small smile appear on Dawn's face.

"Yeah. I feel like you're always texting him. Like, not in a bad way, just like, who is this mystery man who's got you giggling at your phone? I mean, you're literally smiling right now and I barely mentioned him."

Edie raised an eyebrow but remained quiet as they kept walking.

"He's funny and I feel like we're on the same wavelength about a lot of different film stuff. It's like, every time he texts me, I want to read it right then," Dawn began to skip but stopped when she realized Edie was falling behind. "Is that problematic? A friend crush on a person I've never met?"

"It's modern. It's cute. We live in the internet age." Georgia placed her hand on her hip with a shrug. "If you want to have a new best friend in your phone we've never met, go off."

"Georgia."

"I'm just kidding! Is he cute?"

"He's from Austin. He's in college," Dawn turned dramatically to face Georgia as she leaned against the counter, "and yes, he's very cute."

Georgia glanced at her now dinging phone as the group blindly walked towards several houses with the same bricks and windows in all the same places. She let out a small sigh at the notification on her screen.

"What?" Edie questioned.

Georgia quickly shut her phone off and walked ahead. "Nothing."

"Seriously, what?" Edie poked until Georgia let out a slow exasperated breath.

"Sarah Bettelhem just told me Ben is going to be there," she uttered through tight lips.

"It's not that big of a deal. I'm fine." Edie kept walking, her eyes trained on the sidewalk.

"Okay, girl. If you say so." Georgia went quiet.

"She's only saying that 'cause she doesn't want to admit that Ben is the only person who has ever understood any of her family shit," whispered Dawn. " Plus, you act like lying to your parents is such a big deal because you want them to think you're perfect and straight but you actually lie to them all the time."

"What?" Edie stopped in the middle of the sidewalk.

"D," added Geo, shocked at Dawn's sudden bluntness. Georgia was usually the one saying the harshest version of the truth. She waited for something to happen as Edie ceased to move on the sidewalk.

"Are you kidding?" Edie's lips parted in shock.

Dawn stopped walking and turned around to look at Edie.

"Why would I be kidding? Ben went through all that shit for you and you basically made them break up with you because of your parents. I know I'm supposed to be on your side or whatever but like, Ben was fucking cool and you were really rude to them."

"Can you guys chill for like three seconds," Georgia interjected, trying to cool the conversation.

"Sorry. Just forget it," Dawn went quiet. The girls started walking again.

Dawn turned to Georgia after a moment. "Speaking of um, family shit, how did your mom's date go with the mystery man? You never told us."

"No comment," she muttered.

"That ugly? Yikes."

Georgia kept silent hoping the subject would change. The whole thing felt too big and too unreal to utter.

Edie suddenly increased her pace so she was in front of Georgia and Dawn then stopped and turned around.

"You're right, D. Okay? You're right. I was wrong. I did the wrong thing. I messed up." She paused for a long time and let out a small sigh. "Listen, I'm not twelve. If they want to talk, we can talk. If not? It's no big deal."

Dawn chimed in. "I actually just turned twelve yesterday, so despite my earlier statements, I will facilitate and even participate in a confrontation on your behalf if I need to," she said with a laugh.

"No, we're going to be adults." Edie narrowed her eyes at Georgia and Dawn.

"How boring," Dawn sighed. "You know who else is going to be there? Georgia's lover." Dawn drawled out the words and placed a hand on Georgia's cheek.

They laughed and kept walking. Another park floated by and dozens of neighborhoods labeled with carved stones, all named after types of trees and bodies of water. The night went on as they wandered farther and farther into the twists and turns of cul-de-sacs until the muddied sound of teenagers chatting and too loud music came into earshot. Busted cars were parked up and down the street. People were huddled smoking weed and hanging out by the cars in groups of three and four.

The house emerged from the darkness, its interior lights peeking out from small windows smattered across from the front of the façade. The lawn was littered with bodies talking in small circles. The night started within the girls as they moved towards the front door.

Bodies gathered in the living room like ants over abandoned fruit. The party's host, Gunther, was nowhere to be found and the girls tried to ease into the movement of the party. Dawn and Edie disappeared into the crowd to find something to drink. The kitchen seemed to be the pulsing heart of the party at the moment.

Like an arrow, Georgia's body found its way to the bumping center of the living room, which functioned as the dance floor. Georgia wanted to forget everything she'd ever known. She wanted to know nothing about Simone, about school, about who she was or where she was going. She closed her eyes and began to move to the music all around her.

She decided at that moment to permanently keep the situation with Simone to herself. She had been thinking that telling Edie and Dawn would help her figure out what to do, but now she saw that it was useless, another problem on a huge stack of already existing problems. She hated being difficult. She hated being the problem. For her mother, for her school, for her friends. She didn't mind being the problem for herself. She would deal with it on her own. The movement of the music sifted through her limbs and let her be free from the stress of his voice, his smell, his face too close to hers. Somebody's hand brushed against her lower back as they moved through the living room and she flinched. She hated the disgust she felt but kept dancing anyway.

....
....

Edie and Dawn moved to the kitchen, which bumbled with unimportant talk of school and what new album was the best, though

Edie and Dawn thought that nobody at Alsbury knew anything about anything, especially music.

Edie snatched up an almost empty handle of vodka and began to look for juice and sodas on the counter. Dawn eyed her as she moved around the now sticky marble countertops for something to mix her drink with. "You don't usually drink," Dawn said evenly.

"I could though," Edie retorted. She could start right now. For once, she didn't need to ask for permission to do something wrong. Dawn was right. She had been rude to Ben and made them break up with her. She was wrong. She was the mess. She lied constantly and had no one left.

"I don't know, E." Dawn brushed the hair from her face and kept an eye on Edie's frantic movements.

Edie couldn't find the mixer she was looking for and brought the large glass bottle of vodka above her head. She felt drunk on the night without having had a drop. She tipped the bottle towards her lips as Dawn watched in horror. The vodka splashed against her chin and dribbled down to her top, some of it catching in her mouth. It stung and she felt stupid but still determined to make the wrong decision on purpose; to prove to herself that she had control over something.

"Oops."

"Okay then." Dawn reached for the bottle and set it down on the counter beside Edie. Edie picked up a different almost empty bottle of liquor. Probably something from Gunther's parents, it looked too fancy to be corner store trash for seventeen-year-olds willing to drink anything.

Edie laughed lightly as though she was already intoxicated from the one sip. She tilted her head back again and kept drinking.

"Please come dance with me," Dawn grabbed Edie's hand, helping her put the bottle down. "It'll be good." Dawn led Edie away to the living room.

Edie eased into the music, Dawn's hand still clenching her own. She spun and spun in bumbled in circles around her friend.

....
....

Dawn's phone buzzed and she migrated away from Edie to the edge of the room so she could read the text without bumping into all the moving bodies congregated in the center of the living room.

Collin's name popped up on her screen and she couldn't help but smile to herself. She was getting used to their conversations. Not even a mediocre house party would keep her from reading his words immediately.

COLLIN: *Just finished the doc about Charleston and you were 100% right. Too many shots of birds!*
Dawn snickered.
DAWN: *lol right?? at a party rn and you wouldn't believe how yikes things are getting*
COLLIN: *????*
DAWN: *edie is getting Very drunk despite never drinking and i think geo is talking to her secret-not-secret-anymore girlfriend*
COLLIN: *Wow. That does sound yikes. Is Edie ok?? She's the one who just broke up with her partner, right?*
DAWN: *yup :(and yeah she's having a hard time. she's ok. or . . . she will be. i know her, she's totally brilliant and tough. weird u haven't met them but know so much*
COLLIN: *I was just thinking that! Hope I can meet them if you come to Austin for the fest. My friends swear I made you up and am actually just texting myself all the time.*
DAWN: *lol tell them I said hey. really*

COLLIN: *We'll see if they believe me. Collin and the invisible girl. Not a bad movie title.*

DAWN: *Dawn Salcedo Will Haunt Your iPhone Forever! not as catchy :~) k, gotta go but call later! i think i hear edie yelling at someone in the kitchen*

COLLIN: *Oof. Later ghost girl.*

Dawn turned towards the hallway off of the living room and through a cracked door saw Jill and Georgia laying on a queen-sized bed. She turned back to the living room to look for Edie but couldn't spot her in the small crowd. She felt a small panic build up in her chest as she made her way back to the kitchen where she could hear Edie's voice emitting off its tiles.

Dawn found Edie with the same bottle from earlier held in one hand while the other hand raised a white, porcelain plate from the kitchen's many cabinets high above her head.

"Edie, put it down, I'm serious. Put it down." Dawn held her palm out like you would a wild animal soon to attack.

Edie laughed drunkenly.

"Seriously, E. Chill out and just put it down" Dawn begged. She imagined the plate hitting the floor, she imagined the startled look on Edie's face, the night ruined for everyone.

"I'm going to smash it like we're at a wedding!" Dawn watched as Edie stumbled, unable to keep herself from doubling over; it was like her torso had decided it was tired of holding her up, everything slow and uncontrollable. Edie tripped over the hem of her dress and her fingers let go of the plate. It went flying against the hard countertop, and Edie's body bent to the floor like tumbling building blocks, her dress pooling around her knees.

Dawn watched the whole disaster in slow motion, the plate breaking exactly how she'd imagined it would. Except that no flood of realization hit Edie, who looked up at her with a glassy smile from the floor.

"Dawn, will you marry me?" Edie whined out as she began gathering broken porcelain bits from around the floor.

"Edie, please. You're going to . . ." Dawn trailed off as her phone rang on the counter. An old picture of her dad appeared on the screen. Her stomach turned as she picked up the phone.

"E, get up. I'll be right back." She walked out of the kitchen as her thumb slid across the screen to answer the call. She rushed to the bathroom and shut the door behind her. She could barely understand her father's voice on the other end of the line, the steady stream of music blaring against the closed bathroom door. She listened closely as the voice on the other end mumbled words at her.

Dawn emerged from the bathroom, still on the phone. "Okay, Papa, I'm coming. Don't move. I'll be there in just a second." She hung up and rushed out of the bathroom.

The first person she spotted in the now even more crowded living room was Ben.

"Ben, I need you to drive me somewhere. Please. Now." She grabbed their arm as she spoke. Her voice wrenched as she tried to keep herself together.

"Yeah, yeah absolutely." They nodded quickly.

"I'm gonna text Georgia. I think she's in the bedroom. And can you please grab Edie?"

Ben's face scrunched in confusion and Dawn realized they hadn't seen her all night.

"In the kitchen. I'll text Geo and meet you in the car."

"Yeah. Here," Ben tossed their keys in Dawn's direction and she ran out to their car.

EIGHTEEN

March 26, Five Days to Deadline

Edie, Ben, and Dawn took an exit off of 288 and pulled into the large parking lot of an H-E-B. Georgia pulled up alone in her own car next to Ben's, her headlights blaring out into the night.

Edie trained her eyes on Dawn's quickly moving hands unbuckling the seatbelt next to hers and pushing open Ben's passenger door. The car shook Edie's body as Dawn slammed the door and rushed into the store, followed by Georgia.

Edie looked into the rearview mirror and caught Ben's eye as they turned the ignition so only the car lowlights and radio were on. She sat still in the backseat as the radio played a plush song from the eighties Ben hummed a few notes of.

"Ben, I'm really, really sorry." Edie tried to still her thoughts and fill in the quiet with her now much more sober speech.

"I know," they said, turning the radio down to a low hum.

Edie waited. Her mind was in overdrive.

"Do you think we could . . . get back together?" Edie felt the quiver in her voice, the shallowness of every breath scraping its way out.

"No. I can't be with someone so hidden." They turned off their headlights and stared out at the glowing H-E-B plus! sign, the letter *H* flickering so that it showed *H-E-B plus! E-B plus! H-E-B plus! E-B plus!*.

"I can't be hidden, E. I love you. A lot, obviously. " They stopped looking in the mirror at Edie, their eyes moving to the passenger's side window. "I just want to be me all the time. Not just, like, when it's good for everybody else. You don't understand what it's like to be me." Their hands gripped the steering wheel tight.

"That's not true at all. I know you. Of course, I understand—I—of course I—" Edie's words had dissipated into a slumping whisper.

"Why do you always have to turn the conversation around to you? I'm talking about me and you think this is about you! You know what? I have to go. I'm supposed to pick up my brother." Ben turned the key in the ignition and the car huffily rumbled to life again.

"Okay." She got out of the car. "I love you." Her words met their dirty driver's side window as she stepped out of the backseat and closed the door behind her.

As Ben started to slowly pull off into the lot, Edie ran to stand in front of the car. Ben rolled down their window.

"What are you doing? I could have hit you." Their eyes crazed and angry, they stared at Edie just inches from the hood.

"Your headlights aren't on," she said, her words deflated and heavy.

Ben flipped the car lights on and lit up Edie and her dress and her tears and her bare legs. They pulled around her and drove into the night's traffic. As she turned to look, her stomach wretched and puke spewed from her throat and onto the pavement. She wiped the corner of her mouth and tasted the sting of alcohol on her tongue. There was no time to feel sorry for herself, she stumbled dizzily inside to help Dawn.

....
....

As soon as she entered the store, Dawn realized it was far too big and overwhelming for her to look down every single aisle, some sort of mega H-E-B for suburban families who never ventured into the city and needed to get all their shit in one place. She felt agitation creeping up her skin as she spoke to the only person on the registers, a kid who looked too young to be working there.

Dawn's frustration mounted as he absentmindedly fidgeted with the name tag fixed to his bright red H-E-B smock while she tried to talk to him.

"Have you seen anything? Have you seen a man in here or heard from anybody else who works here?" Her words rushed out in panic but the boy seemed unmoved.

"I don't know what you're talking about." He spoke slowly like each word was a dollar out of his paycheck.

Dawn read the name tag he was toying with. "Vernon, I know you are very tired, but I just got a call from my dad. He's here in this H-E-B, and it's an emergency." Dawn pleaded, her eyes never leaving his hooded ones. He looked one heavy blink away from falling asleep while standing up.

"I don't know. I can call my manager though. I'm just gonna call my manager." He began to reach for a machine near the register that looked like a huge walkie-talkie.

"You are fucking useless!" Dawn shrieked, slamming her hands on the register counter.

Georgia appeared beside her and gazed between Dawn and the boy who now stood with the intercom phone in hand looking startled. "I just checked the bathrooms. No luck."

"Let's just do every aisle," Dawn sighed. "I'll take the back."

"I'll start from the other side," Georgia declared, turning away from Dawn. Rounding the last register, Georgia spotted Edie emerging through the sliding doors and grabbed her hand so they could look together.

Dawn ran as fast as her legs would take her. Her heart tried to burst out of her chest again and again as she looked left and right past each row of shelved food.

Head swiveling back and forth, legs burning hot, she remembered all the times she'd felt like this. Her mother's funeral. Staying at Georgia's house for days in the middle of one of those forever summers, leaving her dad at home alone. She remembered thinking about all the things that could go wrong for him every single day she wasn't by his side, and leaving it anyway.

She heard shouting across the store. "Dawn! Dawn, I'm over here! I found him," Georgia's voice filled the aisles as Dawn turned on her heel and tried to locate her.

Dawn came to a row filled with pots and pans. She met the scene with a gasp. Her father was slumped among the remains of a knocked over shelf of wine glasses. He was bloody and cut up as Georgia and Edie leaned over him, picking up glass from around his hands.

"Oh, god."

She rushed to his side and kneeled into the splattered glass surrounding him, pushing Georgia and Edie away. Her knees met the sharp edges and cold linoleum quickly, but her adrenaline didn't let her feel it all the way.

Peter looked up at her and spoke softly, "You are so pretty. So beautiful like your mother."

"Shhh. Quiet, Papa." She began to reach for small shards of glass caught in his pants.

"I never tell you, Dawn. You are so, so grown up now. You used to be so small. My little Albert."

Dawn breathed in deeply to keep from crying, the air in her lungs threatening to transform into a heaving sob. She held back her tears and concentrated on helping her dad.

"Okay, Papa. Be quiet," she said, continuing to clean him up. She caught a glimpse of a few older women staring as they walked past the aisle on their way to check out.

Dawn suddenly felt embarrassed at the scene. Her father was a mess, and she was just like him, both of them spread out across the floor of the grocery store like crazy people, a perfect pair.

"Go away. I can take care of this," she said to Georgia and Edie, who hovered awkwardly beside her. She didn't look up at them.

"Dawn, please. We can help," Georgia said. She and Edie started to bend down again, towards Dawn and her dad.

"I said go away." As she spoke, she looked up at them and couldn't help the tears from rolling thick down her cheeks at the sight of their pity. "Please go away. I'll call for help, okay? Don't worry."

Dawn couldn't tell if she was relieved or disappointed when they listened to her.

Their footsteps retreated down the aisle, across the front of the store, into the parking lot, away from Dawn and her problems. Dawn felt their absence, her full aloneness. She cried for all the times she'd been alone like this with him and all the times she'd be alone in the future.

The grocery store lights flickered overhead, beating down on her and her dad. She dusted the shattered glass away from her father into a small pile by his side. She felt the pain of her bloodied knees as she tried to stand up. Two of the leftover wine glasses fell as she stumbled to her feet.

"Come on, Papa." She grabbed both his hands and urged him to bend his legs and prop his back up against the shelf to stand.

Dawn called no one, so no one came.

NINETEEN

Monday afternoon, Dawn crept through the front door of her home. Everything was quiet and the lamp above the front porch flickered on as she stepped through to the hallway. The two large ice bags in her arms made it hard for her to carry the rest of the groceries she'd bought, so she put them down and wandered into the kitchen to put all of the food away. She stacked several frozen meals into the freezer and slammed the door shut with a suctioning snap.

Wandering back to the hallway, Dawn spotted the bags of ice and attempted to pick them up. The biting pain of the ice clinging to her arms was overwhelming, so she dropped them onto the foyer floor and dragged them across the linoleum and into the bathroom. The bags left a trail of water she'd have to clean up later.

She quickly emptied the bags into her small tub. Her hand wound the shower handle halfway and cold water spilled out onto the frozen chunks.

After she undressed completely, she stepped in. Her limbs settled in slowly, adjusting to the nipping ice cubes. She lowered herself into the freezing cold water, the tip of her nose the last thing to dip beneath the bath.

As the water swirled above her, she fell deep into memories of her mother's funeral.

She was thirteen years old, just barely on the verge of pretty. The day was clear and warmer than any other day that year so far. Dawn and her dad stood towards the front of a small crowd of their family around her mother's casket as it disappeared out of view and into the ground.

The thing was huge and shining. It made her think of her mother as larger than she actually was, some giant, unmoving object. In reality, her mother was petite and shrill as a cicada in summer. Even when she whispered, her words jettisoned into the air and spread out across a room. This is what made people like her, the feeling she emanated that the whole world was in on the joke with her.

Dawn's dress was incredibly itchy. Her mother had thrifted it for her. The inseam pinched at her ribs and scratched up her thighs. Her father cried loudly over the casket, eventually kneeling to the fresh dirt at his feet. Dawn felt her cheeks go red as onlookers watched the display.

"Hold my hand, Papa." She reached out to her father who was now lying still with both hands strained and red around the edges of the plot of dirt. He let go so that they could clasp each other's hands.

The rest of the service blurred by quickly and ended in Dawn's aunt's house. Her Aunt Kay was her mother's sister and bore only a slight resemblance to her mother's tiny frame and boisterous air. Dawn found her stirring something on the stove, pulling spoons and forks from various drawers around the room.

She spotted Dawn out of the corner of her eye and stopped abruptly. She dropped the utensils and they pulled each other into a tight hug.

They held on for a long time, each not letting the other breathe.

"Your mother was all the family your father had. You be kind. Be easy for him, okay?" Kay muffled into Dawn's then shoulder-length hair.

"I know he's been a little all over the place lately, but it's okay. You just be easy."

"I don't know what I'm going to do Aunt Kay."

"If he ever gets in one of those manic states and disappears on you, you just call me, okay?" Dawn knew she wouldn't but nodded anyway. She'd always been this stubborn, wanting to deal with things on her own no matter how bad they got. When she was a kid, her step-siblings were too old to care for her or even be around so she'd had to rely on herself. The isolation had turned into a righteous obstinance she couldn't shake.

Somewhere off in the distance, a voice shouted, "Dawn. Dawn!" Dawn couldn't place it, and her memories of that day started to go blurry and dissipate.

"Dawn! Dawn!!" Dawn suddenly emerged from the ice-cold bath and was startled to hear her father's voice coming from the living room.

"Dawn!" She gasped for air and shuddered at the chill of the bathroom.

Her father continued to shout as she whipped the towel down from the door hook and attempted to wrap it around her body. She stood quickly to dry off and clumsily darted to the living room, freezing water dripping down her face and legs.

Her dad sat yelling her name until she appeared in the doorway. He was slumped over in the dust-brown armchair watching late-night infomercials for products no one was buying. The small, folding table beside the sofa shook under the weight of a stack of books and dirty dishes.

"Did you make dinner?" he asked, looking up at her as he spoke.

Dawn stood in her towel, dark brown hair soaked and curled around her face. She shivered against the emptiness of the room and felt her toes sinking into the puddle she'd created in the shallow shag carpet.

"Papa, don't scare me like that." Her father looked away, seemingly forgetting what he'd just asked for.

"I'll have it ready in a second, okay?" Her father didn't respond, but instead turned back to watching the television.

"Did you like the little patty things last time? They were on sale, so I got some more."

"Uh huh. The juice too." He looked at Dawn for a long time. He seemed to be trying to grasp a thought that was floating too high above his head. His voice quivered and dropped to a whisper above the muffled commercials buzzing through the room.

"I'm sorry about the store. I don't really know what happened."

"It's okay. You don't have to keep apologizing."

Dawn walked to the kitchen and grabbed a meal out of the freezer. The TV dinner made its way around the dimly lit microwave turntable as she stood with her elbows on the counter, her hands over her eyes.

She wasn't going to cry. She couldn't anymore, her body wouldn't let her.

There was too much to do. She hadn't been to school in days and her assignments were starting to catch up with her. Her NYU acceptance sat unreplied to in her email inbox. Dawn hadn't opened up her laptop to edit footage for the documentary. She felt like a mess, not because of the situation with her father, but because of what it meant for her life—that she came from a messed-up place. That no one would want to love her in a meaningful way because she was heavy with baggage she couldn't let go of. That she didn't deserve the love she wanted.

The microwave dinged and Dawn pulled out the now steaming meal as the edges seared her fingertips with plasticky heat.

The seat beside her father was dingy, but she sat gracefully. She fed her father the dinner as his eyes blankly stared at the television set. There was a woman on screen selling him and Dawn a better, skinnier life.

TWENTY

March 31, Zero Days to Deadline

die slipped into statistics class and found her seat towards the back next to Georgia. The usual teacher, Mrs. Beniretto, was out that day and a substitute sat behind the desk, shopping for high heels on Mrs. Beniretto's desktop computer.

"Have you heard from her since Friday night?" Georgia asked, not to Edie but to the empty desk beside her where Dawn usually would have been.

Edie toyed with her pencil and erased an answer she'd already written down. "No, but we should go over there after school one day this week. What about Wednesday?"

"I can't. My mom is having Simone over for dinner."

"That's my only free day. I might still go if my parents let me. I don't want her to think we're going to disappear or something."

"Maybe I could think of a way to get out of the dinner. I could say I have to study or something. I don't really want to see Simone again if I don't have to."

Edie put her work to the side and lowered her voice "I mean, let's be real. Frank will probably be thankful that you're leaving early so she can get freaky with Simone."

Georgia gagged. "E, what the fuck," she exclaimed loudly.

The substitute teacher shot them a look from the front of the classroom then turned back to the screen she'd been staring into so deeply.

"Frankie and Simone sitting in a tree, K-I-S-S—"

"He's actually disgusting. I can't wait until my mom dumps him like the piece of shit he is." Edie watched Georgia's face shadow and then even.

"Jesus. Where did that come from?" Edie folded the worksheet neatly into her bag and turned her full attention to Georgia.

"I don't want to say. I think I might be overreacting."

"You can tell me. I won't say anything. I swear." Edie leveled her voice and tried to meet Georgia's eyes.

"No, it's okay. I'll figure it out tonight."

"You sure?" Edie asked. She waited as Georgia stared down at her phone with her lips pursed in concentration.

"Yeah, no."

"Okay." Edie pulled the worksheet back out and went back to working on it, distracted by thoughts of what Georgia wasn't saying and Ben. The class was almost over and they needed to turn it in before they left. Edie focused hard on the page and tried to put all of her energy into getting the answers right. Ever since her break with Ben, everything in her life was going right. Or, that's what she was telling herself. She studied more, was somewhat kinder to her parents, and had lots of time to work on her embroidery, which she'd essentially quit doing sophomore year when the difficulty of her classes increased. Yet, here she was unhappy and heartbroken. She thought that maybe she was lying to herself the way she lied to her parents. In reality, she didn't want to embroider or study more, she wanted Ben. She wanted them to hold her and tell her they loved her. No grade or stupid yarn hat was going to replace that feeling of want.

"You okay, E?"

"Huh?"

"Your pencil." She looked down and saw that she'd crushed the lead into the page by pressing down too hard.

"Oh, yeah. Just thinking about Ben." She put the pencil between her teeth and started to chew. She knew she sounded dramatic but couldn't help it.

"Shit, I forgot to tell you. They stopped me in the hall to talk after Bio this morning."

"What did they say?" Edie tried to calm herself, bracing for the worst.

"They just asked how you were."

"Oh."

"They seemed pretty messed up. Like, wearing gym shorts," Georgia laughed. Edie tried to join in but couldn't. Ben had worn cut-off jeans ever since she'd met them, no matter the occasion. Edie had never even seen them in anything else until the first night she'd slept over at their house. Edie liked this about them, their predictability, their sense of self.

"Really?"

"Yeah. Total disaster town."

Edie couldn't decide if she was happy about it or not. Some part of her liked that they were unhappy without her. But only a small part. The rest of her was suffering. Ben understood her, saw her for who she was even with their eyes closed.

"I don't know what to do, Geo. I'm such an idiot. I think I really messed up." She dropped the pencil from her lips and rested her head on the desk.

"You're not an idiot. You are a very smart person who said some very dumb and hurtful things."

"But I can't take it back. I can't take anything back. Ben isn't big on letting things go. I think I knew that about them, but I must have forgotten." Edie thought about all the times Ben would recall past conversations in great detail. They never forgot a single thought or idea she'd had. Would this be something they'd remember forever, too? Her hurtful words replaying in their head until . . . until what?

"Edie, you are my best friend in the entire world, but honestly, I can say that Ben was kind of right and you were kind of wrong." Georgia looked up at the ceiling of the classroom. "I'm sorry I took so long to tell you this, but I saw how sad you were and didn't want to hurt you more than you were already hurting. You wanted them to lie, which made them uncomfortable. You made them feel like their identity wasn't valid, like it was something they could just turn on and off."

"I know, Geo." Edie's frown slumped into a pout as she tried to keep herself from crying in the middle of class.

"Does that mean they had to break up with you? No." Georgia grabbed Edie's hands in hers and squeezed them gently. "Does that mean you can control your parents and all their little problems that make them hate people they don't even know? No."

"I just don't know what to do next. I apologized. I mean, I was a drunk mess, but I did. I meant it. I would apologize again and again." Edie let go of Georgia's hands and rested her head on the desk.

"Listen, I know this isn't comforting, but if they won't forgive you, you just have to let it go." Georgia squeezed Edie's hands in hers again and directed her eyes towards the classroom ceiling again. "Let them go, I mean." Georgia didn't meet Edie's gaze.

"I know," Edie whined out.

"Come here." Georgia grabbed Edie around the shoulders. The hug was tight and made Edie feel a little safer than before.

"Holy shit." Edie gasped out, her lashes still wet from tears.

"What?

"You know Dawn never turned in the film." Edie's eyes were wide in panic at the realization.

"Wait, isn't it—"

"Due today? Yeah. She said she was going to upload the final version she's sending to the film fest on the school computers because they're way faster than her laptop. She hasn't been here in days."

"Shit. You know she disappears sometimes when stuff happens with her dad. Remember spring sophomore year?"

"Yeah. She missed like twenty assignments and we stayed up three nights in a row helping her do math. Well, mostly me, but you were there for moral support."

"So, we need to finish it." Georgia said plainly.

"I was just thinking that." Edie scrunched her eyebrows and ran through solutions in her head.

"How do we do that? You know I don't understand computers."

"No idea."

"Love that, honestly." Georgia tried to laugh but nothing came out.

"What about her movie nerd friend Collin?"

"Oh, I think I actually have a screenshot of his number from one time when Dawn sent me a pic of their messages." Georgia whipped her phone out and started scrolling.

Edie lifted an eyebrow and gave Georgia a questioning look.

"What? It was for an emergency! And now look, an emergency. Let me see if I can text him. Maybe he can tell us what to do."

"Okay. Just let me know and I'll make it happen."

They sat in the back of the class and shared another hug as they watched time go by on the huge clock above the substitute teacher's head.

TWENTY-ONE

My name is Cara. I'm seventeen. I guess I'm just gonna talk about the same shit I always talk about. Math, being tired, I don't know. Anime?

Love is weird. I'm a total Virgo. Everything together, everything in order. It's the same in relationships. Well, the one.

So, let me tell you a story. Freshman year, I met Beatriz my first day here. I'm walking down the English hall and I'm eleven minutes late to freshman seminar fully about to have a breakdown because I couldn't find Miss Zigfield's classroom. It's in that nook around the corner leading into the science hall, which I know now, but then, yeah. Dumb freshman vibes. So Beatriz walks up to me, and I was immediately like "oh this is the prettiest person I've ever seen in real life." Like, this girl is going to be a problem for me. Seriously, that's my first thought. We end up in Zigfield's class together. And Biology. And PE.

Anyway, in an attempt to flirt, I ignore her for like two weeks straight even though I'm literally seeing her three times a day. It didn't work at all but luckily we were put together on this super intense project. Do you remember that thing where we had to make a sculpture of a cell

*with like lights and stuff? Yeah, so that one. I end up at
her house and she made peanut butter cookies, which, I'm
allergic, so she's super embarrassed and like saying how
she's so so sorry meanwhile like I would have taken like
an Oreo and a bottle of water so whatever. Anyway, she
literally bakes me another batch of cookies. Like full-tilt
Martha Stewart in the kitchen, flour all over her face,
making me sugar cookies just for a project hangout. So
yeah, we're sitting on her floor eating hot cookies and I
burn my tongue and I feel stupid but I just tell her like I
really like you.*

*Um, so we dated. I guess you know that. Everyone knows
that. It was super intense. I thought we were gonna get mar-
ried or at least like go to the same college. We dated for three
and a half years and then suddenly we just didn't. Like, I
don't think we got in some huge argument or anything, we
just didn't really fit anymore. So, that sucked. You get really
used to someone. I guess especially since we're in school and
we just see each other every day all the time. I don't think
there was a single year we didn't have at least three classes
together, which is kind of wild.*

*This is supposed to be about love though. So, I'll just
say, I really love her. Love. Not, loved. Love. Like, right
now. I love her right now.*

Edie pressed the red record button on the large camera and
stared intently at the lit-up screen with all its glowing icons and
numbers.

"Oh god." Edie saw a blinking red light and started to panic.

"What?" Cara looked at Edie with wide eyes over her
brushed-brass glasses.

Edie was silent for a moment longer as she stared at the camera equipment with a panicked expression.

"What?" Cara asked again. She stood up from her stool and walked around the tripod to look at the screen over Edie's shoulder.

Edie clicked the red button again and the screen returned to normal.

"Oh, oh my god. Nothing," sighed Edie, startled by the girl's voice behind her, "I thought I hadn't turned the microphone on that whole time. That would have been really bad."

Cara crossed her hand over her chest and clutched at her shirt. "No shit. Thanks for interviewing me, by the way. Dawn's project sounds really cool."

"Yeah, for sure. Sorry it was so last minute, we realized we needed one more interview before the final edit. You're literally the last one." Edie continued to squint at the camera in an attempt to find the off button. "Dawn's way better at this stuff. I'm just trying to help."

"You did great! She's seemed super stressed whenever I've seen her in English for the past, like, month. So it's nice that you're helping." Cara walked across the band room to pick up her tote bag, which was slumped against a broken trombone.

"Professional friendship obligations."

"For sure."

"Hey, can I ask you a question?" Edie didn't look up and began to take the camera off its tripod, first fumbling to unplug the microphone attached to the top of it.

"Yeah, sure."

"Was it hard?" Edie breathed out.

"What?"

"Moving on." Edie finally stopped messing with the camera and looked to Cara for some answer she could understand.

Cara swung her bag over her right shoulder and turned back to look at Edie full on. "It hurts. But I'm here, and I'm laughing about it, so it's not an impossible hurt."

She gave Edie a side hug and disappeared out the door before Edie could press for more answers the way she wanted to. She suddenly felt out of breath and completely tired of the day.

Packing up the bags, Edie tried to imagine the next few months ahead. She closed her eyes and strained to picture herself graduating and then the big moving day. She placed herself in a nondescript dorm room chatting with friends she hadn't met yet. None of it made sense. The whole thing was blurred around the edges, missing all the important bits. She couldn't form any single image into a whole.

She opened her eyes and she was back in the dusty band room.

The camera was heavy as she slung the bag over her shoulder. Her backpack got tangled with it and she set everything down again. Edie looked around the room. The instruments had been cleared to make room for Dawn's filming months ago. The backgrounds leaned against the far right wall in dozens of colors Dawn had picked out over a long weekend of intense visits to the craft store. The room made Edie feel warm with love. She admired Dawn's inability to deny her talents. She wanted to make a movie and so it was being made. Full stop. Edie couldn't find the charge in herself but loved it in Dawn all the same. She was a bullet moving fast towards exactly what she wanted. Why couldn't Edie be in control like that?

She readjusted the bags on her back and shoulder and left the room. She had lots of work to do with Georgia and Collin on the final edit of the film.

As she sat in the AV lab's computer room, Georgia thought about how she still hadn't heard back from Kenyon and the anxiety was eating her alive. Every day she would reopen the portfolio she'd sent in with her application and scrutinize every detail. It was too late to change anything; they already had it. She found some comfort in it, though, rereading the pages, seeing what the admissions people were seeing.

Edie knocked on the door to the lab and gave a small wave as she walked through to the row of computers, backpack swinging.

"What's up, nut?"

"Existential dread, babe," Georgia sighed, closing the document of her writing. "But today is not about me, it's about finishing this thing for Dawn."

Georgia pulled up the footage Collin had sent her as Edie settled into the chair next to her. After they'd texted him about the situation with Dawn's film, he'd sent them one of the older versions of Dawn's film she'd shared with him and promised to finish editing the whole thing and send it in if they could help edit some of the footage. He'd sent some video clips and notes for them in the plainest language he could muster. Georgia dropped the videos into the free video editing software on the lab computer and asked Edie to Google how to use it. Georgia had never even so much as made a slideshow for class so she was in for a long night of YouTube tutorials from precocious twelve-year-olds.

She looked to Edie for guidance, but she was busy staring intently at a YouTube tutorial. Georgia looked back at the screen in front of her. She pressed the play button to see what would happen and a clip she had accidentally hovered over started to play. Dawn appeared on screen, in a plain yellow dress, framed against a dark blue background.

I'm having some trouble finishing this thing. There's too much love all over the place. As soon as I finish an interview, I want to start another one. It's actually completely crazy how badly I need to finish this yet how completely unwilling I am to be done. I don't think I'll ever be finished learning all the different ways queer love is all around me.

Like, Edie and Ben. They just have it, you know? Or, Georgia and me. It's literally love. Like, would-do-anything-for-the-other-person love. Or Tessa and Ali or John and Margo or Tavion or Kate and Finley or Shamir and his boyfriend or anyone. It just keeps going like branch off of a branch off of a branch. A big, Texas-sized tree of queerness.

Dawn struck Georgia as someone super easy to like, to love, even. She had a big laugh like double doors opening into a party. She always listened first. Maybe that was the documentarian in her. She never missed an opportunity to care for her friends. She'd bring them gum from the corner store even if she only had fifty cents left. Her generosity was her love. And her love was for Georgia and Edie.

"What if we called Collin?" Edie asked.

"Good idea." Georgia scrolled to their text thread and pressed the call button. He picked up on the second ring and she put him on speaker.

"Georgia?"

"Yeah. Edie's here too."

"Oh cool! Is everything alright? I texted Dawn to ask if I could help with the film after you messaged me but I never heard back so . . ." Georgia heard the concern in the lilt of his voice, the kindness he had towards her friend.

"Yeah, no," Georgia sighed, "she hasn't been texting but she's gonna be okay. We're going to get this thing done for her and get that woman to Austin."

"Alright then, let's do it. I'm glad to help. She's like the coolest person I know."

"Same." Georgia laughed and turned her attention to the screen. "We put the clips in the editing suite but we don't really know what to do next."

Collin's voice came clearly through Georgia's phone as he guided her and Edie through the process of splicing videos into smaller clips, moving them around in different orders, and making sure the sound levels were correct throughout each interview. Hours passed as the girls listened intently, the mouse clicking as Collin went step by step.

They sent the files they worked on back to him in the world's largest email attachment and looked at each other's tired, grateful eyes in the black reflection of the now-off computer screen.

TWENTY-TWO

April 2, Ten Days to Austin Film Festival

Hey, I'm not going to Dawn's tonight. Or, I can't. Parents said no," Edie sighed into the phone.

"Dude, they're so annoying."

"Can you go at least?"

"Simone is already here cooking dinner, and my mom thinks by the time we're done eating it's going to be too late at night." Georgia picked at the carpet under her palm with her lavender acrylic nails.

"Okay. Let me know if D texts you back. I saw she read one of my messages. I'm worried."

"Of course." Georgia heard her mother's singsong voice through her bedroom door and lifted the phone away from her ear. "I gotta go. My mom is calling me." She hung up the phone quickly and pulled herself from the floor where she'd been spread out doing some writing and got ready for dinner. Simone had arrived about fifteen minutes earlier, but she'd been hiding out in her room in the hopes that she could avoid interacting with him as much as possible.

Swirling smells of the roasted duck her mother was cooking wafted into the hallway from the kitchen and into Georgia's room. She followed the scent of the savory spices and found her mother barefoot, leaning over a pot of sauce, Simone hovering uselessly near the dish cabinet.

Georgia couldn't help but think her mother looked like a kid with her hair pulled high into a ponytail and her toes tapping to some inaudible song.

"It's almost ready, Geo. Set the table," her mother said, back still turned towards the food.

The plates made a tinkling sound as they landed on the tiny round table. Georgia made sure to put her set as far from Simone's as she could. Her mother carried the pot from the stove onto the waiting potholder and Simone rushed over with the pan of duck in hand.

Sitting at this table with Frankie was all Georgia knew. As long as she'd been alive, it had always been one plus one. Two plates, two long days to talk about, two pairs of shoes clashing beneath the table. Now, for the first time, here was Simone with his clunky feet and stupid glasses and voice that coiled and slumped like some dead thing at the bottom of a trash can.

They all moved the dishes around the table and grabbed their servings. Georgia shoved the duck into her mouth and spread the sauce over the small potatoes from the pan. Frankie and Simone talked about nothing and she wondered what her mother, the most brilliant and soft-hearted person she knew, could possibly see in him.

"You know, there's actually a poetry reading happening at BookWoman in Austin next weekend. You could read some of your poems. You said you write poems, right, Georgia?" She shuddered at the sound of her name on his tongue.

"Yeah. Thanks."

"Oh, Geo, wouldn't that be nice? You never share your poetry." Her mother added, approving of Simone's suggestion.

"Yeah."

"I would like to hear some of your writing one day." Simone said. Sauce sat messily on his chin and dribbled down his face as he spoke. Georgia kept her head down and tried to force the time to go faster as her mom and Simone began talking about bookstores in Houston they liked.

"Turn on the radio, Georgie." Her mother insisted as dinner came to an end.

She did as she was told and got up to mess around with the buttons on their kitchen boombox, which her mother had referred to as the radio ever since they'd bought it a decade ago. They only had four CDs, two of which were from Georgia's punk phase in middle school. The other two were love songs of the seventies. She slipped a CD into the player and some crooning song about never ever ever ever breaking up began to play.

Her mother cleared the plates and began to move around the kitchen to the tune as it ramped up to the chorus. She swayed her hips and tapped her toes on the little kitchen rugs they had spread out around the floor.

"I used to listen to this song in my bright yellow Ford Pinto," Simone chimed in over the sound of the running water on his dirty plate.

"Oh god, I remember those. I wasn't old enough to drive but my aunt had one when I was a little girl," laughed Frankie, her head nodding lightly to the song.

Georgia watched Simone begin to move to the music, with his perpetually sweaty hands mounted onto Frankie's shoulders. Georgia felt sick and out of place. The song went on and on as they stumbled over each other's feet.

"Too much, too much," Frankie muttered into Simone's chest. "Let me change so we can go out."

Frankie left the room and the air ballooned with discomfort.

"Dance with me," he said flatly.

"No, thanks."

Simone crossed the kitchen in one stride to face her. He reached his hand out towards her.

"Just dance with me." His voice took on an insistent tone as he moved closer.

He grabbed her waist and pulled her body in close. She could feel the chill from his belt buckle rub against her stomach. He swayed and so she swayed too. It felt as though every bug that ever existed crawled up and down her skin with each thump and beat of the music. He dragged his finger up her forearm slowly. She wanted to push him away and stab him with one of the knives on the counter.

But she didn't. She let it happen and felt dumb because she was so sure she was not the type of person that this would happen to. Whenever bad things happened to girls in movies she thought, *well if that were me, I'd just leave*. But here she was, solidly unmoving in his arms.

Her mind went nowhere. Simone smelled like the ginger her mother seasoned the duck with. Something else too, maybe a strong deodorant with illustrations of trees and mint leaves on the label. They moved left and right and she waited until the song was over.

The song ended and he moved away. Frankie rounded the corner in a lavender wrap dress and they were out the door before Georgia could think of anything beyond the kiss her mother gave her on the forehead as she disappeared.

TWENTY-THREE

April 3, Nine Days to Austin Film Festival

Dawn woke up and checked on her dad but had otherwise not left her bed for the last three days. Someone or something invisible was sitting on her chest. She couldn't get up. She couldn't answer the dozens of texts Edie and Georgia had sent.

She was disappearing into herself like an expansive and endless hole. Her heart hurt, the thought of her failure with the documentary pounding in her chest.

Dawn held herself as if she was holding somebody she loved. She had to do it when she got like this, inconsolable from the unfairness of her life. It started in eighth grade. The night of her middle school's Valentine's dance. Annie Jones had spit on her when she'd asked her to dance. It was the worst thing that had happened to Dawn at that point in her life. She ran home, dumb green dress grasped tight in her fists. She just kept running until her house appeared before her, some safe place she could cry out to no one that the world was unfair. She looked at herself in the mirror and wrapped both arms around her that night. It felt nice. Usually, as she brought her arms up around her thin shoulders, she pretended that she was two people. One wanting body, and one giving body.

The days passed as Dawn watched Sex and the City from the very beginning for the third time in her life. She watched every season in order and hated it and loved it, too.

Somewhere between two and three in the morning, Dawn forced herself to look at the old emails she'd been avoiding for a few days.

Among the mess of coupons and subscriptions to film and poetry newsletters, Dawn saw her worst nightmare.

URGENT—Austin Film Festival

She didn't want to open it. She let her mouse hover over the trash can icon. But she didn't usually like avoiding disappointment. She opened it.

Dear Dawn Salcedo,
This is an update regarding THE QUEER GIRL IS GOING TO BE OKAY. The Documentary Student Films deadline was March 31st. Please send the film and a biography as soon as possible or your position will be forfeited and your film disqualified from competition. We look forward to your final submission.

Thank You,
Austin Film Festival Committee

Dawn shut her laptop with a flourish and closed her eyes until the blue glow of her screen disappeared into black behind her eyelids. She was too tired to care. It didn't even matter anymore. She would not be the best filmmaker or the best writer or the best anything. She would stay home and take care of her father and be just okay at that. She might even end up being good if she worked at it.

Dawn tried convincing herself out of her lifelong dream. College was dumb anyway, she thought. It wasn't hers anymore. It belonged to somebody else. Somebody with talent and money and a lusciously boring family.

She couldn't even make the one film that meant something to her. And what did that make her? Not an artist, not a friend. She wasn't some hero of queer representation; she was tired.

She couldn't even begin to name all the things that wanted to harm her.

She touched her ribs one by one trying to imagine how small she had become in such little time. Her sadness had shrunk her. She felt like a tiny bug soon to be crushed beneath the foot of the world. She must be at least the size of those dark glass-backed beetles that crawled all across the kitchen linoleum in the summer, she figured.

If she could just origami fold herself up into something minuscule, soon she'd disappear and not have to do anything or help anybody or have to look anyone in the eye as she disappointed them for the third or fourth time.

She began to imagine it, floating away, forgetting her father, forgetting any man who didn't love her, really, gone. She'd float to some cliffside and call Edie and Georgia from a payphone by the sea. She'd repair bicycles and forget she even liked learning and movies and kisses that stung like cheap, stolen wine.

She opened up her laptop again.

Another old email popped up.

Dear Dawn,

I sent a few texts but never heard back, so I thought I'd email? I hope it's okay your friends told me about your doc not getting finished. Let me know if there's anything I can do. Not even just about the doc. Anything.

Yours,
Collin

Yours, Collin? What did he want? What did this boy want? Dawn wanted to cry just thinking about all the things men in her life had taken from her. She let herself feel pathetic and weak and incapable. She sunk into it and nursed the bad feelings like a fresh bruise.

She stared at the screen and typed out a message.

Thank you. For everything.
Dawn

No truly, no yours, just Dawn. She closed her computer and let the world happen without her.

All week, Dawn had slept until it didn't make sense to anymore. She hadn't heard again from the film festival and accepted that she was out of the running for good. Edie and Georgia had left her messages and she tried to text them back but couldn't muster both communicating with them and focusing on taking care of her dad.

Finally, Dawn pulled on blue sweatpants and a crumpled shirt from beneath her bed. She swung open her closet door behind all her clothes to reveal, hidden in the back, the glittering black dress.

It hung on a too-small bent plastic hanger. Dawn reached up and slid both arms off the hanger in a slow, somber motion. Above her head on the shelf sat the white shopping bag, still taut and filled with the wrapping paper and receipt.

The soft fabric felt nice laid across her arms as she began to fold it. She didn't cry or even think. The dress went back into the bag in a neat rectangle. Dawn checked on her father then walked to the corner to wait forty-five minutes to board a bus to the Galleria.

She kept her head down and tried not to mind the bumps the bus driver seemed to be intentionally hitting every three seconds. She didn't have her phone and decided to look out the window as it began to rain. She tried to listen closely to the sound the city made when it was filling up with water.

Small rivers swishing down storm drains, the bus's incessant screeching as it approached puddles—she wanted to hear every note. When she exited the bus, she paused to listen to cars inching down Westheimer, a woman yelling at her dog named Sunny, the small trees rustling their new, barely green leaves. She wanted to know and remember it all, fall in love with it. This is where she would spend the next few years. Maybe forever. She belonged to the city and she was trying to let it belong to her too.

The saleswoman was kind to her despite the dress getting a little bit of rain on it. She brushed her hand over the dress's pleats as she squinted at Dawn's receipt over a pair of honey yellow–rimmed glasses.

"It should process in three to five days, and the amount will be returned in full to your account."

"Okay, thanks." It came out in a scratch, so she cleared her throat and repeated herself. She hadn't heard the sound of her own voice in days.

Dawn left with no dress and enough money to start working on a plan to get her dad some home care. She started thinking about what she could do while she saved up for college, maybe community college classes.

She straightened her back as she stepped back onto the bus. The bus driver removed his dark blue cap to scratch his head for a moment then turned to her.

"It's coming down today, huh?"

Dawn didn't know if it was a question directed at her or the world, so she smiled and began to walk towards the seat directly behind him. Her sweatpants were itchy and soaked through in small patches from the rain.

"But it doesn't matter," he echoed, again to no one in particular. "It's going to be a great day today."

Dawn looked out the window. "Absolutely."

TWENTY-FOUR

April 4, Eight Days to Austin Film Festival

Cars rushed past Georgia and Edie as they kept their eyes focused on the street corner. The morning bus came hurling around the stop sign, and the short woman who had been standing next to them boarded but no one got off. The bus made a terrible screeching sound and pulled off slowly down the road.

"Damn it," Georgia said looking down at her watch. "She's not coming. That was the 7:52. The next one's not until 8:35."

"We can just wait a little longer. Dawn said she was coming," Edie offered.

A week had passed, and Dawn hadn't been to school. It was Friday, and she had promised over text to both of them that today she was coming back. Dawn finally started to respond to their texts on Thursday night but wouldn't talk about what happened with her dad. Georgia and Edie called her after school Thursday, their bodies huddled over Georgia's phone with Dawn on speaker phone. They talked about homework Dawn had missed but that was it.

"Fine, but let's sit."

Georgia shrugged her backpack off and threw it onto the sidewalk. They'd picked up two jumbo-sized sweet teas from a gas station on their way and now held them to their lips, sipping down the cool.

They talked about college and Georgia felt embarrassed. She had nothing to share. She hadn't heard back from Kenyon yet.

Georgia silently realized Edie hadn't even asked about the fact that they were missing the first part of school. She was usually such a stickler. A lot of things had lost their importance lately.

"What kind of writer do you want to be?" Edie asked, gazing off into the distance.

"What do you mean?" Georgia asked. She'd always shared her writing with Edie, so it felt strange, almost random, that she would ask.

"Like, what kind of person do you want to be?" Edie stared out at the road as she spoke. "Are you going to tour the country or live in New York and complain about how busy you are every day or be happy in a cabin in the country with your wife and dogs?"

"I don't know." Georgia felt dizzy just thinking about the future.

"But pretend you do." Edie looked at her with wide eyes waiting for a response. They used to play games like this a lot when they first met. She, Edie, and Dawn would sit in a circle asking each other questions about what the others thought their future would be like. Georgia remembered Dawn telling her once that she was destined to win a National Book Award. *It's just the type of talent you are*, she'd said with great certainty.

"I want to live in Chicago or maybe Portland. I want to go to museums every day and write about my life, my friends."

"Sounds cold. Love that for you though." Edie took a sip from her drink and turned to look at Georgia straight on, her expression turning serious. "I want that for you, you know. I want people to read your writing and see how amazing you are."

"Thanks, E." Georgia smiled and took another sip of her sweet tea.

After a while, Edie rested her head on Georgia's lap as car after car passed. They talked about an assignment neither of them had started and listened to a podcast about movies, the earphones straining to reach so that they could both comfortably listen with one pod.

Another city bus finally bounded from the corner and stopped in front of them. A man with red hair and a work jacket tightly tucked under his arm got off the bus. Dawn was behind him.

She was wearing ratty jeans and a lime green t-shirt. The shirt was too small and announced in bold print *Perkins Middle School Field Day*. Her hair was tied messily into a ponytail tight and low behind her ears so that if she looked at you straight on it would seem as though she had almost no hair at all. She wore no makeup, not even her usual lip gloss and NYX blush she'd stolen from the CVS down the block from Alsbury sophomore year.

As she stomped off the bus, her eyes met Georgia and then Edie and she began to cry.

"I love y'all so much," she gasped out through tears.

They opened their arms to her, and the girls hugged in front of the stop as the bus pulled away. The hug lasted too long and devolved into tears and messy mumblings into each other's shoulders.

They walked to a diner a block away from Alsbury with their hands linked in the early April warmth.

They slid into a red booth towards the back. They ordered fries and pancakes and talked to Vincent the waiter about what they were doing out of school at this hour. He'd been there since they were freshmen and had crooked teeth like a picket fence blown over during a bad storm. His kindness had landed them dozens of free root beer floats over the years.

As he walked away, Georgia shared a look with Edie before they both turned to Dawn. She was quiet, her hand toying with the saltshaker on the end of the table.

"How has everything been with your dad?" Georgia waited as Dawn seemed to drift off in her mind, her eyes wandering from the diner ceiling and back to the table.

"He's okay. Things are going to be okay." Dawn placed her palms flat on the table and Edie reached up to rest her hand on top of Dawn's.

Georgia thought it was better not to push her until she was ready to talk. Dawn would tell them how she was feeling when she was ready. Seeing Dawn so quiet, so stoically going through the situation with her dad, Georgia wanted to tell the girls everything about Simone. She was tired of holding on to the secret. These were her friends and she knew she could trust them with whatever the world threw at her.

"Is it okay if I tell y'all about something?" Dawn and Edie nodded, their hands still touching on top of the table.

Georgia began to recount what happened with Simone, frequent pauses for when Dawn gasped and said *shut up*, which really just meant to keep telling the story. The food was set down on the table as she finished up the details.

"Geo, that's really weird." Edie licked syrup off of her dull knife and set it down beside the plate of pancakes.

"I know, but technically nothing happened," Georgia offered quietly.

"If something's happening you should tell Frankie," said Dawn over an already half-empty strawberry milkshake.

"Nothing's happening!" Georgia erupted. She took a deep breath and drew back. "I just don't know what to do. That's why I'm even telling y'all about this. I need help."

Without a pause, Dawn spoke. "You should kill him." She sat up in the booth with a serious face. She dipped her fry into the ketchup pile with a measured movement. Georgia watched her as she stuffed the fry into her mouth without smiling.

"Dawn," Georgia whined.

"Kidding, duh," she expressed through a full mouth.

"Honestly Geo, you need to tell Frankie," Edie said evenly. "He's gross and she deserves the best, yes or no?"

"I know," resigned Georgia. "I know."

Dawn told the girls her dad was waiting at home and she needed to leave.

"Want to talk about the English homework from the few days you missed?" Edie asked, setting her fork down and looking up as Dawn stood up to leave.

"I'll just text you. Bye, cuties." She walked away and the small bell hanging over the door rang as she walked out.

Edie looked at Georgia as she started to shimmy out of the booth.

"Sorry, Geo, I gotta go too. I'm doing dinner with my family and I have to go pick up groceries."

"Okay. Did you notice?" Georgia cut her eyes to the door where Dawn had just exited.

"What, that she didn't mention the film? Yeah. Don't worry, Collin sent in the final version after we sent in the parts we edited. Sorry I forgot to text you. He said they got back to him like right after he sent it saying the submission was still accepted even though it was late. Teamwork made the dream work." Edie adjusted her bag on her shoulder.

"Oh good." Georgia sighed, grateful that everything went according to their last minute plan. "I'm going to stay here a little longer." She looked up from the table as Edie left a small pile of one-dollar bills.

"Okay, G. Seriously though, you have to tell her." Edie swung her bag over her other shoulder and gave Georgia a quick hug before turning around.

"I know."

Edie disappeared out of the door as Georgia buried her head in her arms on the table and took in the stink of grilling meat and tile floor cleaner. She pulled out her phone.

She typed up a long message in her Notes app. She explained Simone and her mother and the feel of his hand on her arm. She typed what Edie and Dawn said and then wrote her own feelings. How she wanted her mother to be happy, how Simone was the first man who'd made it to a second and even third date. When she felt she'd written the entire situation, she ended with a question. *Should I tell my mother?* She copy-pasted it into a message to Jill.

A few seconds passed and she got a reply from Jill. Three words glowed in her inbox. *Yes, call me.*

TWENTY-FIVE

April 5, Seven Days to Austin Film Festival

Edie propped her feet up against her bed as she lay on the ground scrolling through her phone. Nothing was new or interesting to her and she kept opening the same three apps over and over again hoping that fact would change.

She'd been trying to look forward. Even if she'd ruined things with Ben, she needed to be a person and keep going. Her stomach had been empty for days; eating took up as much energy as running a thousand miles. She called Georgia every night trying to get the hours to pass before she could go to sleep and forget who she was and what she had done.

Edie tried to avoid her parents as much as possible. She didn't want to accidentally say something she regretted just because she was sad. She figured they thought she got a bad grade at school or was tired from all her classes and extracurriculars. Not that it mattered to her what they thought. The anxiety of keeping secrets from them while going through a breakup was beginning to weigh on her more heavily by the day. She wanted to go to sleep and wake up in a new place, far away from her parents and her friends and anybody who knew her.

No matter how hard she tried to pick herself up and do her homework, she couldn't remove the blanket of sadness that enveloped her every day since the drunken apology she gave

Ben. Edie was behind on everything and she couldn't work up the energy to care.

A light knocking rattled her door open. Marvin entered her room shyly. He still had on his uniform from karate and stank in the way that only sweaty eight-year-olds can.

"What's up?"

He did a running jump onto her bed. She figured it must be something serious. He never visited her room unless he wanted to talk.

"Something bad happened at school the other day." She put her phone down by her side and looked up at him.

"Yeah, what?"

"Alex says he doesn't want to hang out with me anymore." He looked down at his hands and then looked up at her again.

"Best friend Alex, or Alex from karate?"

"Friend," he let out softly.

"Why would he say that? Were you being mean?"

"No!" He paused and began to pick at the strings in the blue belt loosely tied around his waist.

"We were at recess and Sarah said that since we're in the fourth grade, we have to kiss somebody." Edie held in a laugh as she thought of what to say.

"Icky. Kissing is gross." She propped herself up on one elbow and held her nose with the other hand, playing the part of knowledgeable big sister.

"That's what I said. But Alex said that he wanted to kiss Nicholas, and I said that Nicholas is a boy and you're not supposed to kiss boys. And then he said he doesn't want to hang out anymore."

Edie's mind raced. What was she supposed to say? She could feel her jeans pressing into her tummy and then separating again and again as she breathed quickly. She couldn't find her balance and spoke before she could think it all the way through.

"Well, it doesn't matter who Alex wants to kiss." Edie treaded lightly into her next words, "For example, let me guess. You want to kiss Sarah, right?"

"No! Okay, a little. But only 'cause she's really cool and nice and has nice hair."

"Exactly. Maybe Alex thinks Nicholas is really cool and nice and has nice hair." Her voice shook as she tried to keep her speech even and unsuspicious. Marvin seemed to be thinking over what she'd said.

"Oh. Yeah, I guess. It's like in the video games when you play the boy character instead of the girl character." His voice rose in understanding.

"That's not the same thing." Edie sputtered out with a small laugh.

"Why not?" His head flinched to the right then the left.

"I do that because the boy characters have better weapons. Which is dumb, by the way."

"Okay." Marvin's shoulders dipped. "I'm gonna say sorry to Alex tomorrow 'cause we have soccer Friday and if he's not on my team we're going to lose really bad." He hopped off of the bed and skipped to the door.

Before she could regret anything else, Edie spoke, "Wait. So, what if I wanted to kiss somebody who was not a boy?"

"Like Alex?" He tapped the door a few times in thought.

"Yeah. Kind of like Alex." Edie waited for his next words like she was waiting for the end of the world.

He tapped the door a few more times. "Hm, that's okay. You should kiss who you like the most, like Alex."

"Okay." She could barely mutter anything else. "I-I'll see you at dinner."

Marvin left and the door shut behind him quietly. He was out of the door before Edie could warn him not to bring the conversation up at dinner. He always told their parents every-thing. She could already imagine it, her parents going from brown to a deep red. Anger.

They would be angry. They'd say something ridiculous about taking him out of school or making sure he never went to Alex's house again. She hoped he wouldn't bring it up.

Edie suddenly felt the weight of the day on her back. She stuffed her notebook and a few homework assignments into her bag and rushed out of her room and into the kitchen. She lied to her parents again about an emergency test she had to prepare for. She wasn't sure if she liked that she was getting better and better each time she told an untruth. The early evening sped past her as she biked to Georgia's.

Everything looked the same but glimmered with a hue of hope it'd refused to have before this exact moment. Edie's thoughts tangled into the moss hanging off the perfectly manicured trees across every lawn. A single shining phrase pulled from one end of her mind to the other as she reached Georgia's front door and swung it open.

"I came out to my brother," she yelped as she crossed the threshold and whipped into Georgia's bedroom.

"Well, I think I did. Kind of. I think I just had a heart attack." She tossed her backpack onto the blue shag carpet and grabbed her friend by both shoulders. "Geo, this is the only good thing I've done all year."

"Congratulations! What did he say? I mean, what did you say? What happened?"

She recounted the short conversation to Georgia and col-lapsed onto her bed in one flourish.

"E, I'm not sure that counts."

"What do you mean?" Edie rose up on one elbow to look at Georgia straight on.

"You didn't really tell him anything." Georgia let her face ease into a sympathetic frown as she watched Edie lay back down again.

Edie let the words sink under her skin so she could feel their full meaning. "You're right. I just got excited because I thought I was taking control. I thought I was doing something good for myself." She pouted at the ceiling. She had said it, but she hadn't.

"Baby steps." Georgia laid down beside her and looked up too.

"I know. Baby steps."

They watched old episodes of *Pose* and complained about school until the room became dark around them and they became exhausted with themselves. Homework laid blank and undone next to the bed they'd made into a theater with Georgia's laptop. The night blanketed them and made Edie forget that she was newly out, newly brave.

Edie fell asleep. Georgia moved from the bed gently attempting not to wake her. She snuck into the hallway and made her way to her mother's bedroom where she found Frankie watching a cooking show on her small television. Georgia stood in the doorway and watched as a woman folded dough into a heap over and over again on the fuzzy screen.

"Mom?"

"Hi, sweetie. Edie asleep?"

"Yeah," She hesitated to enter the bedroom. She crossed her hands behind her back. "Can we talk about something?"

"Always, G." Her mother patted a space on her bed so Georgia could sit down. She walked in and tried to settle into a spot on the mattress. She crossed her legs on the sheets like she'd been doing since she was little. Her mother scooted over so that they were touching leg to leg.

"It's about Simone." Georgia ran her hands over the sheets and tried to get the right words to come.

"Kind of a nerd, huh?"

"Yeah," she let a moment pass. The quiet floated between them, her mother's smile expectant. "Actually it's nothing." Georgia slipped out of the room before her mother could say anything and snuck back to her room. She felt disappointed in herself for not speaking up, scared to tell the truth. She snuggled into bed next to Edie as moonlight sparkled through her bedroom into the next day.

The morning came slowly. Georgia looked over at the clock and saw that it said seven. Frankie opened up the bedroom door with a whisper.

"Edie, your phone has been going off all morning. I just saw it on the counter. I think it's your dad."

Edie opened her eyes and let them wander over the room that wasn't her own. Everything was blurred at the edges and she was unsure of what was going on.

She noticed Frankie holding her phone out towards the bed. "I think your parents have been trying to call you, sweetie."

Edie focused and everything became clear. She had slept over without telling her parents. She'd kind of but not really come out to Marvin. Her chest tightened.

"Oh my god, thank you." She grabbed her phone from Frankie and skimmed over the dozens of missed calls and texts. "Shit shit shit."

They were all exclamation points and questions with two and three question marks. She saw Marvin's name mixed in with all the messages. Her stomach hurt and she felt as though she needed to throw up.

"E, are you okay?"

"Yeah. I think my life is over. I don't know what to do. I don't know what I'm going to do." She was breathing hard. Nothing made sense.

"Hey, calm down. It's going to be okay." Georgia grabbed her into a hug as her breathing increased. "It's going to be okay." She just kept saying it again and again as Edie tried to slow her heart rate.

"Okay. I'm going to go home. I'm going to deal with this. Everything is going to be fine." She repeated this in her head as she grabbed her backpack and walked out of the front door of the house. Georgia stood in the doorframe watching her pick up her bike.

"Call me, please. You can stay with us as long as you need no matter what happens." Frankie stood behind her echoing the sentiment with a nod.

She settled on her bike seat quickly and pedaled down the street back to her home.

"I'm going to go home. I'm going to deal with this. Everything is going to be fine. I'm going to go home. I'm going to deal with this. Everything is going to be fine. I'm going to go home. I'm going to deal with this. Everything is going to be fine. I'm going to go home. I'm going to deal with this. Everything is going to be fine. I'm going to go home. I'm going to deal with this. Everything is going to be fine . . ."

TWENTY-SIX

April 6, Six Days to Austin Film Festival

E die closed the front door of her house behind her quietly. She
didn't want to run into her parents on the way in. She shuffled
silently into the living room to find her father seated on the couch
reading the Bible. She was trapped. The scent of almost-burned
eggs spilled over from the kitchen where her mother was cooking
breakfast.

Her father's thumb caught at the curling edge of a single page
of the huge book. "Edie, where have you been?"

There it was. She instantly knew that they'd found out. She
could hear it in the staleness of his voice. Her mouth went dry as
she tried to stay calm. She placed her hand to her chest to make
sure her heart was still there. It hurt so much.

Her queerness was finally on full display. She felt it all the
time, but now, so did everyone else in her house. Maybe they had
seen it all along. When you avoid something so intentionally,
every conversation cannot help but be about it. It stuffs itself into
the small spaces.

"Ronald, I got this. Edie, come to your room," her mother's
voice swam in from the kitchen.

The hallway to her room stretched out far before her. Green
carpeting ran down the hall, far into the future, and even beyond
that. She saw herself coming and then going, dragging her bags

behind her, not sobbing but accepting the separation from her family. She saw her life plan changing so fast, turning itself upside down in a split second. She scraped her fingernail along the wood paneling along the walls to remember the sound in case she never returned to this house.

Her mother's back was perfectly straight as she opened the door to her room. Her pecan-shell skin glowed as morning light slipped in through Edie's window.

"Shut the door." Edie did. Her room felt foreign and messy to her. She looked up at the posters she hadn't picked out and the fluffy comforter she didn't buy covered in clothes that didn't really make her feel like herself. It was as if someone else had been living there all this time, all seventeen years. Someone Christian, and straight, and really into science, and loved by two perfect parents.

Maybe this was the exact right thing for her. This was supposed to happen. Maybe it was in God's plan for them to find out about her. Edie always did this: thought of God, who she didn't entirely believe in at this exact moment but still held on to like a childhood toy. If this was going to happen, then it was going to happen. She closed her eyes and waited for her mother's fire.

"Now, your brother told me something, and I just need you to tell me if it's true or not." Edie couldn't muster up the energy to feel angry with Marvin. All she saw was his two eyes like honey-colored marbles staring up at her, asking questions about things he didn't understand. She would miss him. She felt in her heart that this was the end of the line.

"Are you—"

"Mom—" Edie choked on her words and forced herself not to cry. Even when her mother's eyes drifted out the window and refused to meet her, she didn't cry.

"—Gay?"

"Yes." She knew that this wasn't technically true but thought explaining the nuances of her queerness to her mother was years or even lifetimes away. The air in her lungs flew out and she stiffened against the oncoming storm of words. She tightened her fist until her nails dug into the palms and began to sting.

Her mom moved to the bed where a pile of clean clothes from the laundry sat at the end of the bed. She began to fold a t-shirt almost mechanically and looked up at Edie's bedroom walls. The silence was painful. Edie could hear how much she hated her in the silence. Her mother was quiet for a very long time, the sound of fabric moving in her hand filling the room aggressively.

Finally, she spoke: "No, you're not. And I don't want to hear about it again, okay?"

Edie took in a sharp breath and felt a pang below her ribs. It wasn't relief, it was disappointment. She was being shut down to maintain her mother's idea of who she was instead of who she actually was. After a moment of quick anger, things became clear and Edie wondered why she'd expected anything else from her mom. This was just like her mother, like her family. It was all one big game of let's-never-talk-about-anything-real-and-hope-that-everyone-turns-out-well-adjusted. She knew that and had let herself get caught up in the fantasy of getting to tell her truth, and actually have it be heard, of the liberation that would come with finally just knowing if she would be rejected or not.

"Okay?" she asked again, her lips a flat line.

Luckily, Edie had mastered the game a long time ago. "Yes, okay."

And that was it. Her mother placed the stack of folded shirts on her unmade bed and left the room without looking back. Now the truth was out, whatever that meant. Even if her mother refused to acknowledge it, she had some clue. It would come up later, and she would try to express herself again. Maybe she wasn't big enough yet. Maybe she wasn't stronger than the walls of her home yet.

She stood up and moved to look at herself in the full-length mirror at the far right corner of her room. She looked the same as before. Simple, ordinary. Somehow though, she knew she was unlike every other obedient woman in her family. She'd always known. They folded inwards and agreed and loved openly and folded back in again. In her early childhood, she'd tried to trace the movements of her mother and grandmother and the beautiful women of her family, but every soft pirouette like trying to flex a muscle she didn't have. So here she was. Unseen and still standing. She was going to be fine.

Before the tear threatening to drop to her chest spilled out, she dug her phone out of her back pocket and called Ben.

They Facetimed. Edie wanted to leave and see them in person but felt too tired to lie or even face her parents at all. As the image on the screen opened into a picture of Ben's just-opened eyes, Edie felt the weight of her mother's rejection. She felt so weak. She wanted to be powerful and say what she felt. She wanted to own her words and identity in at least one part of her life.

"Ben, can you forgive me? I really need you to forgive me."

"Of course, I forgive you." They looked away for a moment, unable to meet Edie's gaze. They ran their hand over their dark hair once, twice. "I actually forgave you two weeks ago after you got out of the car, but I wasn't sure how to say it. I was afraid. I don't know."

"Oh. Thank you."

The silence buzzed between them, their phones portals into each other's not-at-all-separate worlds. Edie could hear Ben's dog howling for attention from some far off room in their house.

"Edie, I know that you understand who I am. Maybe more than anyone. It's not always safe to be out to everyone all the time. My parents are cool and yours are not. I should have understood that."

"No, it's not okay. I'm a weak person. I can't stand up to my parents, I can't be honest with my brother. I can't even make you happy." Edie began to cry harder than she'd ever cried.

"You're not weak." Edie didn't believe it. She had no agency. Not a single choice she'd made up to this point in her life had been truly her own. "Come lay down with me," they whispered. Edie listened as Ben shuffled their phone and pushed around the pillows on their bed. They propped the phone up on something so that Edie could see them with their head resting on a teddy bear, the one she'd gotten them as a present.

Edie lay down in her bed as well. She rested her phone against a stuffed animal Ben gave her on their second date. They both closed their eyes and listened to each other's breathing.

"You're not weak," Ben said, eyes still closed. "I love you."

They stayed still with each other for a long time. After a while, Edie's phone buzzed as it was starting to die so she plugged it in. She watched the light outside of her window grow yellow then a dull orange again as Ben snored with their lips curled at the edges into what was almost a smile.

She closed her eyes again and let the day pass by locked in her room with the love of her young life.

TWENTY-SEVEN

April 7, Five Days to Austin Film Festival

Okay, so, you're a young kid trying to figure out what you're feeling. Find some friends who get it. And if you can't because you're afraid to express yourself or your friends don't accept you, first of all those people aren't your friends. Second of all, I swear there are so so so many more people out there who you'll meet who have your best interest at heart. And even though it may not seem like it, they are out there. You need people who care about you if you are going to succeed in accepting yourself fully. And yes, you can have self-acceptance and learn who you are as a person alone but having people there who really really want to see you do well is just the greatest little feeling.

Click.

When I was younger, I would constantly tell my friends I was a fairy. Like daily. I would tell them that if they didn't believe me it didn't matter because no matter what I was going to fly. I was going to disappear and live in a tree or something. I totally believed that I didn't need anyone else. I think that's what queer love is all about. It's about seeing yourself before anyone else.

Click.

I'm in love every day. I kiss my friends. I kiss myself.
Every corner I turn is speeding towards beauty and light.
Nothing stops me. Nothing fills me with fear. I'm a beam
of light.

Click.

When I was in middle school, I didn't realize I was
queer. I thought I was just a really big fan of gay men. Like,
I would check out all these books from the library about
two boys falling in love and be like, I am just so happy for
them. Stupid. I mean, maybe I loved the idea of being an
outsider. Being strong in the face of people who don't want
to see you have something as basic as love.

Click.

I have love. I have it in every corner of my life. It makes
me stronger, more caring, less afraid. I know who I am
because of all the people who love me. That's it. It's that
simple for me.

Dawn watched the interviews over and over again and moved
her mouse between each clip, clicking and cutting the clips as
she went along. It was perfect. She'd given up completely on her
film being accepted to the final round of the fest but was still
proud of the incomplete version she'd made regardless.

It was Monday again, and the middle of April was coming
around. She sat in the library waiting for Edie and Georgia to
come eat lunch with her. Her final plan was coming together.
Three tabs were open, two of them job listings for different
restaurants downtown. She'd take a year or two off before college to take care of her father and film a new project she had an
idea for. Something about intimacy between parents and their
children. The idea had been floating around in her head for some

time. Looking at her father night after night, so despondent and completely dependent on her, it made her want to explore how other people were navigating such a warped relationship to the people that were supposed to be taking care of them.

She'd finish it while working two or three jobs around town, saving money, then maybe submit to a few film schools when she'd gathered up enough money for a nurse for her father and tuition.

It wasn't perfect, but it was possible.

Her computer dinged with an alert in another window, another email, probably spam or some other newsletter she'd signed up for a long time ago but neglected to read every week. The preview flashed in the corner of her screen.

Subject: Austin Film Festival—Final Submission

Dawn sunk into the stiff wooden chair. They were probably messaging to say she'd been officially disqualified. She didn't want to deal with the weight of the words but clicked to open the message anyway.

Dear Dawn Salcedo,

Your final submission for the Student Documentary Feature category has been accepted. Thank you for your completed submission and we look forward to seeing you at the award ceremony this Saturday, April 12th. Please find details on your arrival time and place below.

"No fucking way," Dawn choked out loud to herself.

"What?" Georgia said as she walked up. Edie trailed not too far behind alongside Ben.

Dawn could barely get the words out of her mouth. It was too unreal.

"What? What is it? Are you okay?" urged Edie at Dawn's paling cheeks.

"I'm in. My film is in the final round. I'm up for the scholarship." Dawn picked up her computer with the open email towards the center of the table.

"Oh my god, D. This is wild," Georgia gasped, her hand reaching to bend the screen back for a better view.

"Congratulations," said Ben from the other side of the table.

"I sent the clips to Collin. He—he must have put them together for me. He must have sent them." Dawn felt herself beginning to tear up.

Dawn couldn't believe it. Who does that? Who takes the time to finish something that's not their own with care and kindness? She didn't know what to say. She didn't know what she'd say to him, how she could thank him in any real way that was good enough.

"Actually, he helped us all work together to finish the film. I personally love him already," Edie said between smacks of peanut butter and jelly.

"Who, y'all? Like you and Georgia?"

"Of course, girl," said Georgia.

"No you didn't." Dawn began to cry, an uncontrollable, quiet stream of tears falling down her cheeks. Edie and Georgia scooped her into a quick hug.

"Well, we have to go to Austin. Obviously," said Georgia.

"You think?" Dawn looked up through her tears. She had already given up in her head. Her father needed her and now was not the time to get her hopes up.

"Fuck yes. We have to go. Are you kidding? I think we could skip class Friday and just drive. What are we gonna tell our parents?"

"Wait, I don't even know if I want to yet," Dawn insisted.

"Want to? Dawn, your genius movie is in a *real* film festival. Of course we're going." Georgia's voice rose as she spoke, insistence building up in her words.

"Okay, okay, relax. It's just the student film category," Dawn muttered.

"Just the student film category? Dawn, I'm going to say something and it's absolutely for your own good. You are a bullshitter. You are someone who undersells her fabulousness and you know what you gain? Absolutely nothing. I have sat by as you have accomplished thing after thing and totally put yourself down for it or acted like it meant nothing. We are going to Austin and you are going to win another fucking award because you are brilliant and deserve it."

"Okay, geez."

"D, I'm serious. You have to let yourself feel like a winner sometimes."

Dawn looked out past the stacks of books to the window on the back wall where the afternoon's yellow melted into a soft pink. "I know. You're right."

"You don't have to tell me that. I'll text you both tonight what the driving situation is. Three girlies on a road trip," shrieked Georgia.

"You know I hate when you say that," Edie moaned.

"What, girlie? You don't want to ride in the car with the girlies?"

"Yes, Georgia. I just despise 'girlies' as a term. It scratches my brain."

"Okay, girlie." Georgia swiped her bag from below her chair and pranced out of the library.

"Ugh."

"You need to loosen up, girlie." Dawn laughed at her own joke and took a deep breath. "Also, I'm going to call you tonight. You busy?"

"For you? Never. What's up?"

"I don't know, I just need to like, digest the fact that everything is happening and you're like, the reasonable, logical one of all of us. I need your words of wisdom."

"Whoa. Pressure." Edie took on a serious look. "I can do this."

"Relax, E. I just need you to like, tell me I'm not a flop making a huge mistake."

"Oh, yeah, I can do that." Edie thought for a moment and stared at the leftover crust from her sandwich. "You're not a flop. You're like, the least flop-inclined person I know."

"Thank you."

"No problem. And I can tell you again tonight with slight variation."

"Bless you. I have to go work on a project before class."

Dawn gathered up her computer and shoved her books into her bag as Edie and Ben started to slowly pack up their lunches. She walked away from the table and pushed hard against the library's heavy doors.

Everything that happened to her for the rest of the day barely touched her. She walked like she had somewhere to go. Classes rolled on without her; her thoughts lived in another city, another world, even. Hope and excitement built up in her heart high and unyielding like skyscrapers.

Even at home, the walls didn't seem so dim, the carpet as dingy as it was just that morning. She held her breath as she passed her father's room wanting to avoid a reminder of what was at stake if she didn't win.

She dumped her bag on the floor and let her phone bounce onto the tiny twin-sized bed.

Dawn picked it up and tapped on a name she'd come to love seeing notifications from.

It rang four times and Dawn started to lose her nerve after the fifth. Was it aggressive to call? What if she had to leave a voicemail like a grandma?

The ringing clipped off and Dawn heard a rustling sound on the other end of the line.

"Hello? Dawn?" She froze.

"Hello?" Collin echoed out again.

"Hey."

"Oh, wow. Hi." He sounded surprised. Dawn realized she'd never called him for anything except to talk about movies.

"I just wanted to call and say thanks." Dawn silently waved her hands in the air in a frantic back and forth motion as if to push herself to say something more brilliant, more put together. "I wanted to call and say thank you. So, thank you."

"For what?" Dawn thought about the right response. *Everything? Saving my life?* "Oh! The editing," he breathed out. "Yeah, no problem. I mean, it was mostly Edie and Georgia. They're great. Plus, it's a really incredible documentary. Did you ever hear back from the fest?"

"Yeah. I heard back today. I'm in." Dawn looked up at the cracks in her bedroom ceiling and tried to come up with something better to say. She needed to say thank you in a bigger way than just the two words.

"Congratulations! Hey, can you give me a second? I'm walking home and I just need to get my keys out of my bag real quick."

"Yeah, no problem."

She pressed her ear to the phone waiting for Collin to say something. She heard the jingle of keys and then the sound of a door squeaking on its hinges. Another door opened and then another and Dawn wondered if he'd put his phone down and forgotten they were talking.

"Okay, I'm in bed," he breathed out. Dawn heard the distinctive sound of two shoes hitting the ground. "Did you see the new trailer for *The Departure*?"

"With that girl that was in *Tell Tale*? Absolutely, it was horrible," Dawn sputtered out through a laugh.

"Okay, that's exactly what I thought! But all these forums were talking about how great it was, so I felt like I was the crazy one."

"No, it was terrible. I can say that without hesitation. Plus, it's coming out on Christmas." Dawn walked up and then back down the hallway of her home for the fourth time, a hamster on a wheel. "Who does that?"

"Um, I came out on Christmas. Take that back," Collin laughed, and Dawn couldn't help but mark the cadence of it, its music.

"You're a person, not a movie," she countered.

"And yet people line up to watch my drama all the time. Weird."

"You're an idiot."

"You're friends with an idiot," he retorted.

"Are we friends?" Dawn ran her hand along the wall as she asked, letting her fingers catch in the grooves of the wallpaper.

"Well it would be weird if we weren't, especially since I'm inviting you to stay at my place for the film fest."

"Wait, really?" Dawn stopped pacing and gripped the hallway wall.

"Yeah. Bring your buds, it'll be fun. I can show you around Austin and take you to all the breakfast taco places. Plus, all the hotels are probably booked and like a hundred dollars a night whereas my house is free and there's a dog. Basically, a win-win."

"Collin, that's way too nice. I mean, we can figure something out. I might have a cousin or something I could ask?" Dawn waited for his answer, excited at the idea but not wanting to let it come through in her voice.

"Don't even worry about it. My parents are gonna be taking my brother to some sleepaway camp for talented prodigy artist kids or something, so we'll have lots of room. It'll be like a big party all weekend."

"I don't know what to say," she breathed out. She noticed she'd been holding her breath for the last few moments.

"Say yes. It'll be cool! We can put on our fancy outfits and go to a bunch of film screenings."

"Fine, fine. You've convinced me."

"Good."

Dawn heard the sound of her father's voice coming from his bedroom.

"Oh, I gotta go." Dawn bit her bottom lip tight between her teeth. She realized she didn't want the conversation to end. "I need to take care of something."

"Your dad?"

"Yeah," Dawn breathed out, grateful to be known by this boy, to not have to explain.

"Did you tell him about the fest?"

"Not yet. I-I'm about to."

"This is gonna be unbelievable."

Dawn couldn't help but notice how much he cared. About the movie, about her. She didn't want to get hurt again, she couldn't handle it. She had leaned in too many times and landed flat on her face each and every attempt. Somehow, though, she couldn't pull herself from small, good thoughts of him.

"Yeah. Hey, Collin?"

"Yeah?" She listened to the quiet, his breath and the silence of his life in the background.

"Thank you so much for your words and your time."

"No problem. Thanks for yours. I'll see you this weekend."

"Yeah. Bye."

Dawn waited until she heard the click of Collin hanging up and closed her eyes as she lowered herself to the bed. How did she stumble upon the kindest person in the world and why did he like her? She had never had a friendship like this with a boy. He was so involved yet so far away. They barely knew each other and yet he knew more about her and her likes and dislikes and moods and family shit than almost anyone in her life. She liked him too much and wanted to guard herself from falling in too deep. Friendship is a kind of love too, she reminded herself.

Dawn pushed away her thoughts and moved to get up. Her father's voice was still echoing through the hall like some withering ghost.

She rested her hand on his doorframe and leaned into his dimly lit room. It smelled sour like milky tea left in the bottom of the cup. Her father was wrapped in his blankets staring at the empty ceiling above his head.

"You eat yet?"

"No."

"Want something?"

"Ramen, please. The shrimp one." He reached for the nearly toppling stack of books next to his bed, engineering and butterfly entomology, hobbies dead and dying. Before settling on one, his hand retracted back beneath the blanket, an unfinished thought.

Dawn turned her back and slunk to the kitchen. She poured a cup of water from the sink over the dry cup of noodles and stuffed the Styrofoam container into the microwave. She tapped out a beat on the counter as she trained her eyes on the ramen circling around and around. The repetition of the motion scared her. This would be the rest of her life if she didn't go to the festival and see what her future could be. If she didn't go, she would always be sliding ramen into the microwave and waiting for time to pass. That was it. That would be her story. The timer went off and she pulled the cup out with both palms.

Dawn felt the dirt in the carpet beneath her socks as she walked back to her father's room.

She pushed the door back and sat the soup down on the small empty space next to the bed amongst all the trash and projects and dirty dishes.

"Dad, I'm going to Austin. I have a chance to win a really big scholarship that's going to help us." Dawn tucked her thumbs into her fists and squeezed as she waited for his reply.

"That's good, Dawn." His words clipped off as if he was going to say something else, but then he didn't.

"No, Dad, this is really important. I'm gonna get us some money so someone can come here and clean up and get your food and stuff."

"I don't need anything. I'm okay. You're always worrying too much."

Dawn looked up at the mountains of garbage around them, the food wrappers and shoes without matches in every size.

"If I win, someone's going to come here and help you remember to take your medicine and get out of bed sometimes. It's going to be really good for you."

"Okay."

"Dad, please. Just say something good. Say something nice to me, please." She hated to hear herself whine and beg like a kid. But she needed this. She needed him like he needed her.

He turned towards her: "I don't want to need help, you know? I don't like being like this for you."

"I know, Dad. But I have a chance at something big. I can go to college and help you at the same time."

"Okay." He turned his head back to the ceiling and closed his eyes.

She didn't know what she expected. Of course, his words fell flat against her head. She wanted a congratulations or maybe tears of joy. But that's not how it worked. That's not how he worked, not anymore, at least. She started to leave the room, disappointed in herself for wanting more from him.

"Dawn?"

She turned on her heel, looking back into the dim room one last time. This is where her father would be when she was in Austin, in school one day, out in the world figuring out her life without him.

TWENTY-EIGHT

April 11, One Day to Austin Film Festival

Georgia sat down at her desk where months' worth of unread books stacked up waiting to be flipped through by her greedy hands. Poems by Saeed Jones, Tarfia Faizullah, and Fatimah Asghar rattled around her head; the poets kept her clean, kept her head fuzzy with delightful words like *plumed* and *tendril* and *mote*. She liked it this way, the unpredictable song of words on the page filling her up like a child gorged from dinner with the grownups.

Georgia had a bad habit of asking words to do too much. She wanted her words to be good, to say all that she couldn't out loud. Georgia had to tell her mom that things with Simone were not going to work out. Even if it hurt her, she would have to speak up.

She had always had a hard time facing the specific look of pain that sometimes etched itself across her mother's face. A loan she'd applied for not going through, Georgia not getting accepted to some wonderful private middle school she'd eagerly tried to get her into. The crinkle at the edge of her eyes, a sign that tears might come, made Georgia want to look away, not in embarrassment but in genuine hurt for her mother like the sight of a wounded animal. She'd only seen it a few times in her life but that was enough.

She pulled out her pen and a journal. The journal was blank, a mark of Georgia's habitual need to start new, untouched, whenever she was writing. She had notebooks that had four pages or even two sentences scrawled in them and nothing else. Then she was done with them, exhausted by her presence on the previously perfect paper.

But with time and dedication, words somehow always did what Georgia needed them to. She had to write this note so that she could explain what happened with Simone without seeing that dark look on her mother's face like a waning moon.

She brought her pen down and ignored the growing splotch of ink as she left the pointed nib down for too long in one spot without moving her hand.

Dear Mom,

She scratched it out and turned the page.

Hi Mom!

Scratch, again.

Dear Mom,

She started again. She wrote the letter for everything she had been unable to say in the past few weeks. She wrote what couldn't just pass quietly in the cushioned air between them over dinner tables or late-night movie binges on the couch.

Here she was trying to speak as she'd never spoken before. To risk hurting her mother was a crime she'd never known herself able to commit, but here she was. The pen splotched at some points as she tried to track down a thought.

She ended the letter softly, the only way she knew how.

Love, Georgia

Georgia liked to think that she was a good daughter, that her kindness spilled from her like milk over the lip of a full glass. She hoped that when her mother looked at her, she saw love. That she saw a flower still trying to embrace the honeydew at its mouth. When she looked at her mother, she saw a woman attempting happiness. Sometimes failing, sometimes succeeding, but always bringing her daughter along for the try. Georgia admired this in her, her willingness to see the world as a series of opportunities to feel better than the day before.

She didn't want to hurt her mother the way life had hurt her. The things she hid from Georgia so that she could have a joyous life suddenly seemed innumerable and vast to Georgia, some great depth so far beyond her she could hardly imagine it. But still, she strived to help Frankie by hurting her slightly. She bit her lip as she reread the message once and then once more.

She tore the note out of the journal with a quick rip and folded it into three tight panels. She wrote *Mom* on the opposite side and placed the paper on her mother's bedside table. Her backpack, filled with provisions for the trip to Austin, felt immense as she swung it over her shoulders. Georgia grabbed some fruit from the kitchen and hopped into her Camry. She drove to pick up Edie and Dawn for their final trip together, her windows rolled down to catch the sound of the city behind her.

TWENTY-NINE

April 11, One Day to Austin Film Festival

For Dawn, the drive to Austin was short and long. Short, because three hours sitting down was just two class periods at school, but long because the sun was out and she was impatient and the beauty of Texas roadsides and their unending wildflowers required a lot of stops.

"Are you guys ready?" Dawn asked.

"For what?" Edie groaned, a frequent and extremely vocal victim of motion sickness.

"Our cinematic teen movie moment, duh." Dawn lowered her sunglasses to the bridge of her nose.

"Hell yeah." Georgia pumped a fist out of the open driver's side window.

Dawn fumbled around looking through Georgia's CDs. She finally slid one in and pressed play, and soft guitar streamed into the backseat.

Georgia and Edie exchanged a look in the rearview mirror.

"How dare you," Georgia laughed as the first verse started.

A folk song from their *Country Girls Make Do* playlist streamed through the speakers. Dawn wasn't exactly sure what the song was about, but she knew the chorus mentioned being from Texas, having a little drink, and flirting with cowboys.

"Dawn, you've got to be kidding," Edie sighed, already popping her third ginger candy.

"Just lean in, Edie! Forget that we're moving! Forget about your stomach. Think about the words and just fucking lean in." The song continued and Dawn turned around to lip-sync at Edie as she pouted.

"Are you playing air accordion?" Edie asked as Dawn raised her arms into a strange gesture.

"Babe, I think it's a banjo and a violin," Georgia sputtered out with a laugh.

"Sorry, I'm from Texas, but I'm not from *Texas* Texas." Dawn lowered her arms from the bent position where she'd been pretending to play. "I'm a woman of suburban experience."

They all laughed and let the wind from the open windows whip their voices into the road.

After an hour and a half, they stopped at Hruška's, a gas station and bakery buzzing with University of Texas moms looking for sustenance and souvenirs to remember dropping their kids off at college for the first or seventh time.

Dawn remembered stopping here on a choir trip to San Antonio in elementary school and eating what she believed to be, at the time, the best cinnamon roll she'd ever tasted. She also remembered Clara Getty asking her if she wanted her to get Dawn a Honey Bun on the way back and feeling like it was the key to her adolescent happiness. First a Honey Bun then her hand in marriage. The thought made her laugh, how everything was so important to her as a kid, every look from a girl or boy that lasted a second too long, the subject of dozens of pages in her diary.

"I'll get gas. Can y'all get me a coffee?" Georgia unlocked the car door and Edie and Dawn emerged in a road trip haze.

"Of course. Sugar, right?" Dawn asked, though she already knew the answer.

"You know me too well," drawled Georgia, already pulling the gas nozzle from the pump.

Dawn and Edie wandered through the front door of the building and let the cool rush of air conditioning hit their skin and instantly dry the thin film of sweat on the back of their necks.

Edie peeled off to the bathroom and left Dawn to browse the aisles of old-fashioned candies and Texas-themed knickknacks.

Her eyes landed on pralines and she suddenly remembered her dad at home again. It was his favorite candy—brown sugar, cream, and pecans combined into the perfect confection. It used to be an easy way to make him happy on birthdays and Christmas. Dawn remembered how he would break off a piece and pop it in his mouth with a smile, tilt his neck back, and close his eyes. *Just amazing*, he'd say. Every time. Even if it was from some candy shop they'd never tried before. Even if the flavor was bad or the candy was old. *Just amazing*, his head bent back to the sky as if god herself had sent the candy to him personally and he wanted to send back a thank you.

She picked up two of the candies and held them close to her chest.

Dawn heard Edie come out of the bathroom after a moment, her crowded carabiner jangling loudly against her pants.

"That bathroom always smells like my grandma's house in California. It's just always so clean," Edie beamed. "Kind of giving that little Buc-ee's beaver a run for its money."

Dawn laughed and grabbed Edie's now floral-scented hand so they could walk around. She liked Hruška's kitschy southern decorations and signs for sale declaring SAVE A HORSE, RIDE A COWBOY. A mural spanning the entire store displayed what the store would have looked like in its early days, men in denim and pinch-front hats manning soda machines and cowgirls dancing around a jukebox.

"Did you get Georgia's coffee?" Edie asked, fiddling with a windup snake in a barrel toy.

"Can you get it? I forgot about kolaches," Dawn exclaimed.

"Absolutely. Peach, please?"

"Anything for Selenas." Dawn crooned, trying out her best impression.

"Love that in this scenario I'm JLo." Edie laughed, turning towards the coffee machines.

The bakery line was only two people deep and moved quickly. Dawn spoke to the woman behind the counter in slow Spanish, embarrassed at her plodding tongue. She handed her the fruity treats in a white bag already splotched with grease.

Dawn met Edie at the cash register and paid for the pastries and candy.

"You ready?" Edie asked as she tucked her debit card into the wallet hanging off her carabiner.

"For Austin?"

"Everything. The competition, the drama, the movie stars."

"Okay, drama queen." Dawn grabbed her receipt and stuffed it into her pocket. "Yes and no." Dawn grimaced at her own answer as they started walking out to the car.

Up until now, Dawn had been a stone at the bottom of some huge river. She was molded by whatever crashed into her. She was smooth in some places and rough in others because of the people around her. What they said, what they did, it all affected her at every turn. Now, she was creating her own shape. She was taking hold of what she looked like next. The festival was the first step and everything after was determined by its outcome. The pressure was immense and scary.

"I want to want it, but I don't want to be disappointed, you know? I mean, I haven't even seen the final cut because I trust you guys so much. Like, I feel so tied to this movie and winning and if it doesn't happen there are so many things that have to end."

"Like what? Also, look."

Edie motioned towards the car where Georgia was flailing her body in the front seat, a Yellowcard song playing way too loudly through the open windows.

"No, right. Of course," Dawn laughed watching Georgia's slow head banging. "But really though, E. School has to end, making movies kind of has to end, being free has to end. We have to end."

"This," Edie waved her finger between the two of them as they got to the car and opened the doors, "will never end. I'll annoy you until the grave. And when I die, I'm coming to haunt your ass."

"You good in here?" Dawn asked, reaching to turn down the dial.

"Yes. Just getting rid of some energy with the *Girls Should Be Allowed to Be Weird* playlist," Georgia sputtered, breathless from her car dancing.

"I fucking love that one," Dawn exclaimed, shutting her door.

"Wait, didn't you make it?" Georgia asked.

"Exactly." Dawn turned the volume up and leaned back in her seat as Georgia pulled back onto the road.

She stared ahead at the sun-sparkled highway. Outside the window, green fields full of calves and their mothers in every imaginable shade of dark brown rushed past. When Georgia ripped around a curve on Highway 71, Dawn's body shifted towards the door, her ear pressing into the glass, the sound of Texas humming just beyond its surface.

Austin appeared on the horizon just beyond the maze of exits outlined by sprawling trees.

Dawn could feel the potential energy buzzing inside her chest. She sensed that good things were meant for her in this city.

THIRTY

The girls stared in awe as Georgia's car careened through pockets of Austin neighborhoods laden with odd modern architecture, lawns littered with liberal political signs and bright burnt-orange University of Texas flags.

As Georgia steadily crept along, her phone alerted her that she was approaching her final destination. They looked around for the address numbers on the sides of houses and suddenly saw a boy waving them down wildly from one of the driveways.

"That's him," Dawn let out a snort at the chaotic waving motion Collin was doing to get their attention.

"Aw, he's cute," Edie cooed. "Like a 1920s Columbia English professor and a Care Bear had a baby."

Dawn had imagined him based on the silly pictures they'd sent each other just like this: golden skin like first place, kind green eyes, and a pillow-soft smile of pink and strawberry red. Even better than the pictures. His tight dark curls had grown out since the Halloween photo he'd sent her, now descending to his shoulders like a halo around his perfectly freckled face. He wore loose jeans and a striped green pullover.

He was taller than she'd imagined; his head grazed the ceiling of his garage as he waved the car towards the driveway.

"Edie, you're so weird. But also? Extremely accurate assessment."

Georgia pulled in and put her car in park with a sigh. They all tumbled out of the car sweaty and exhausted from the drive.

The girls dragged their suitcases through the oak-floored halls as Collin led them on a rapid tour of every room in the seemingly endless two-story home. Dawn kept her eyes on him as he occasionally wiped his dark curls from his eyes and pointed to different rooms, explaining that they could go anywhere and look at anything.

His house was charming, everything painted white like a Pottery Barn catalog.

Edie and Georgia disappeared into the guest room and left Dawn and Collin in the kitchen with its white cabinets and big granite island.

"Did y'all want to go out for food? I know you just got here." Collin leaned against the counter as he spoke.

"Yeah, the troops are starving." Dawn patted her hand over her stomach. "We only ate granola bars and bananas on the way here. Oh, and the best kolaches ever, but still. Starving."

"There's a really good taco place down the street. Or, you know, you can choose whatever you want. Just a suggestion."

"Sounds good."

"It's just the nearest thing I could think of that's good," he laughed. "I feel like going to school here forces me to eat the same three things again and again. Stuff near campus."

"Do you like it?" Dawn tilted her weight against the counter so she could face Collin and rest her head on her hands.

"The food?"

"School," she remarked with a quiet laugh.

"No, yeah. I love it here."

"Really? I can't imagine going to college down the street from my house. I mean, if I don't win, I guess that's exactly what I'll be doing." Dawn quieted down. "But, you know what I mean."

"It's nice. I like hanging out with my parents and my brother. I have an apartment on campus that I share with five other people, but I spend a lot of time here at the house. Especially since I started shooting the documentary."

"You think they're sick of you?" Dawn teased, giving Collin a look.

"Yeah right. If I weren't here, who would wash the dishes and drive Lane to art classes?"

"Ah, the duties of an older sibling."

"It's a very luxurious life." He grinned.

"I bet."

Quiet passed between them for a moment and Collin scuffed his shoe into the tiling of the kitchen as if waiting for something to happen. The sound of a far-off washing machine whirred and cut up the silence with its humming.

"Hey, would you want to hang out after the fest?" he asked, not quite meeting her eyes.

"What do you mean?" They had already agreed to hang out all weekend. Dawn could tell that Collin was nervous, his words more spaced out than before.

"Like, just us? After the festival tomorrow?"

"Oh. I mean, yeah. Sure. Yeah. We can do that." Dawn suddenly felt stuck. Here was a lovely boy. The nicest she'd ever met, probably. But she felt guarded. Knox, everyone before him, it all hurt too much. She needed to be by herself for a while. She didn't need crushes running every second of her life.

"I just realized you've been like my best friend for the past few weeks. Like, I talk to you more than anybody, which is weird but very true. I just think it would be cool. Hanging out, I mean."

"Okay." She looked him up and down. She looked really hard. Could you see it in someone's eyes if they're a bad person? She thought back on their two months' worth of texts and late nights watching bad French films over Facetime. Maybe he'd be a good friend. A best friend. "I'd love to."

"Cool," he spoke through a smile.

The sound of Edie and Georgia walking down the hall, grumbling about how hungry they were, interrupted their conversation and all the weight that came with it.

They all piled into Collin's beat-up Civic that seemed like it had been pulled straight from the year 1995, dusty red paint and all. Every seat was covered in cracked gray vinyl and the windows had cranks that required a little extra effort to get them turning. He told the girls he'd bought it on Craigslist himself from a guy named Keto.

The drive was short, just two Beyoncé songs long. and they pulled into a parking lot filled with food trucks.

The lot was packed with picnic tables, the perimeter lined with food trucks advertising cross-cultural food combinations only Austin could boast: kimchi fries, Korean tacos, vegan barbecue. All of the trucks were decorated with bright, outrageous illustrations of dancing burritos and mustached men holding ice cream cones three times the size of their head.

"It's that one." Collin pointed to a truck on the corner of the lot.

They wandered through the tables and craned their necks to read the handwritten menu hung beside the small open window.

"You have to get the tacos. I mean, you don't have to, but, you *should* if you want to have the best possible culinary experience." Collin furrowed his brow and nodded solemnly.

They stood in line for fifteen minutes, chatting about their excitement for the festival, hoping all the while that the satisfaction for their grumbling stomachs was worth the time spent shifting from foot to foot. Collin asked Dawn about what she planned to say during her acceptance speech. "Since you'll obviously be winning thanks to my incredible editing skills," he added.

"I would like to thank the Academy," shouted out Dawn, one hand outstretched graciously at absolutely no one.

"And my lovely friends for feeding fries directly into my mouth so that I wouldn't have to get my laptop keyboard greasy while cutting clips together. Also, our Lord, Lorde," Dawn winked at Edie. "For creating sad queer hits for me to cry to while thinking about how I still don't have a man."

"Seriously, D."

"What? I don't want to get my hopes up. I feel good having made it this far. I have no idea what I'll say if I actually win. What about you?" She gestured towards Collin.

"Me, what?"

"What will you say if you win? I saw your film. It was incredible."

"You're going to win, so I don't plan to say anything." He squinted up at the sun then back down to the group again with a smile. The way he said it wasn't malicious or even joking, he just spoke as if it were an absolute truth. His earnest tone startled Dawn. "Plus, I already go to UT on scholarship, so if I won, the scholarship funding would go to another student anyway."

"I hadn't even thought of that. Maybe if you win they'll slide the money my way." Dawn let out a half laugh. She was so nervous for the day of the festival to arrive.

The tacos were impossibly good. Barely a minute had passed before the tacos had disappeared into their stomachs and the group was back to discussing the festival.

"I saw on Twitter that a bunch of celebrities come into town for the fest. See, like this." Georgia turned her phone towards the group revealing a tweet of a blurry picture of what could have been either Emma Stone or Margot Robbie ordering a coffee at some café.

Collin squinted at the picture trying to make sense of the odd angle the person had shot it from. "Oh, yeah. I saw Timothée Chalamet at the capitol last year. It was wild."

Edie gasped. "The gays love Timothée."

"It's the pallid cheekbones," offered Dawn.

"Oh for sure," Collin laughed. "I mean, I've already seen a famous person this year, though."

"Who?"

"Dawn Salcedo, award-winning documentarian," Collin said with a smirk.

Dawn faked a gag and laughed.

She liked his overt compliments, the obnoxiousness of his jokes, but she didn't want to let herself like it too much. She was not going to go through anymore boy-related shit this year.

The table quieted down. Dawn crumpled the foil from her tacos into a little ball the size of her palm.

"I have another place we can go," Collin said. "It's just up the road and I feel like y'all would really like it."

"Do we at least get a hint as to what this mysterious place is?" Georgia asked.

"There will be books." Collin arched a single eyebrow and knocked his fist on the table.

THIRTY-ONE

April 11, One Day to Austin Film Festival

The bookstore was small, split into two sections divided by long shelves with the cash register shyly tucked into a corner next to a series of "guide to LGBT parenting" books. The cashier was resting their elbows on the counter, eyes tilted downward towards a book splayed open to its last pages.

"Welcome to BookWoman," they muttered, distracted.

The girls gave their obligatory thanks as they waded with Collin into the messily organized displays of glossy books, their bright covers still perfectly intact, not yet flipped through and bent backwards.

"Guys, they have a queer graphic novel section," Dawn whispered in amazement. "A whole section."

"Did you see this?" Edie pointed to a button section with buttons declaring things like *douse me in honey and throw me to the lesbians!* and *I'm not gay but my boyfriend is.*

"Oh my god, I need one of those," exclaimed Georgia.

"Girl, you sound like your mom. Remember we went to Target that one time and she kept saying *I need those curtains, I need this moisturizer, I need this blender.*"

"'Want' is not a concept my mother is familiar with, and I'm at peace with that."

As Edie looked at the shelves and shelves of queer literature, she reflected on her bookshelf at home. She owned two books with queer main characters in them, both white gay boys from tiny towns. She'd turned the binding around on her shelf so that her parents wouldn't see the titles and ask her about them.

Here, they were freely out and on display, just another part of the store. The point, even, was their queerness.

Maybe there was hope. Maybe she could go to college and be okay. She wouldn't have to tell her parents everything. She could turn the binding with them at home and still be herself at school.

Dawn wandered around shelves and pulled a few graphic novels from the shelf about lesbian ballerinas.

"I think I want to live here," Dawn called out.

"Austin?" asked Georgia from across the room.

"No, this store. I want to die here and have my ashes spread in the parking lot."

"No kidding."

Edie picked up a book off the shelf and turned over the cover. She began to read the back cover to herself.

Abigail Reyes is at the top of her game. An early acceptance to Harvard, captain of the winningest high school soccer team in Connecticut, and two parents who loved her more than life itself. But when nonbinary new kid Sid Valentine comes to town to stay at her parents' house, she loses her grip on good grades and begins to spend all her time thinking about them. Can she maintain her perfect life and find love for the very first time?

"Jesus Christ," moaned Georgia, reading over her shoulder.

"Well I'm not *not* gonna get it."

"No, I absolutely love the concept and need to borrow it as soon as possible, please and thank you. It's just, I can already tell that it's one of those books we're going to hate to love. You know, first dates and prom nights and all that gooey stuff that just eats you."

"I know. I can't wait," Edie laughed out loud.

She dropped her book at the cash register and waited for the cashier to look up from their book.

"Oh, I just read this," the cashier said. "It's actually super cute. Like, unbearably so."

"Good. I'm shooting for mind-numbingly charming." Edie smirked.

"We don't really have many books about nonbinary people. Maybe fifteen, so it was really cool to get this one in." She scanned the book and waved it back down to the counter as they spoke.

"Weird. Is there something happening here?" asked Edie, gesturing to a line of plastic chairs at the back of the store.

"Poetry reading. It's in twenty minutes if you and your friends want to stick around."

"Yeah, absolutely." The cashier stuffed a bookmark with a purple giraffe on it into the fresh pages and slid Edie's book back across the counter to her.

Edie took the book and tucked it under her arm as she walked back to a stack of paperbacks Dawn and Georgia were flipping through.

She thought about the space she was in and how it was so different from anywhere she'd been in Houston. Here she was buying queer literature amongst her very queer friends. She was in love and the world was set out in front of her for the taking. She felt like she could breathe for once. Being away from her parents was easy and nice and let her try new things, new ways of being. She started to think about the years ahead in college and all the ways she would change for the better. She could become more herself without judgement or the harsh emotional weight of always doing things right.

....
....

Dawn disappeared out of the store into the parking lot and left the girls and Collin to keep looking around.

Dawn felt the heat lap at the back of her neck as soon as she stepped outside. She kicked a few stubs of gravel and let her eyes glaze over at the rainbow flags and freshly stacked books decorating the storefront window.

A few minutes went by with the hot air brushing her skin a darker brown and the sound of two men arguing in the gas station parking lot across the street. Dawn couldn't hear what they were saying but one of the men, clad in an acid-washed Grateful Dead shirt, kept pointing to a beat-up red car as he barked at the other. Dawn decided to sit on the curb and watch cars pile up on North Lamar.

Her lungs filled up slow and then quick with warm air. She crossed her arms and grabbed her shoulders then closed her eyes until everything was black with silver and green spots punching in and out of view.

The pressure of her own nervousness filled her up like a balloon at the edge of bursting into a hundred messy rubber pieces.

Her panic was interrupted by the sound of the bookstore's front door opening and then the soft scuff of shoes next to her on the paved lot.

Collin bent down beside her and let a couple moments of silence go by without making a sound or movement.

"Collin, I am freaking the fuck out."

"What's going on?" He reached his right hand out above her head to create a shadow across her eyes.

"Thanks." She looked at him for a moment in thought.

"I really want to win. I want to be here. Austin, I mean. I want to make movies and pretend to be normal and eat tacos and just exist. Is that insane? Am I the person who thinks they're really good but really I'm just okay and shooting too high?"

"No. Of course not."

"I don't think I've ever wanted something so badly." She looked down at the pavement. "I mean, I really *really* need this to happen. It's just . . . I feel like I'm setting myself up for a thousand-foot fall to the ground."

"You're being hopeful. That's important." Collin smiled but she couldn't relax.

"Yeah but it's also stupid and a terrible thing to put myself through if I don't win."

"Or a wonderful thing if you do. You'll have proved yourself right. That you *are* an incredible filmmaker who deserves a huge opportunity." He let his hands fly through the air as he spoke, a parade of excited gestures.

"I know. I just don't want to fall. Or fail. I don't want to fail and then fall." Dawn bent over and let out a deep breath.

"You're not going to fail."

"How can you say that?"

"I believe in you."

"I hope this doesn't come off mean, like, at all, but I can't go on belief." Dawn took a deep breath and looked away from him. "Not yours. Not even mine."

"I know, but it's still true. No matter what happens, you will use your hands and your heart and your huge brain to make great movies. You could go home, take care of your dad, and write scripts or develop documentary ideas. At the end of the day, you are a star who will make incredible things happen. Look at what you've already done. You're going to be okay no matter what."

"I want to believe you."

"Dawn Salcedo, you are the most talented person I know, and the world will see your work and grow from it. Please know that." Collin reached his hand out and put it over hers.

Dawn felt like the quaking feeling in her head was settling down to stillness. Her nerves dissipated at his touch then picked back up slightly when she realized she might like the feeling of his palm on hers.

The store's door squeaked open and Georgia peeked her head around the glass. Collin kept his hand firmly on top of hers and turned his head.

"The reading is about to start. Are y'all good?"

"Yeah, just a second." Dawn waited for Georgia to disappear behind the door again then swiped at the single tear making its way down her cheek.

"You want a hug?"

"Yeah." She settled her chin into his blue cardigan and noticed that he smelled just like his house—comfortable, clean sheets and sesame oil.

"Thank you, Collin. For everything."

....
....

As the reading began, Dawn and Collin squeezed into the tiny arrangement of chairs beside Georgia and Edie. The once distracted and quiet cashier was suddenly alive, announcing the start of the poetry reading with an enthusiasm and verve that delighted the small crowd that was beginning to gather.

"Welcome to Campfire! I'm Allison and my pronouns are they/she. If you're new here, Campfire is a monthly poetry reading featuring queer poets of Austin. This afternoon we have Oscar Huerta, Gemma Hoit, Penelope Stoner, and two free slots for any brave poets in the audience."

The small group clapped and looked around.

"Don't worry folks. New poets can hop in any time after the featured poets are done reading."

"The rules are simple. Poets must introduce themselves, read a poem they love, then proceed with their own poem. Be respectful, snap if you're feeling the vibe, and have fun." People snapped in response and Allison smiled.

Georgia looked around and tried to figure out who the poets were, her people. The room was filled with thrifted clothes and haircuts her mother would call "unique." It was lovely. People in their twenties and thirties pushed up against the shelves of queer, colorful books and held notepads and slung hand-painted canvas tote bags over their hunched shoulders as they tried to get comfortable for the reading.

"Alright, first up, I am so happy to introduce local beekeeper and lowkey icon, Oscar Huerta!"

The girl in front of her was leaning on her friend's shoulder, so Georgia could just barely see someone inch towards the front of the audience, a deep green flannel tied around their waist.

"My name is Oscar Huerta. Thank you so much for the kind introduction, Allison. My pronouns are he/him. Um, I thought for a long time about which poem I would read first. Because there's this inherent pressure with picking a poem you love. Too many favorites and all that." He rubbed his finger against a plain blue notebook as he spoke.

"I ended up picking a Nathaniel Mackey poem that's been playing through my mind lots this past month. I feel like it's following me around so maybe it's the right one. Not something I love but something that loves me enough to trail my thoughts."

He started in on a poem Georgia recognized from *Nod House*. She closed her eyes to listen and snapped every time the words moved her to. The poem ended and the poet wrenched his hands around his notebook, explaining that the poem he was about to read was part of an upcoming chapbook.

His poem was slow, line after line about his boyfriend, his likeness to bees, how spring brought him out like fresh spilling sap. As each poet read, Georgia snapped like she had a right to be in the room, unselfconscious of the sound or the effect the words had on her. She belonged.

"Are you gonna go up there?" Dawn whispered as Allison made their way back to the front to ask for volunteers.

"I don't know. I don't have a poem picked out that I love. You're supposed to read the work of someone else first."

"Just pick something. You're always sending Edie and me stuff. What about that Richard Siken you memorized last year?"

"That's not bad. Yeah, I could do that."

Allison's voice came back to Georgia as she tried to gather up the courage to volunteer herself.

"Any new or old poets want to get up here? We have time for two volunteers. Please remember that Campfire is a space for both new and experienced writers. We would love to hear your words."

Dawn raised her hand high and waved it frantically.

"Dawn!" Georgia uttered as she swatted her hand down.

"Looks like we have a volunteer! Please come to the front and introduce yourself."

"Dawn, I will kill you and I will like it." But, of course, she was thrilled and almost grateful for the push towards the uncomfortable.

She grabbed her phone out of her bag and walked to the front.

"My name is Georgia Graham and my pronouns are she/her. I'm from Houston. I'm visiting for the weekend, because my best friend is in the Austin Film Festival. Thanks for inviting me into this space." Polite claps dispersed. "I actually have a poem I like so much I spent a few weeks last year memorizing it. Here we go."

She started on the Richard Siken and quickly grew comfortable in the words. They spilled easily from her mouth like a friend's phone number or dearly loved song. She closed her eyes and the lines flowed from her without thought. When it ended, she opened them and stared out at the rapidly snapping group of people who were older and maybe better than her.

"The poem I want to read is one I wrote for my friends who are here with me. Edie, Dawn, you've already heard this one, but I love you so much."

She opened the poem she'd read to them at the beach on her phone and began to read.

She tried to ignore the crowd and instead focused on her voice, the curve of the stanzas on her lips. It felt like she was writing the poem as she read it out loud, wanting to cut certain words here and there as she listened to herself. Snaps came from the chairs sporadically, but Georgia tried to zone them out and kept reading until the end.

The room swelled with claps when she finished. Her chest tightened at the sight of all the strangers applauding her.

Georgia uttered a breathless thank you and scurried back to her seat.

"Geo, that was amazing," poked Edie. She reached over Dawn to squeeze Georgia's arm. "I mean, really great."

Georgia smiled and folded her arms over herself. One more person from the crowd stood up to read, but Georgia could barely pay attention. The rush of the reading filled her head so that there wasn't room to take in much else.

"I really liked your stuff. Keep it up," a girl nodded to Georgia on her way out. Georgia could barely utter a thank you before she was gone, bubblegum pink hair swaying over her shoulders as she opened the door.

Georgia's phone started ringing and she hurried to answer it, embarrassed she'd forgotten to turn it down during the reading in the first place.

"Hello?"

"Georgia, you got a letter," the voice on the other end shrieked.

"Mom?" She thought of the note she'd left for her mother at home but quickly interrupted her own thinking as her her mom's words sunk in. "Wait, what letter?"

"It's from Kenyon College, Georgia baby. It's a *big* envelope." Each word was a star shooting bright through the phone. Georgia felt dizzy and wonderful.

"Oh my god. Open it." She pushed her way to the door and planted her feet on the pavement just outside. Cars rushed by as she waited for the news on the other end of the line.

"You sure? I can wait until you get home." Georgia could hear her mother practically tap dancing over the phone.

"Nope. Just rip it open." Georgia closed her eyes and tried to pay attention to the subtle sounds around her, the feeling of wind and heat on her skin. Her anxiety died down a little as she found the sound of birds, the crosswalk ding, and chattering voices in the parking lot. "I honestly feel like I'm going to die, so just do it."

"The dramatics, G."

"Mom," Georgia whined. "Please just take me out of my misery."

She heard the envelope ripping and the sound of paper being shaken out on their dinner table. The pause her mother took was excruciating.

"You got in, baby."

"I did?"

"You got in, baby girl!"

Georgia started jumping up and down in the parking lot. Her bag jolted on her shoulder and shook as she punched her fist into the air.

"Mom, I'm going to college."

"I know. I'm so proud of you. I knew you could do it. When are you girls coming home Sunday? We should have a party."

"Oh, I don't know. I'll ask Dawn when the festival stuff is over. Maybe a party before graduation."

"I'm so proud of you, Georgia."

"Thanks, Mom. Okay, I gotta go. I think Dawn is trying to get my attention." Georgia laughed at Dawn waving through the display window.

"Okay, honey. I'll see you as soon as you get home."

She hung up and walked back into the store. The cool air swept over her body and she felt lighter than ever.

"You okay? We were just getting ready to leave." Dawn and Edie held the books they'd bought as Collin swiped his card at the counter.

"Yeah, that was my mom. I got into Kenyon." She smiled huge getting to say it out loud.

"Geo, you star!" Dawn's paper bag of new books split wide open as she dropped it onto the ground to pull Georgia in for a hug.

"It's in Ohio," Georgia murmured over Dawn's shoulder.

"Queen of sowing her wild oats in nature," Dawn said into Georgia's hair as Edie joined the already messy hug.

"Something tells me you have no idea where Ohio is." Georgia laughed, the tears just barely escaping her bottom lashes.

"Shut up. It's in nature. It's in America. It's where you're going to write your debut book of poetry," Dawn laughed.

"I'm gonna be so far away." Georgia wiped at her eyes as she felt the girls' arms tight around her shoulders.

"We'll write letters to each other. We'll kiss the envelopes and put stickers on every sheet of paper. I mean, video chatting too, duh. But the letters feel like an important element."

They all pulled away and Edie grabbed Georgia by both shoulders.

"You are incredible. I love you and your words so much."

"Thanks, E. That means so much. I mean, I think you guys literally read my first poem like sophomore year."

"Oh yeah. 'Leaves of Grass,'" offered Dawn.

"That's Walt Whitman."

"No, that's you. Your poem was called 'Leaves of Grass.' I remember that day in English like it was yesterday."

"Wow, exposed," added Edie. "I'm sorry, G. It was definitely called 'Leaves of Grass.'"

"Jesus Christ. I've grown, people. I got into a writing program. I'm better now!"

. . . .
. . . .

Back home, Dawn and Edie stripped down to their underwear while Georgia hogged the hot shower water in the guest bathroom. Something about feeling too sweaty to sleep.

Edie got under the covers and waited for Dawn to curl up next to her like they did at every sleepover since the beginning of time, or at least sophomore year. They were the perfect heights to cuddle each other comfortably just like everyone is if they try hard enough. Dawn's hands and thighs were cold, so it felt like being held by ice itself. Edie was used to this, the chill and then gradual warmth that eventually came with sleep.

"You're gonna do great tomorrow."

"I hope so." Dawn's words could barely be heard over the sound of the air conditioner flowing through the room. "I don't want to go to sleep. I feel like the world is going to burst into flames overnight if I close my eyes."

"Think of the sea. Think about sheep. Oh! Think of that ASMR video you like where the hot guy pretends to be your flight attendant."

"I love that one."

"I know." Edie went quiet and settled her limbs over Dawn's like water over stone. Things became blurry and dark and the night came onto them without warning.

"Are you guys cuddling without me?" Georgia's voice rang from the bathroom.

Edie just barely opened her eyes enough to see the silhouette of Georgia's body in the doorway.

"Come here," Edie moaned out in her best zombie impression, her voice scratching with sleep.

Georgia tumbled into bed and joined the pile of warm bodies.

"What's up?" she teased, evidently energized from the warm water.

"We're asleep," Edie groaned, words long and heavy from the day.

Edie wrapped her arms around Georgia's waist as she plopped into the cuddle pile. Georgia fidgeted for a moment beneath Edie's hands.

"Georgia, just close your eyes. Think about the future. Think about Ohio. Think about writing beneath a tree so huge you can't even begin to see the top of it."

THIRTY-TWO

April 12, Zero Days to Austin Film Festival

The evening of the ceremony came quickly, much quicker than Dawn expected.

Dawn stared at herself in the guest bathroom mirror. She looked okay. The green dress she'd worn on her date with Knox suddenly stunk with bad memories. She could barely stand to face her reflection.

Knox on her skin, Knox with his stupid words. When she looked at herself in the mirror, there he was with his tongue like the tip of a knife. Dawn couldn't help but feel the ugliness of the past all over her.

"Hell no." Edie swung the unlocked bathroom door open to reveal an already sullen Dawn pouting at her reflection.

"Is it that bad?" Dawn didn't really want the answer but braced herself for Edie's unwavering honesty anyway.

"Yes, it is." Arms crossed, Edie met Dawn's gaze in the big bathroom mirror.

"E!" Dawn's bottom lip quivered slightly as she began to tear up.

"Which is why," Edie interrupted, "we got you something."

"Who is we? What?" Dawn turned away from Edie's reflection in the mirror and met her, eye to eye, leaning against the bathroom door.

"Bring it in, Geo!" Edie opened the door all the way to reveal Georgia standing in the frame, her arms full with a long black garment wrapped in plastic.

Dawn braced herself against the counter for balance as she struggled to keep upright.

"It's the dress." Dawn could barely get the words out. The air in the room felt so limited, barely enough to keep her standing and alive.

"Hell yeah, so you can look like Selena's long-lost fabulous cousin when you win tonight." Edie laughed.

"Gomez or Quintanilla?" Georgia asked.

"Quintanilla, obviously."

Dawn brought one hand up to her mouth as she reached to touch the plastic bag with the other. Tears began to stream down her face.

Edie handed Dawn a crumpled ball of tissue from the Kleenex box on the counter which she smushed in her hand and patted against her red skin.

Dawn squealed and they started jumping up and down. It was the biggest night of her life and nothing could hurt her. Excitement rushed through her like a soft hand through thick, tangled hair.

Georgia slipped into a silver dress with dark blue beads hanging off its hem. She looked like a disco ball had kissed a windchime. Edie's dress wasn't a dress but a flowing orange jumpsuit with fabric that swirled around at her ankles and made her look taller than she really was.

By the time their liquid lipsticks had dried and they'd placed their makeup brushes down, it was 6:00 p.m., just thirty minutes before the start of the awards ceremony

Collin yelled from the kitchen to ask if they were ready and Dawn hurried to find their bags as Edie and Georgia checked themselves in the mirror one last time.

Dawn swung Edie's fanny pack at her and told Georgia she could use her purse to hold her phone.

"Are you sure this is good?" Dawn asked, seeing herself in the mirror. Georgia walked behind her and put her hands on Dawn's nearly bare shoulders.

"I don't mean this as a drag, but you have never looked better than you look right now in this exact moment."

Dawn smoothed her hair down flat against her palm on both sides and placed her already sweating hands on top of Georgia's.

"Drag accepted. Thank you."

They pooled into the hallway and met Collin, who was dressed in a white button-up tucked beneath a moss-green blazer and gray suit pants. Dawn looked at his matching ginger-colored tie and pocket hankie and smiled. He was like a finely dressed mouse, adorable and charming.

"Snazzy." Dawn walked towards him and tugged lightly at his tie.

"Oh, thanks. I basically just put on my clothes from high school graduation."

"Come on. We're gonna be late," Edie scolded, ever the group mom.

They a ll w andered o ut o f t he d oor a nd i nto C ollin's c ar, careful not to let their clothes get caught beneath their shoes or on any stray branches reaching towards them in the driveway. Aus-tin's spring wind whipped against their nicely combed hair and reminded them that something magical could happen to them at any moment.

THIRTY-THREE

April 12, Zero Days to Austin Film Festival

The award ceremony was downtown at the Paramount Theater; film fest attendees could turn to the right and see the state capitol then turn left and see the edge of Lady Bird Lake.

Dawn stepped onto the fresh yellow carpet roped off with yellow cords and was met with the flash of a camera. She had her festival pass around her neck but swung it around to her back for pictures.

Dawn tried to take in the grandeur of the theater but was quickly overwhelmed by the people crowding in behind and in front of her. She tilted her head up and was met by angelic scenes painted onto the cylindrical ceiling in swathes of pastel high above her head.

Edie and Georgia sat on Dawn's right while Collin's thigh just barely touched hers on the left, their heads tilted up slightly towards the stage.

A man took the stage, a smart black suit and tie tightly pressed to fit his body. He introduced himself as the emcee and began thanking the festival's sponsors. He talked for a long time and Dawn tried to clap when everyone else did but got lost reading all the fascinating biography paragraphs in the program pamphlet. So many people had gone to UT's film program. She began to sweat. For the first time, she recognized how close she was to her dream. Mere moments away, even.

"And now, the part you've all been waiting for!"

Cheers and whoops burst across the audience.

"In addition to the standard film awards, we have a few special categories being announced tonight. The student awards! We have the three categories of best student narrative feature film, best student short film, and best student documentary film. One of these awards, the documentary category, will have a full scholarship to the Department of Radio, Television, and Film at the University of Texas attached, generously provided by the University of Texas RTF alumni in collaboration with the department."

"Hook 'em horns!" A stray voice yelled out from the crowd and the crowd burst into cheers as people threw up their hands into the school's symbol, the pointer and pinky finger up in the shape of horns.

"Alright! For the student narrative feature film category nominations, we have: *Golden Sun* written and directed by Solmaz Sahani, *Camp Tango* written by Ben Apoly and directed by Gordon Watts, and *When You Find Me* written and directed by Jennifer Waters."

Short flashes of the films projected onto a screen hanging above the stage. Dawn noticed the row in front of her buzzing with movement, they'd sat all the nominees together in rows towards the front of the theater.

"And the winner is," the emcee paused for far too long as the audience held its silent excitement. "Jennifer Waters with *When You Find Me!*"

A girl in a flouncing orange dress shot up from her velvet seat in front of Dawn and shuffled past her row. The fluffed-out skirt of her dress whipped against both sides of the aisle as she made her way to the stairs then eventually the stage where she was handed a small statue of a golden roll of film and a microphone.

She spoke into the mic and it squeaked at the boom of her voice.

"Hi, Mom!" She waved into the audience of thousands of people.

"I just want to thank my producer, my whole team, and every single actor for their hard work. Christopher, thank you for keeping me motivated and sane."

A single whoop emerged from the crowd. Christopher, Dawn figured.

She went on talking for a short while. The crowd erupted into applause as she finished off her speech and descended down the stairs again, trophy in hand.

The emcee announced the winner of the short film category, and Dawn grew nervous as she realized her category was the only one left. Handing a boy with nearly ankle length blonde haire a trophy for his short film, the emcee stepped up to the podium and spoke again.

"As I mentioned before, tonight, we have a very special award in the student category." Dawn gripped the arm of her seat. "One lucky student director will be receiving a full scholarship to UT Austin's Radio, Television, and Film department."

The room filled with applause and Georgia squeezed Dawn's hand so hard it went white.

Tonight's nominees for best student documentary are: Dawn Salcedo with *The Queer Girl Is Going to Be Okay*, Harusha Kan with *Surviving Belmont, Texas*, and Collin Rees with *Meeting Lane*."

"The winner of best student documentary and the recipient of a full scholarship to the University of Texas is . . . !"

The pause was so long and deep it could hold every single one of Dawn's hopes. She waded into that quiet and slowed down her breathing to almost nothing. This was it, the difference between having everything and having nothing.

Dawn looked around and saw a room full of strangers either about to witness her fail or fly. The seat beneath her felt itchy and hot suddenly. The lights from the stage reflected back onto her skin and she couldn't take the overwhelming warmth in the room. Her vision became dark as she tried to concentrate on anything but time passing. She could feel the fabric of her dress moving up and down slowly as she breathed.

"Dawn Salcedo with *The Queer Girl Is Going to Be Okay!*"

She couldn't think. The applause closed around her body like a hand.

Numbness. The world couldn't touch her, the wave of voices shouting her name couldn't touch her. She put her hands on both armrests just to feel something beneath her fingertips, just to steady herself.

Georgia patted her thigh and pointed forward where the emcee was holding a trophy and a piece of paper out towards the audience, towards her. Georgia kept saying something but Dawn couldn't understand over the sound of her own disbelief.

"It's you! You won!" Georgia rapidly tapped Dawn on her thigh attempting to grab her attention.

"Huh?" Her lip dropped gently to her chin in shock.

"Go up there! You won. We won." Edie pointed to the stage where the host was standing with the mic outstretched towards her, a smile spread on his glistening face.

The words glided into her mind, slow and real all at once.

She'd done it. She was going to go to college to make movies.

She stood up and looked at her palms, where a thin layer of sweat had gathered. She wiped her hands along the back of her dress and began to move through the row. Edie squeezed her hand as she shimmied into the open aisle. Her dress ran smooth against the back of her legs and all along her skin just like she imagined it would.

The applause kept going as she ascended the steps. She turned around with her hand on the rail and saw nothing but light. It hit her eyes and turned her vision into a white blur as she continued to the mic. The emcee handed her the golden trophy and certificate and gave her a quick hug and congratulations. He gestured towards the podium and shifted over so she could stand behind it.

Dawn squinted out at the audience and took a breath. She tried to find Edie and Georgia and Collin. It was easy since Georgia was still whooping and clapping though the applause had subsided moments ago.

She'd never felt this way before. She tried to spin the words on her tongue but nothing came out. Dawn steadied her breath and tried again.

"Hi." She cleared her throat at the reverb.

"I didn't really think I was going to win, so I didn't really prepare anything." A little pool of laughter rose from the crowd and she relaxed into the sound.

"*The Queer Girl Is Going to Be Okay* is a film that is more important to me than anything. It's about the queerness of love. Queer love. Queer personhood. It is a story about my friends and my chosen family. It's also about the universality and specificity of the queer experience. I am so honored to win this award with this film, a project I believe in with my whole heart."

"When I started making this documentary, I had no idea that I would end up here in front all of you. I thought I was making a film for a few of my friends so that I could remember who I am and where I came from. I wanted to document young queer people and their stories today. I wanted to give importance to some infinitely tiny piece of history. I'm so glad to have our stories illuminated in this huge way."

"I want to thank Georgia Graham and Edie Cypress. They are the only reason I am standing on the stage. I want to thank my mother for giving me a stubborn attitude and the ticket guy at AMC who let me into movies for free since I was thirteen. I think his name is Michael. Thank you to every friend and stranger who sat down to talk to me about the wonderful, sometimes sad world of experiences they've had with such a brutal honesty I couldn't even believe. Finally, I want to thank Collin Rees, who I believe more or less saved my life even though he did not have to. I will not stop telling queer stories and letting LGBTQIA people speak up. Thank you."

The rain of applause fell over her head and drenched her in good feelings.

Before the moment had even begun, it was over. Her thoughts were completely frenzied as she was applauded back to her seat, where her friends waited for her with congratulations and smiles stretched so far that she'd remember them forever.

A few more rounds of applause later and the ceremony was over. People bumbled into the lobby, where so many people spoke simultaneously that all the sounds blended into a single rustling hum.

Dawn kept her eyes on Georgia and Edie as they tried to meet towards the front. As they were passing the bathrooms, she felt a small tap on her shoulder. She turned around to find the source and was met with a thin man in gray glasses the same shining shade as his hair.

"Dawn?"

"Yes?" She didn't recognize the man but he seemed to know her.

"I'm Jeff. I teach a few of the documentary courses at UT. I just wanted to say congratulations. I loved your film and I am looking forward to having you and your work in some of my classes in the upcoming years."

"Oh my goodness. You're Jeff Morales." She'd watched his film one late night over Facetime with Collin. She couldn't believe he was standing right in front of her. "Thank you so much. Thank you. Really."

"Great to meet you. Have a wonderful evening." He shook her hand as he spoke then disappeared into the crowd again.

Dawn turned back around and tried to find Georgia when she was stopped again by another person. This time, it was a junior in the radio, television, and film department. He congratulated her and said her film was one of the best he'd seen all year.

It kept on like this, as Dawn was ushered from person to person hoping to shake her hand; she was completely dazed and overjoyed at the same time. She didn't know what to say to anyone besides thank you.

Bodies flooded out of the theater and onto the streets of Austin. Dawn wandered around for a few moments looking at street signs and trying to orient herself. She saw the water to her left and the capitol to her right and her heart burst at the potential of learning the ins and outs of a new city. Already she wanted to have a favorite coffee shop and bike trail all her own. She wanted Austin to be hers.

She pulled out her phone and typed out her dad's number. She bit her lip and pressed the call button. She turned around and kept an eye on the theater's bright marquee as she waited for the line to ring. The rings started and kept coming. It felt like the phone rang longer than it ever had before.

A crunching sound tickled her ears and she was afraid she'd got his voicemail. Then she heard his voice.

"Dawn?" It came out low and aching. He sounded tired.

"Dad." Dawn breathed slowly and listened to the sound of home in her father's voice.

"Where are you?"

"I'm in Austin. I'm at that film festival I told you about." A few people bumped into Dawn's shoulder lightly as they rushed by to a restaurant across the street. She took a few steps towards the street to get out of the way of the sidewalk. The other end of the line was quiet.

"Oh." Empty confusion tangled itself in his voice.

"I won, Papa. I won the award." A few police cars crept by as Dawn's bottom lip began to quiver in that way she hated.

"Oh, that's good." He made it sound like a question he didn't know the answer to.

"I'm gonna get someone to take care of you."

"Thank you, Dawn. Thank you for being a good kid."

Dawn raised her head upward to the sky to catch the tears that threatened to spill out. The marquee glinted against her eyes and then the moon. She kept her composure as she thought of all the times she needed to hear thank you but hadn't.

"You're welcome, Papa." The last word caught in her throat and she choked on it.

"Thank you. Okay, goodbye. I need to watch my shows."

"Okay, Dad. Goodbye. I got you some pralines. Goodbye."

Dawn wiped her eyes, tired from all the feeling she'd done that day.

Georgia and Edie emerged from the still buzzing crowd and hooked their arms into Dawn's on either side. Collin trailed behind and smiled at the girls as they started down the street. They were practically vibrating with excitement from the night. They walked down Congress Avenue unsure of where they were going but elevated on happiness, nonetheless.

THIRTY-FOUR

April 13, Forty-Two Days to Graduation

Collin nervously handed Dawn a pair of socks as they stepped in front of a sculpture in the center of a hilly park next to Lady Bird Lake. The socks were a cream color and had small red apples embroidered on the ankles.

"I saw them at a Korean beauty store downtown, and they reminded me of when you said you liked, um, some Korean soap. I couldn't find it, but I thought the socks were pretty cool." Dawn melted but kept her cool. She had to have mentioned it the second or third conversation they'd ever had, but he remembered. He liked her enough to pay attention.

Collin tucked his thumbs in his front pockets as they began slowly circling the park. They'd both arrived in the late Sunday afternoon and the sun was beginning to go down all around them. The soft rattling of hidden snakes echoed through the park, the soundtrack lovely and frightening at the same time.

They talked about Cate Blanchett and the best brand of spaghetti sauce and came up with a list of seventeen ways to escape a conversation you didn't want to be a part of anymore (Dawn's favorite came from Collin and involved faking an emergency heart surgery). Dawn laughed more than she had in weeks. She wanted to hold Collin's hand.

Dawn stopped walking and suggested they sit in the grass. She pulled out a big red blanket from her bag she'd grabbed from his house and spread it out on a small spot at the far end of the park, away from a crowd of rowdy teenagers yelling at the sky or maybe each other.

Collin dumped out the contents of his bag and filled the blanket with juice boxes and fruit snacks. They collapsed onto the ground and stared up at the sky, the darkness starting to take over the night as the sun disappeared and was replaced by stars.

Dawn rested her hand on her stomach and looked up blankly at the sky as she spoke, "Do you have a favorite French movie?"

"Yeah. My brother really likes *Jean de Florette* for some reason, so we watch that a lot. I don't think it's my favorite in terms of content or anything, but I like feeling close to my brother and it reminds me of him now."

"That's so sweet." Dawn thought of the smiling boy in Collin's documentary. Seeing Collin take such good care of him made her like him even more. "Wait a minute, isn't that movie kind of sad and slow for a kid?"

"Yeah, I guess. I think he just likes the vibes. It's very yellow. Lots of flowers and fields of grass."

"A child who understands vibes. Love that." Dawn shivered as a gust of wind chilled the air around them. The park was getting colder as light disappeared from the sky. "I guess I used to watch *The Picture of Dorian Gray* whenever I was sad in elementary school, so that feels like the same thing."

"I don't think so." He sat up and turned to look at Dawn with a laugh. The feeling of his eyes on her went straight to her stomach.

"Why not?"

"That movie has no vibes." He laughed again, arms stretching out, almost touching Dawn.

"A man literally rots because of his narcissism. How is that not the ultimate vibe?"

"You're so right. I'm a fool." Collin laughed and Dawn joined easily, her breath drawing in sharply at the sudden shaking of her ribs. She was relaxed. She liked him. She could breathe.

"Speaking of Dorian Gray, I have a good would-you-rather." He met her eyes again with the question, a sudden intensity glowing behind them.

"Shoot." Dawn didn't break eye contact. She could do this.

"Would you rather be super pretty, like, extremely symmetrical or whatever scientists say makes a person nice to look at, but nobody knows who you are, or"—he looked up into the sky as he tried to form the words—"kinda be average-to-below-average-looking, by societal standards, of course, but you're, like, Beyoncé-level famous."

"Pretty," Dawn answered swiftly and without hesitation. "I'd rather be pretty."

"Really?" He chuckled at the quickness of her words." I was thinking you'd say famous. You could make movies and everyone would watch them because you're you."

"Everyone will watch my movies anyway because they'll be good." Dawn smiled at her own words.

"That's true. It's still surprising though." Night wind chilled against them harsher now and Collin offered his jean jacket to Dawn. It had flags sewn into its back and was far too big for her, she realized, as she slipped it on. "I'm on my way to figuring you out, Dawn Salcedo."

They let the silence pass between them slowly. It was comfortable, the nothingness. He searched her eyes as she tried to stop shivering.

"I guess I just like the idea of being beautiful."

"You are." He brought his arm around her, warm against the cold Texas night.

Dawn's phone rang out into the quiet, breaking the spell that had cast itself over them.

"Oh, just a second," Dawn grabbed for her phone. "It's Georgia." She awkwardly moved from beneath his arm and pressed the phone to her ear, trying to look anywhere but Collin's mouth, a pink envelope, soft words folded inside.

"Hey. Yeah of course, I'm coming. Okay. I'll be there in a second. Yeah, I just lost track of time. Okay. See you. Bye . . . okay, love you, bye."

"You have to leave?"

"We all still have homework to do before school on Monday. We're driving back to Houston before it gets darker than it already is." Collin nodded.

Dawn felt a sudden sadness overcome her. She realized she wanted to hang out longer. Something was tugging at her, telling her to spend more time with him. She looked at the time on her phone and knew it wasn't possible, but being aware of the feeling of want was still important.

They picked up the uneaten snacks and the blanket and carried them under each arm. Collin reached his f ree hand out to Dawn. They held hands and walked to the parking lot beside the park where Collin had parked his car. She burned up inside, Collin's hands cool and soft in hers.

They had to separate hands when they split to opposite sides of the car and Dawn wondered if holding hands was a one-time thing. Her hands were cold again as she opened her door. They settled into their seats and Collin turned the key and waited until his car bucked into motion. Outside the window, the whole city somehow appeared much brighter to Dawn now that Collin was there with her. Now that she had a future beneath its lights. Collin slid his palm over Dawn's hand. Dawn looked over to smile at Collin and saw that he was smiling too.

THIRTY-FIVE

May 24, 1 Day to Graduation

Georgia's house was yellow with warmth and good news. Cars were lined down the street blocking neighbors' driveways, their bumpers just kissing.

The lights were on out front and the window shades were pulled all the way up so that even from the street you could see that something lovely and fun was going on inside. Music spilled out of the front door like an open invitation.

Frankie decorated like it was the last party the girls were ever going to have. Streamers hung from every surface strong enough to hold them, making the ceiling look like a rainbow spiderweb.

Ben and Edie arrived together, and Georgia hugged them both as they stepped through the front door.

"Hello! Congratulations!" shrieked Edie. A graduation card from her parents weighed down her hand awkwardly as she threw her arms up into the air in celebration. She handed the card to Georgia quickly, and Ben's arm snaked around her waist.

"Thank you." Georgia bowed ceremoniously towards the couple. "Everyone's in the living room playing board games."

She was wearing a plain, light blue dress that stopped suddenly above her ankle in a perfect line. It was her mother's, something she'd lovingly pulled out from the back of her closet.

"Please tell them I said thanks." Georgia waved the card in the air and it shook with the sound of a few dollar bills.

Edie and Ben walked into the living room to find Frankie judiciously watching over a deeply involved game of Sorry! Some of their friends from school were bent over the board while others talked on the couch, by the stereo, on the floor. A few of their parents also stood at the periphery.

"Finally, the happy couple has arrived," announced Frankie. They laughed and she kissed them both on the cheek like they were in a foreign country and not a Texas suburb.

"Come here." She gestured to a table in the corner. "I'm about the start a card game before I get Georgia's cake out of the fridge. Try to get people to join in."

Edie bent to sit at the table and Ben plopped beside her, kissing her sloppily on the cheek. They smiled into each other and shuffled the cards out of the pack. They began to play and tried to pull Jill in from the corner where she was staring at childhood photos of Georgia hung on the wall.

Georgia retreated to her room and sat on her bed holding the card and staring at the landscape of her room. She scanned the messy surfaces in her room for every detail of her childhood. The worn pages of her middle school notebooks. A picture of her and Frankie many years before at the rodeo was pinned to the wall. It all seemed so recent, so fresh in her memory. Somehow, it was all going to be behind her soon. She could see her life going forward. Her friendships were loose soil in a tight fist, the fragments of earth dropping out between dirty fingers. She smiled to herself as Frankie edged open the door.

"Geo, we're doing the cake," she whispered with a smile.

"Okay. I'm coming."

Georgia stood up from the bed and looked at one of the pictures tacked to her wall. She brought her finger to it.

"I think that was taken when you were seven," her mom insisted. "I looked good. So skinny."

In the picture, her mother stood in a pale red button-up top in the front lawn of a house. Georgia was standing balanced on Frankie's feet, just barely reaching her waist, bundled up in a pullover and overalls of the same color. Frankie must have made the outfit; she'd always been good at sewing. The picture was faded, but Georgia could just spot the front door of her house, familiar and a dusted gray in the photo rather than its current bright yellow.

Georgia observed her own face, focused, joyful. Her mother's smile was bright, a woman alone in her singular home with her singular child, the daughter she held everything within. A neighbor or maybe Frankie's sister must have taken it.

"I think that's exactly what I'll look like." Georgia kept looking at the photo.

"If you're lucky."

"I'm sorry about Simone, Mama." Georgia took a sharp breath in, nervous at having brought him up not just in a letter but to her face.

"It's okay. He always smelled like market fish." Georgia could see her mother's sadness clearly— it flickered, the slight downturn of her lips pulling so that small creases formed at the edges of her eyes. It flashed on her face only for a moment. Georgia wouldn't have caught it on anyone else. It turned into a smile as she grabbed Georgia's hand. Her grasp was strong, a mirror to the softness of her skin.

"You are the most important thing to me in this world." She didn't let go as she said this, squeezing Georgia's hand once, twice, as though she needed Georgia to see and feel the truth of the statement. She could feel in her palm that they were one and two, Georgia and Frankie.

Georgia nodded.

"Come one, all your friends are waiting with the cake."

Georgia settled onto the couch next to Jill as the party continued on around her. Jill grabbed her hand and squeezed and squeezed.

"You are so wonderful," whispered Jill. "Everyone here thinks you are wonderful. I love you."

Georgia smiled at the admission. She beamed and said it back, her heart flipping in her chest as the house buzzed quietly around them.

Her mother gathered people from every room, the small vanilla-iced cake cradled in her hands. Slowly, the party moved into the living room, an organism of conversations. Frankie settled the cake into Georgia's lap and excitedly yelled the word *cake!* high above the collective muttering. Her balance wavered as she tried to stuff candles into the cake with her left hand and light them with her right. Georgia reached out with a laugh to set her upright again.

Edie squeezed in next to her on the other side of the couch as everyone started singing "for she's a jolly good fellow." The flame from the candles warmed up Georgia's face, her cheeks taking on a deep red from all the attention. Dawn pushed through to the couch everyone was crowded around as the song gained momentum, Collin trailing closely behind her. All the notes were wrong, and nobody cared.

Georgia never knew what to do when people sang to her—well, at her. Appreciation for her friends filled her. Here was a room of every person who ever cared about her. The song ended and she was stuck thinking of a wish.

"You guys should blow them out with me." She turned her head to Edie then Dawn. Dawn's hand was intertwined with

Collin's, but she let go and leaned into the cake just as Edie did too. Georgia counted down to three and they all puffed up their cheeks to blow the flaming candles to smoke. Georgia hoped they'd all wished for the same thing.

"I have a surprise for you, Geo. We can cut the cake after." Dawn knowingly nodded at Collin and excitedly grabbed Georgia's hand. "It's outside."

Everyone shuffled out into the warm early spring night. The wind was blowing hot over the stars. Orange and yellow front porch lights glimmered up and down the street. Lightning bugs swirled around people's lawns, flickering off and on in an illuminated dance.

Georgia and Frankie's garage was completely covered with two white sheets sewn together into one large one and duct-taped to the metal. Dawn had propped up a table with a mini projector connected to her computer. The projector glittered bright onto the sheet. Dawn leaned towards her computer screen and pulled up a file. A still image of Georgia with a play symbol over her face popped up onto the projector.

"Collin sent me the final version of the documentary you all worked on. I wanted to show it to all of you guys. I think it's actually about all of us. I mean, it's about love, but, really, it's about our love for each other."

She pressed play. Georgia appeared on the screen and began to speak.

I think love is impossible. It's like the Earth spinning. Like, you know that it's happening all the time, but you don't remember or recognize it until somebody brings it up and you're like, oh yeah, this incredible, unexplainable science is going on all around me.

The words *THE QUEER GIRL IS GOING TO BE OKAY* flashed across the screen in red letters on a black background.

Suddenly, there was Dawn, her hair pulled back tight into a high ponytail on top of her head, little ringlets falling into her eyes.

I want to be in love. I want the impossible. I would wait a million years for it. So, what is it? What is queer love?

There were quick snippets of kids from their school, phone videos sent in from Dawn's friends from her online film forums, Georgia, Edie, Ben.

Images from every day of their lives: two boys holding hands in the hallway of Alsbury, Georgia laughing as she drove down 59 and sang to a Robyn song, a boy winking as he slipped a note into a locker covered in hearts, two girls running down a parking garage decline holding hands in the middle of the night somewhere in the city, Ben and Edie kissing each other lightly in some crowded living room. These were snippets of their love, their friendships with each other.

It's a marshmallow sucked in slow between a boy's lips at summer camp.
It's resistance.
Your best friend in the entire world telling you something at 3:00 a.m. Something they've never said out loud before.
Yearning, dude, Just yearning.
It's loud and angry and in your fucking face.
It's their pajamas cool against your skin under the covers. It's their nose just grazing your cheek.
It's sweetness, sweet things. Sending a letter through the mail when you're in the same city.

People think it's the same. They want to say we're just like everyone else, but we're not. Queerness is itself. Queer longing is specific.

Everyone was drawn to the bright light across the garage and settled into watching. Edie, Georgia, and Dawn sat down in the driveway and leaned against each other as the clips kept coming. The film played across their backs and made their skin and clothes glow with the past and the present and even the future of their loves. They had each other. They had love and life stretched out in front of them in a thousand different directions. They held on tight to each other's waists, long after the credits rolled to black.

ACKNOWLEDGEMENTS

I owe several people for the existence of this novel. First, I want to thank my endless slew of kind and deeply encouraging English teachers who pushed me very early on to embrace writing. Thank you Michael Seckman for telling me I should keep writing weird, melodramatic poems. Thank you Erica Harris for everything you've ever done and for basically gifting me and everyone that hung out in your classroom good taste in indie music. Thank you to my homeschool teacher Adrianne Bailey for all the kindness and attention you afforded my developing mind. Thank you to my parents for allowing me to learn what and how I wanted to learn.

Thank you to my literary agent Garrett Alwert for calling me and telling me you liked my writing so much you'd read my grocery list. This book would be an idea of an idea without you.

Thank you to my editor Irene Vázquez as well as the entire Levine Querido team for believing in my book and bringing it into the world.

Thank you to my best friends who enabled the idea of this novel to flourish in small moments of awe in Carothers dormitory. Sidney Primm, Julian Merville, Abby Evans, and Libby Carr, you are my stars! Also, thank you to Daria Lourd for giving me lots of squeezes as I nervously awaited this book's arrival into the world.

Thank you to The Davidson Institute, Momentum Education, and Knight-Hennessy Scholars for the financial support and showing me that my writing could exist beyond my laptop.

Thank you, finally, to my sister Joi Walls for her unending support as my confidante, co-conspirator, and unofficial-official manager.

ABOUT THE AUTHOR

Dale Walls is a culture writer, curator, and art historian based in San Francisco. They are currently pursuing an art history PhD and are a Knight- Hennessy Scholar at Stanford University . Dale has written for Teen Vogue, Artsy, and Google Arts and Culture and is a 2022 Lambda Literary Fellow. The Queer Girl Is Going To Be Okay is their debut novel.

SOME NOTES ON THIS BOOK'S PRODUCTION

The art for the jacket was first created by Kameron White using a digital layout and programs such as Procreate and ClipStudioPaint. The text was set by Westchester Publishing Services, in Danbury, CT in Adobe Text pro. The display text was set in BC Alphapipe, by designer Radek Sidun, derived from the font Alphapipe by Czech graphic designer Jiří Rathouský and ATF Railroad Gothic, introduced in 1906 by the American Type Founders Company.

Production was supervised by Freesia Blizard

Book jacket and case designed by
Kameron White and Casey Moses

Book interiors designed by Lewelin Polanco

Editors: Meghan Maria McCullough,
Madelyn McZeal, & Irene Vázquez

LQ